The Talisman of Darktree Hollow

E M McIntyre

The Talisman of Darktree Hollow

Book 3: The Red King Trilogy

Copyright © 2018 E M McIntyre
Cover design © 2019 K A Denver

Edited by Phyllis Entis

United States of America

ISBN-13: 978-0-9988993-4-3

ISBN-10: 0-9988993-4-8

For my Papa, with love...

Book 3

The Red King Trilogy

1

A soft thrum filled Abby's ears. She stared at the remains of the Red King, mystified by the magic allowing his body to float in the air. She peered into the glowing, red emptiness of the gateway through which they stepped only moments ago. *I hope Rory and Finlay are sure about this.* With no visible way out, she eyed her magical wolfhound. Attempting to keep her thoughts private from the dog, she contemplated their situation. *The Red King came from the land of Shay, so if Finlay were bound to him as an animal guide hundreds of years ago, I wonder if he remembers things about Shay he's not telling me.* Abby glanced at the young Scotsman. *And since Rory is distantly related to the Red King, does that mean whoever is on the other side of this portal — if we ever find an exit — will expect him to rule the land? Or what if they're hostile and afraid of Rory stealing the crown?*

An eerie sound gave Abby pause. "Hey guys," she gulped, darting her eyes to either side at Finlay and Rory. "Did you hear that?"

Rory grunted in reply. "Aye, A-by. Sounded like someone tellin' us to 'complete the circle' and 'protect the fallen.' "

Abby rolled her eyes. "Don't know why they keep saying that. We already completed the circle when we fixed that megalith with the broken top. But what's 'protect the fallen' supposed to mean? Protect the body of the Red King?"

Finlay nudged Abby's backside with his muzzle. *Let us worry on this later, lass. A more important task is at hand. I would prefer not to spend the rest of my days trapped inside this portal.*

Okay, okay, fuzzball, you're right, Abby snorted, pushing the Red King's body forward with renewed vigor.

Moments later Rory thrust a finger straight ahead. "A-by, do ye see it?"

"I think so," Abby replied, squinting toward a distant point. "Maybe it's an exit. Let's go!"

They pushed the remains of Rory's kin as fast as they dared, slowing as they neared the opaque outline of a fiery, red tree shimmering in the air.

"Looks just like the tree we stepped through a minute ago." Abby drew a deep breath, "Sure hope it leads where we think."

Finlay loomed over Abby's shoulder. *Time is short, we must take him home. On with the two of you, child.*

Heeding her massive wolfhound's words, Abby looked to Rory. "You ready for this?" she asked, her stomach churning with a myriad of emotions.

"Aye. Let us see what lies beyond."

Forestalling further indecision, Finlay snorted, strode around the floating body, and stepped through the portal.

Abby chuckled, "Okay then, guess we're following Finlay."

With one last glance at Rory, Abby squeezed her eyes tight and pushed.

***

A short gasp prompted Abby to open her eyes. By her side, Rory stood mouth agape. Blinking at the stark change in surroundings, Abby followed his gaze out onto a deep valley; a vast sea of trees climbed its sides, their height dwarfing even the tallest redwoods Abby once visited. "Whoa," she exhaled, "everything is so big!

Welcome to the land of Shay." Glancing over her shoulder, Abby considered the portal. A momentary emptiness consumed her as she envisioned her parents, her sister, Agatha, and Mrs. MacTavish. *Will I ever see them again?*

Finlay pawed at the ground before nuzzling his snout into Abby's armpit. *Let go of your sadness, lass. Be assured you will see your family again. But, for now, the boy must close the portal. It would not be prudent to leave such a thing open to anyone's use.*

"Rory, Finlay says you have to close the portal."

Rory pulled his gaze from the impressive landscape and examined the gateway. "Aye, would be wise." After a moment of consideration, Rory removed the Rose of Shaeron from its pouch. With the stone outstretched, the Scotsman closed his eyes and scrunched his brow.

"Nothing's happening, Rory."

With a deep groan, Rory stared at his magical gem. "I'm no' sure what to do."

"Hmm. Well, when we were in the stone circle, the moon had to shine through it just right," Abby contemplated the mid-morning sun, "but I'm pretty sure that's not going to work right now."

Rory shrugged. Retracing his steps back to the crimson tree, he gripped the end of the Rose and inched it toward the glimmering field. Just as the gem made contact, the portal collapsed into a fiery ball and rocketed into the air. All eyes followed its path as it swirled higher and higher before plunging toward Rory. The Scotsman shrank back as the stone swallowed up what was once their path between worlds. He glanced at Abby with raised eyebrows before slipping the Rose back into its pouch.

"Huh. That worked well. Nice going, Rory."

With a goofy grin, Rory moved to stand once again next to the body of his long-dead kin.

Abby edged up to her companion as she looked down upon the body. "So now what?" she asked, shifting her attention to Finlay. "You used to live here, where do we go now? And," she continued, hand on hip, checking in all directions, "where in the world did that deer go? Can you smell Guido anywhere, Finlay? I'd think he'd need to be nearby for his magic to keep the Red King levitated."

The dog paced, nose to the sky. After several moments of silence, he looked at Abby. *I was but a young pup when I last set paw in Shay, bound as guide with the Red King for mere moons before Sylvan Myst beckoned us to your reality. Alas, I am afraid any memories of this land are lost to me in this moment. And,* he projected after sucking in a breath, filling his deep chest, *the stag's scent dissipates. I believe he has moved on, but to where I know not.*

"Fabulous," Abby groaned. "Guido up and leaves us, you don't remember anything about Shay, and we have no idea where to go or what to do with the Red King's body. I'd say we're off to a great start."

Rory pivoted to face Abby. Placing his hands on her shoulders, he turned her toward him. "Do no' fill yerself with worry. Me gut says we shall find our way." The Scotsman stared off into the valley, a sense of peace filling his eyes. "I feel a grand pull inside me. We must go this way," he finished, pointing to the tree-lined gorge.

Abby glanced from the valley to the Red King and back. "Maybe it's a bad idea to go pushing him around all over since we know nothing about this place. I think we should hide him. But where?"

Only then did Abby digest their new environment in full. They stood in a clearing of short, fuzzy grass tinged with orange, facing a steep drop several feet ahead into the valley of unbelievable trees. A canopy of enormous plants with gigantic, floppy leaves acted as a backdrop to where the group had emerged from the magical gateway. Abby spun around in awe. "It's like we stepped into the Jurassic period for plants," she said nervously, "dinosaurs excluded, I hope."

Confused by his companion, Rory raised an eyebrow. "Yer speakin' strange things again, Lass."

Abby groaned, having forgotten his 14th century origin. "Right. Sorry, Rory. Never mind. Help me search for a hiding place, like a cave or something." Abby reached out and ruffled Finlay's fur. "Mind watching over Mr. Mummy while we search?"

Finlay scratched at the ground. *We do not know what dangers may exist.* He lowered his head and stared deep into Abby's eyes for several quiet moments before puffing dog breath in her face. *As you wish, but stay close to the boy. If danger arises, do not hesitate to call out.*

Abby smiled, pleased by her animal guide's growing willingness to trust in her ability. "Thanks, fuzzface," she said, patting him on the head as he curled into a ball next to the Red King. Cinching her backpack, Abby motioned for Rory to follow. "Let's try through there," she said, pointing to a gap between two monstrous plants.

"Aye." Rory swept an arm forward, "Lead the way, A-by."

Approaching the strange plants with caution, Abby reached out and parted the leaves, revealing a path of sorts into the unknown. *Here goes,* she thought. Stepping into the dim forest of greenery, Abby absorbed the many exotic sounds and smells, similar to, yet different from, those of her parent world. An unusual insect, much larger than she cared for, hovered in front of her before darting off. Abby scrunched her face, unsure of what she'd just seen. Looking down, she noticed the same strange, fuzzy grass as in the clearing. Brushing her foot through it, Abby paused for a closer look.

"Whoa, did you see that?" she asked, pointing toward the ground.

Rory tilted his head curiously for a moment before shaking it.

Abby toed the grass again. In response, flecks of bright orange lit up the space through which her boot passed. Abby bent over, reaching a finger toward the fading lights.

"A-by!" Rory grabbed her elbow and stopped his eager sidekick's actions. "Ye should be more careful. We know nothin' of this land. I do no' want any harm to come to ye."

Abby straightened, considering the Scotsman's words. A fleeting moment of stubbornness rolled through her before common sense asserted itself. "You're right," she sighed. "I'll try to remember not to touch any ole thing. But you have to admit," she continued with a smile, "that was pretty cool."

Rory grunted as he ushered her forward with a grin. "Let us continue, Lass. We do no' want to keep yer grand beast waiting."

Abby snorted. "I'm sure Finlay won't mind. He's probably snoozing."

A tickle caressed Abby's mind. *You presume wrong, child. Listen to the boy — best not to keep the beast waiting.*

Abby shook her head and chuckled to herself. *Yeah, yeah. We're going, we're going.*

Rory pointed over Abby's shoulder as she continued picking a careful path through the maze of plants. "Over there."

She followed the line of his finger to a fallen log leaning against a mammoth tree stump. "Wow! That's got to be the biggest tree I've ever seen," she exclaimed over her shoulder as she headed toward it.

Nearing the stump, Abby froze. "Uh, I must be seeing things."

"What do ye mean, A-by?" Rory asked, coming to a halt next to her.

"I mean those eyes," she said, raising a shaky hand to point at the stump.

Just as Abby described, a large pair of eyes wavered in the air, blinking at the onlookers. An equally large mouth opened with a bellowing croak, belching a glob of sticky, black goo to the ground.

Cringing, Abby inched forward, straining to comprehend the mystery before her. "It's a giant, camouflaged toad! And it must be sick. Don't know what that black stuff is, but gross! Better watch our step."

Without warning, the toad leaped into the air. Abby and Rory ducked in unison as it sailed over their heads and landed with a thud before hopping away into the shrubbery.

"Okay then," Abby drawled, stepping up to the three-foot stump, wondering what else might jump out at them.

Rory remained silent, his attention now captured by the eight-foot section of fallen tree.

Abby watched as he jumped atop the stump and examined the end of the log. "What's so interesting?" she asked after hearing a soft grunt from the Scotsman.

"It has no innards."

"Yeah, so it's a hollow log. What's the big deal?"

"Do ye no' see, A-by?" Rory gestured, sticking an arm inside the log and moving it around in a wide circle. "Is big enough to fit a man."

"Let me see," she replied, hoisting herself up. Abby peered into the rotted core of the once impressive tree. "You're right! Smart thinking, Rory. I bet if we push this to the ground we could stick the Red King inside and no one would ever know."

Rory's face reddened at the praise. "Aye, Lass. Yer words are sound. Let us do as ye say."

Abby nodded, and with four hands placed firmly around the perimeter of the log, the pair pushed. With a second effort, their newfound hiding place landed on the ground with a dull thump.

Abby brushed her hands against her jeans and jumped to the ground. She motioned for Rory to follow, and squatted to peer into the log one last time. "Yep, I think this is perfect. Let's go tell Finlay."

Rory signaled for Abby to lead the way as she stood and adjusted her backpack.

"I hope everything else is as lucky here in Shay, land of giant, belching toads," Abby mumbled. As they retraced their steps, she reached back absentmindedly to intertwine her fingers with Rory's. Watching where she walked, Abby lost herself in the warmth of the Scotsman's hand. Glancing up, she stopped with a gasp. "How did we get to the middle of the clearing so fast? I'd swear just a second ago we weren't far from the log."

"Is peculiar, Lass," Rory agreed with a bewildered tone. Pulling Abby toward Finlay and his kin, he eyed the dog. "Perhaps yer white warrior played a trick on us, used his magic because he was tired of waitin'."

"Of course not," she said, watching Finlay stand and stretch. "We weren't touching him, remember? You have to touch him for it to work."

Finlay smacked his lips. *What are you children going on about?*

"It's nothing, Finlay," Abby replied, brushing off the strange moment. "But wait until you see what we found. It's the perfect solution." She gestured for Rory to help her guide the floating body into the sea of plants. "Come on, this way," she said, wiggling her nose at the dog before setting off.

Finlay followed along, stopping to sniff the many curiosities.

"Almost there," Abby hollered over her shoulder. When no reply came, she glanced back to see Finlay entranced by the glowing, orange grass. Abby giggled at the vision of her monstrous wolfhound nearly the size of a horse swatting at the tiny, star-like lights. *Finlay! Eyes up here, silly.*

The dog halted, paw mid-swat. Trotting to catch up, he nudged Abby's backside. *I believe you found it just as alluring.*

Abby snorted in reply as they came to a stop before the log. *You have a point.*

"How shall we do this?" Rory asked, touching Abby on the elbow to gain her attention.

Abby looked back and forth between the log and its soon-to-be occupant. "Well, only one way to find out if he'll fit. Let's start by getting his feet just above the opening."

Rory nodded, and the duo aligned the body of the Red King with the end of the log. "Shall we push down on both sides, A-by?"

"Yeah, then let's see if we can slide his feet into the hole."

With a further nod from the Scotsman, the pair pushed against the force of Guido's magic. After a moment of resistance, the body hovered in line with the hollow interior of the log.

"Okay, keep pushing down, but now let's guide him forward. Hopefully he'll slide right in."

With the Red King's feet swallowed by the hollow tree, the rest of his body followed with ease. She looked up at Finlay with delight. "See, the perfect hiding place. No one will ever know he's there!"

Finlay circled the log, inspecting it from every direction. *It seems you have indeed found a safe place, child. Though I am reluctant to leave him, we must ensure his safety as we discover our true purpose here.*

"Finlay's good with this, Rory. You're sure too, right? I don't think we have a choice."

Rory placed a hand on his hilt and studied their surroundings one last time. "Aye, Lass. Is the best thing. Let us be on our way."

Abby took Rory's hand with a gentle squeeze. "Okay then," she said, sinking a hand into Finlay's thick coat, "to the clearing, my fine hound."

2

As the travelers neared the floor of the valley, Abby stopped to lean against a random boulder. "We've been hiking for hours," she said, rubbing her protesting belly, "anyone else hungry? It's got to be way past lunchtime." She swung her backpack around when neither companion objected to the suggestion. After rummaging through all the pouches, Abby frowned. "Guys, there's nothing left. We've eaten everything Mrs. MacTavish packed for us." She pulled her mini water bottle from an outside pocket and examined its contents. "At least we have a little water left, but we definitely didn't plan well enough." Frustrated, Abby returned her bag to her back. "Now what?" She pointed at the closest plant. "For all we know, everything here is poisonous. And I really don't want to do any taste testing."

"Do no' worry, A-by," Rory replied, standing tall and puffing out his chest with a wide smile. "I shall catch us a kinnen!"

Abby laughed at his comical face. "And where exactly do you think you'll find a rabbit, let alone catch one? We haven't had a single animal cross our path since that giant toad. Besides, you don't have a bow anymore."

Rory's shoulders slumped. "Aye, yer words are wise. I fear I have no answer then."

Finlay moved to stand between the two. *I shall hunt for our meal, into the depths of the forest ahead. Though unfamiliar to me, my nose tells me many options await.*

"Finlay says he'll go catch us some lunch, but," she scrutinized his size, "how do you plan to sneak up on anything? You're not exactly invisible, you know."

Finlay flicked his tongue along Abby's chin with an exaggerated slurp. *Do you forget my abilities?*

Abby wiped her chin against her shoulder. "Gross, Finlay." Abby gave in to his playfulness after ruffling his chest and sticking out her tongue. "You're right, you'll be the sneakiest of us all. So, what are you waiting for?" she asked with a smile. "I'm starving."

Finlay tilted his head, winked, and disappeared suddenly.

"Don't know what he'll find, but whatever it is, we'll need some way to cook it."

Rory grunted in agreement. "If ye gather some stone for a pit, I shall collect fresh wood for makin' a fire."

"Works for me." Abby searched the area for small stones and began tossing them to an open spot suitable for a tiny fire pit. After amassing what she thought to be enough rocks, Abby set about arranging them into a ring. She looked up as Rory approached with a handful of kindling. "Cool, thanks," she said as he created a small pile in the middle of the ring. "See any good branches on the ground anywhere?"

"Nae, A-by, and I do no' want to venture too far into the forest. I shall cut down a low limb from there," he said, drawing his sword and pointing toward a nearby sapling.

She watched as Rory strode to the young tree, sword raised. The Scotsman inspected the limbs and nodded to himself as he gripped a likely branch with his free hand. Just as he lifted his blade, an ear-piercing shriek rang out.

Rory whipped around, sword ready, searching the landscape for the source of the cry.

Abby jumped up, uncertain what to do, and froze when a female voice called out.

"Aaauuuttt!" the unseen being screamed.

As she composed herself, Abby locked eyes with Rory, who only hinted a shrug in response. "Hello?" she called out. "We don't mean to cause any trouble, just trying to start a fire."

One of the many giant bushes rustled a short distance away. Abby held her breath, afraid of what might materialize from within the plant. Branches parted and out stepped a girl no older than herself holding a bow with arrow notched and pointed straight at Rory's heart. She wore clothing made from what Abby guessed to be animal hide of some kind, its earthy color blending in with the surroundings. The girl moved several feet closer to Rory. She growled, pulling back even further on the bow's string.

Abby's heart fluttered at the sight. "No!" she cried, "please don't hurt him." Images of Rory grasping his chest, holding tight to an arrow shaft filled her head.

The girl motioned with her weapon for the Scotsman to move away from the tree. Once satisfied with Rory's compliance, the newcomer shifted her attention to Abby.

Abby called out in her mind. *Finlay! Now would be a good time to come back, food or no food. We have a problem!*

The girl cocked her head once locking eyes with Abby. Lowering her arrow several degrees, she relaxed her posture.

Abby studied the strange girl more closely and gasped. "Your hair!" she blurted, "you..., you have a golden curl just like me!"

The girl eased her stance, bringing the point of the arrow to the ground. "Of course. All women in Shay are born with the golden drop." She eyed Abby with suspicion as she moved closer. "But you would know this, because you are a member of the Manta tribe. Correct?" She narrowed the distance between herself and Abby. "Though, you are unfamiliar to me," she said, furrowing her brow while considering Abby's clothing.

Abby's stomach turned upside down. *Did she just say golden drop! That's what Mavis and Tavis called my gold curl. How would they know that? How would she know that!* Confusion roiled Abby's mind as she pictured the gem embedded in Rory's sword. *My amulet was the golden drop in the prophecy, wasn't it? And Manta? That's what that creepy Mallena kept calling me. She must have thought I came from Shay! That I was part of this Manta tribe.*

The girl studied Abby's face. "What is your name?" she demanded.

Abby stuttered in reply, "Abby Fletcher, but you can call me Abby." She then motioned with her head toward Rory, "And that's Rory. Rory MacKay."

The girl tilted her head as Abby shifted her weight from foot to foot.

"I am called Wren."

"Wren," Abby repeated softly, distracted by a distant movement over the girl's shoulder. She gulped. *Finlay!* Abby called out in her mind as the dog stalked toward the stranger. *We don't know what she wants, but I think she's friendly. Please don't startle her though, I'd prefer not to have an arrow in the foot.*

Finlay relaxed his muscles as he continued his silent movement forward. *Very well, child. I shall heed your instinct. But if I sense she means to harm you, it will not end well.*

Abby stared at Wren and smiled, hoping she appeared friendly and at ease to the stranger. "So, Wren, I have a dog named Finlay. He was out searching for food but is on his way back right now. He's behind you a little way," she explained, bobbing her head forward briefly while darting her eyes over the girl's shoulder then back. "I don't want you to get freaked out or anything, but he's really big, like, unnaturally big. He's a softy though, so you don't need to be scared."

Wren tilted her head even further, her eyes filled with amusement, then turned her head for a glimpse over her shoulder. "He is your guide," she stated, looking back to Abby, seeming unalarmed by Finlay's mammoth size.

Abby opened her mouth but shut it promptly, taken aback by the girl's reply. "Well," she said finally, "yes. But how did you know that?"

"You are connected with him, here," Wren said, releasing her right hand from the bow and touching Abby's temple, "and here," she continued, making a fist with her hand and holding it level with Abby's heart.

Abby stood speechless, overwhelmed by the girl's knowledge and her touch. *Who is she? How could she possibly know that!* She glanced at Rory, who now stood only several paces away, his hand on the hilt of his sheathed sword. "Um, Wren?" she asked, bringing her focus back to the girl, "how come you screamed at us?"

"All trees in Shay are sacred. He," Wren said, staring at Rory, "showed intent to violate the Law of Souls. Why do you not know this?" she finished, gripping her bow anew.

Confused, Abby stared at Wren while holding back a groan. *Law of Souls? What the heck is that?*

Wren raised an eyebrow. "All Manta are sworn to the Law at birth. You do not know what I speak of?"

"I, uh," Abby stammered, praying she wasn't about to make a huge mistake, "well, you see, we're not from around here. And we're really sorry we almost broke your law. We didn't mean to, honest."

Wren stepped back, watching as Finlay butted up to his protégé, and Rory walked around Abby to stand by her other side. The girl's eyes widened after a moment of thought. "You are from the Other."

"The Other?" Abby echoed, exchanging a bewildered expression with Rory.

"The place to which many Manta disappeared during the Great Crossing. A place where only those wielding a Talisman may venture." Wren paused, a hint of realization washing across her face. "You must be a Protector. Please," she continued, bowing her head, "show me your Talisman."

Abby cast a further confused look in Rory's direction. "Protector? Talisman? I'm sorry, Wren, but we're not sure what you mean."

Wren studied the trio in front of her before closing her eyes and lowering her head. After several moments of silence, Wren looked up. "It is not you, Abby, but you," she said, focusing on Rory. "You, Rory, are a Protector. You possess a Talisman of great power. I must see it."

Abby reached out to Finlay as a proud grin announced itself on Rory's face. *What's your feel for her, Finlay? Can we trust her? She seems friendly enough, I guess, even though I have no idea what she's talking about.*

The dog fixed an eye on Wren. *I detect no ill will.*

You sure? That's what you thought about Aillig.

Finlay swung his head toward Abby. *His case was unique, lass. He was well practiced at deception. This Wren, however, smells of nothing but purity to me.*

Abby gave Finlay a mental shrug before elbowing Rory. "Go ahead, show her."

Rory sidestepped away from Abby, pulling his sword in dramatic fashion. "Perhaps this is what yer speakin' of, Lass." He swung the blade around for show before summoning flames to dance along its edge. "I can create fire with me sword," Rory finished with a gallant smile.

Wren tipped her head. "Impressive. But no, this is not what I wish to see. Your Talisman is a powerful stone. Do you still not know of what I speak?"

Rory sheathed his sword and glanced knowingly at Abby. Reaching toward the pouch secured at his waist, he paused, only to continue after seeing Abby mouth words of reassurance to him. Rory placed the Rose of Shaeron in his palm and held it out. "I do have this, Lass. We call it the Rose."

Wren leaned forward, drawing a sharp breath. "The Stone of Enlightenment! For time untold its powers have been lost to Shay."

Abby gazed at the Rose and whispered its rightful name. *Wonder what that means...*

A powerful screech sounded in the distance, pulling all eyes from the Rose and into the air. Rory slipped the stone into its pouch and returned to Abby's side.

Wren smiled deeply and her eyes seemed to shine as she looked back to Abby. "Rowen. He comes. He will be pleased."

"Rowen? Who's that? And why are we looking up at the sky?"

"He is my binding and a Protector."

Abby wrinkled her brow. "Your binding? What does that mean?"

Wren turned her attention to the sky again. "Just wait."

Abby shrugged and mouthed the words 'her binding' to Rory. He replied with an equal shrug, then pointed to the sky.

In the distance, Abby could make out the hint of a dark figure soaring above the tree line. A second screech ripped through the air. Abby gasped. "Is that a giant bird?"

"His name is Riffin," Wren replied, keeping her eyes on the creature.

The mysterious figure flew closer and closer at an alarming rate. Abby could now see the form of an enormous, tawny owl. *Is that a person on its back?*

The owl circled overhead three times before gliding gracefully to the ground near the group. The raptor squawked and proceeded to preen as a slender, young man slid from its back, releasing a set of reins that seemed to pull back and dissolve into the owl's feathers.

"Rowen," Wren sang as she rushed to his open arms.

Rowen touched his forehead to Wren's. "You have made new friends?" he asked after a moment of embracc. "I have not seen them before."

"They come from the Other," Wren whispered in his ear.

Rowen straightened, his eyes full of curiosity. Taking Wren by the hand, he headed toward the strangers.

Abby inspected the young man further as the couple approached. Standing a bit taller than Wren's five and a half feet, Rowen wore similar, earth-colored clothing, yet appeared to be clad in an unusual outer layer of unknown material. *Armor perhaps*, Abby thought, glimpsing the tip of a bow beyond his shaggy, strawberry blond hair.

Wren carried out introductions after slowing to a stop. "Rowen, these are Rory, Abby, and Abby's guide, Finlay. And he," she said, pointing to Rory, "is a Protector."

Rowen raised his brow. "A Protector? This is a fortunate happening, Wren. Please, Brother," he requested, turning to Rory, "tell me, what Talisman is entrusted to your care?"

Abby sensed Rory could not remember the strange name Wren gave the Rose, for he simply pulled it from its pouch for all to see.

"The Stone of Enlightenment! It is as I hoped," Rowen exclaimed. "But you are from the Other. You must explain how you came upon it. It has been lost from our land since the crossing of Redwin."

Abby's stomach rumbled a long, slow growl loud enough to elicit a chuckle from all present. "Uh, sorry about that," she blushed. "It's been a little while since we've had anything to eat."

"Of course," Wren said, "let us care for your immediate needs, then you will tell us about the Talisman and how you came to be in Shay."

Abby lifted a shoulder, "Sure, okay. Finlay was about to catch us something to eat, like maybe a rabbit if he could find one. Should I tell him to search again?"

Rowen and Wren froze in horror. "All life is sacred in Shay, Abby. It is Law. You must never slay an animal here," Wren stated with a shiver.

Abby glanced at Finlay. *Oh boy, guess it's a good thing I called you back when I did. First the trees, now the animals. How do they even survive here!*

"So, what do you eat then?" Abby asked, trying not to show her frustration.

Wren released Rowen's hand and walked toward the tree from which Rory had intended to scavenge a limb. "Come, I will show you."

***

As Abby and Rory watched, Wren knelt in front of the sapling, closed her eyes, and raised her hands, palm down.

"What is she doin', A-by?" Rory whispered.

"I have no clue," Abby replied softly, "let's just watch and see what happens."

After a long silence, Wren gently dug her fingers into the soil at the base of the tree. When she freed her cupped hands from the dirt, they held three pulsating, green orbs.

Abby craned her neck for a better view. "Whoa. What are those?"

Wren held the orbs to her stomach and walked back to the group. "Bria," she said, holding one out carefully for the trio to see.

Abby reached out hesitantly to touch the sphere.

"Yes," Wren nodded, "take one. It will not harm you."

Abby smiled and scooped up the offering, surprised by the warmth of it in her hand. "Bria," she repeated as

Rory also accepted one. "What is it though?" she asked, her eyes fixated on the pulsing.

Wren smiled. "Bria is the land's offering to us. If you fall weak from hunger, it is food. If thirst is your enemy, it gives you fluid. If you follow the Law, Shay will always help you when you are in need."

Abby looked at Rory with wonder, recognizing equal excitement in his eyes. "But what do we do with it?" she asked, turning back to Wren.

Wren tipped her head back with a laugh. "Why, you eat it, of course."

Abby straightened up, trying not to blush. "Oh, of course. That makes perfect sense. But," she paused, "what does it taste like?"

"Do not worry yourself, Abby, it tastes as whatever you wish," Wren said with a wink before tossing the third Bria into the air towards Finlay.

The wolfhound lifted up onto his hind legs and snatched the orb out of the air. Chewing twice, he swallowed with an exaggerated gulp. *Just like your shopkeeper's stew, child. Have faith in our new companion. Or shall I eat yours too?*

Abby rolled her eyes at the dog and clutched the Bria to her chest.

Wren laughed. "Finlay finds it satisfactory?"

Abby snorted. "Yeah, so much so, he offered to eat mine." Abby raised the Bria to her mouth and sniffed. "Well then how about a slice of my favorite pizza?" she said just before popping it into her mouth. Abby chewed and closed her eyes with a sigh of satisfaction. "Wow. You weren't kidding. That tasted just like pepperoni-pineapple, deep-dish pizza!"

"I do not know what this is you speak of, Abby, but I am pleased it suited you. Thanks to the magic of the Bria, you should feel nourished for many days to come. Please, Rory," Wren continued, motioning to the Scotsman, "you can see your binding and her guide have fared well."

Rory shrugged and popped the Bria in his mouth. His eyes grew large as he tried to chew and smile at the same time. "Aye," he said after swallowing, "is good, but do ye no' eat anythin' else in the land of Shay?"

Rowen's smile held a tinge of sadness. "Though once our only source of nourishment, Bria have become rare in recent times. Law allows us to take sparingly from plant life, so long as we cause no harm to the mother being, but we find it is not so filling. And only if an animal is at the cusp of completing its circle do we feed on its flesh."

Abby suppressed a frown. *There's that phrase again, 'complete the circle.' I'd really like to know what it means, but do we dare tell them about the Red King?* Drawn back to the moment, Abby glanced up to see Finlay nose to beak with the owl. *Oh geez, don't get yourself into trouble, fuzzface.*

Rowen followed Abby's gaze. "Riffin has taken a liking to your guide."

"May I say hello to him?" Abby asked with an uncharacteristic shyness. "Owls are my favorite, and I've never seen one so big."

Rowen chuckled. "Of course, just be wary of his talons."

Abby nodded and approached Riffin with caution. She marveled at his size once standing before him. The complex mixture of earthy colors in his feathers created a beautiful, marbled display. Letting her eyes follow his impressive frame to the ground, Abby cringed inside as her gaze reached his feet. *Rowen wasn't kidding about his talons. He could take down just about anything without a problem.*

"Hey big fella," she cooed, looking into Riffin's yellow eyes. "Mind if I pet you?"

Riffin rotated his head around and down toward his feet while making a 'whooo-winnie' sound.

Abby laughed as she reached out to stroke his feathers. "You remind me of a barred owl. Of course, only in sound," she continued as if talking to a baby, "you're the most impressive owl I've ever seen. Aren't you, Riffy boy?"

The owl cooed back in response, nuzzling its beak against Abby's shoulder.

Abby eyed Finlay over her shoulder. She sensed a wave of jealousy touch the edge of her mind. *What,* she thought, playfully narrowing her eyes at the dog. *I can't have a favorite owl?*

Big dog stinks.

Abby giggled at the funny voice, "Yeah, he can get a little stinky at times. Isn't that right, Finlay?"

Drawing back, Abby paused, her laughter dying off. "Hey, wait a minute!" she exclaimed, looking from the bird to the dog. "Did you just say Finlay stinks? You can talk to me too?"

At the rise in Abby's voice, Rory, Wren, and Rowen gathered around. From the corner of her eye, Abby caught Wren and Rowen staring intently at one another.

"Abby," Wren asked with apprehension, "did we hear you correctly? Riffin can communicate with you?"

Abby's eyes darted from one person to the next in a moment of trepidation. *Don't freak out, Abby. If you tell them the truth, maybe they'll help us with the Red King. We certainly aren't getting very far on our own.* Inhaling slowly, Abby calmed herself. "Well, yes. But I don't see what the big deal is. There's a giant deer around here somewhere named Guido that talked to me too, but that was back home."

Rowen cleared his throat and frowned. "You have seen Guido? He was in the Other?"

Abby swallowed nervously. "Um, he helped us with something. Is that bad? Was he not supposed to be there?"

Rowen shook his head. "It is more confusing than anything." The Protector stood silent as if considering how to respond. "Guido was guide to Pixius, a brave and loyal Protector of the Stone of Wisdom. He met an unfortunate death not even a full moon ago." Rowen sighed before continuing. "The only way for Guido to have crossed to the Other is for a stone bearer to have opened a portal. It could not have been Pixius and there are few Protectors left. There is only one person careless enough to do so." Concern filled Rowen's eyes. "Come. We must return to Willow Wood at once."

Abby could feel the urgency in Rowen's words. "Willow Wood?"

"Our home," Wren answered with a gentle touch to Abby's hand. "We will be safe there. And," the girl eyed Abby's clothing again, "Emi will make you something more suitable to wear in Shay."

"Wait. We're not safe here? And who is Emi," Abby blurted with a sudden unease.

Wren left Abby's questions hanging in the air. She reached out to Rowen, touching her forehead to his. "In life and in death," they said in unison as he stepped away.

Rowen sunk his left hand into Riffin's feathers and pulled himself up onto the owl's broad back in one fluid movement. Reins appeared in his hands as the bird hopped forward and ruffled its feathers. The Protector leaned in, whispering something into his guide's ear. Riffin chirruped as he beat his powerful wings, launching into the air. With a last glance at the group, he called out, "To Willow Wood."

3

Following Wren's lead, the group hiked into early evening through a vast expanse of forest. Abby remained baffled by and in awe of the size of the trees, plants, and insects. She cringed when imagining how large a spider might be in the land of Shay. Shaking off the thought, Abby realized she could not recall seeing any other animal life in the forest. She pondered potential reasons as they stepped out of the woods and into a clearing filled with more of the funny, orange grass. Strange flowers of vivid colors dappled the meadow, consuming Abby's attention until she searched the sky, spotting the dark form of Rowen and Riffin circling overhead.

Wren pointed into the distance across the clearing. "Willow Wood is just beyond. Soon we will rest our feet."

"Hey, Wren," Abby called, jogging to catch up and match the girl's pace.

"You have many questions," Wren said with a knowing expression. "I will do my best to answer them now."

Abby scrunched her brow, confused by Wren's strange intuition. "Well, yeah, I guess I do."

"You are perplexed by our binding custom, are you not?"

Abby shook her head in disbelief. "How do you do that? Can you read my mind or something?"

Wren smiled. "It is my gift. Let us say I am often as one with my surroundings."

Abby nodded though she did not understand. "You called me Rory's binding. What exactly did you mean? We're not married or even dating or anything."

"I do not know these words you speak but I will tell you what it means in Shay. Protectors are not whole until they find their true match, the person they are destined to become one with. Only then are they able to wield their given Talisman."

Abby glanced over her shoulder at Rory. The Scotsman had been able to use the Rose from the moment he first held it. Feeling a rising heat in her cheeks, she gulped. *Does that mean we're destined to become one?* Abby looked back to Wren. "So, what happens then, once they find each other, I mean?" she asked shakily.

"The binding ritual, of course."

Abby's eyes widened, "Binding ritual?"

Wren brushed her fingers along the underside of Abby's chin. "It is a ritual of words, spoken in unison while standing beneath the Great Willow."

Abby's shoulders relaxed. "Oh, I see. Sounds somewhat similar to what we call a wedding ceremony."

"Would you like to hear it, Abby?"

"Uh, sure, why not?"

With her eyes, Wren followed the soaring path of Rowen and his guide as the words rolled from her lips. "All that was, all that is, all that will be. Bound by touch, bound by soul, bound by eternity."

Abby walked on in silence considering the weight of the words. *Do I really feel that way for Rory?* She peered over her shoulder again at the young man.

"What was in life will be in death. It is our belief in Shay." Wren smiled and eyed Abby before continuing. "You are already bound in here, Abby," she said, reaching out to indicate Abby's heart, "you have yet to say the words."

Abby turned her head away and studied the ground, embarrassed by Wren's statement and the growing realization she knew the girl spoke the truth.

Wren grinned at Abby's reaction. "Tell me, Abby, what is it like in the Other?"

Abby sighed, thinking of her family. "It's not as peaceful and quiet as it is here, that's for sure. And everything is much, much smaller," she chuckled, watching the tree line ahead grow taller and taller with every step.

Wren nodded in reply, increasing her pace toward their final destination. After several minutes of silent travel, she slowed to a stop, motioning for Rory and Finlay to join them. "Welcome to Willow Wood," she said, pointing to the massive wall of trees filling their view ahead.

Abby squinted into the distance. "That's weird, I could swear it looked like a tree just moved."

"Your eyes see the truth, Abby."

"Really?" Abby strained her eyes again and focused on an undulating pattern among the trees. "What the..."

"The magic of Shay is what you see at work. The Mantara, they protect our ancient home."

Abby stopped short from biting her tongue. *Mantara! This is getting way too weird. How on earth did the Mantara get here? Or, maybe I should be asking how the Mantara got into that little hollow near Caledonia!*

Wren seemed to ignore Abby's reaction and raised a hand in the air, signaling for Rowen to descend.

The group watched as Riffin circled slowly, lower and lower, until landing without a sound. Rowen hopped from his bird's back and with eagerness touched foreheads with Wren.

Rowen stepped back, excitement filling his eyes. "Welcome to our home, Brothers and Sister. Please, follow me." Rowen took off toward the towering wall of trees, whistling at Riffin as he did. The bird looked up from preening and squawked before following. Abby thought she heard the owl mumbling about never having time to clean its feathers, but after a quick glare from Rowen, Riffin continued in silence.

Upon reaching the fortress, Abby stared upward, gawking at its enormity.

Rory whispered in her ear. "A-by, does it no' remind ye of where we discovered the Rose?"

"That's exactly what I was thinking too, Rory, except way taller."

Ignoring their whispers, Wren stepped away, motioning for all to watch. She placed her hands upon the closest tree and closed her eyes. Moments later, the ground rumbled. Wren backed up several paces and bowed.

"Whoa!" Abby gasped when branches and roots swirled high and low. "Mantara," she whispered to herself, only then believing it, "but how?"

The snake-like movement continued with added snaps and cracks until a parting of the trees appeared as if to beckon them inside.

Wren and Rowen passed through the opening, with Riffin hopping behind. Wren stroked a tree with her fingertips and looked over her shoulder. "Come," she directed, "you will see no harm inside these walls."

Abby stretched an arm out to connect with Finlay's lush coat. *That's more than once now Wren has mentioned things not being safe outside of Willow Wood. Seems a little weird. Nothing out there has felt dangerous.*

Finlay prodded Abby forward with his muzzle. *Do not be so quick to judge a situation, child. Remember, we have only just arrived in this place. Sometimes things have a way of hiding themselves. All may not be as it appears.*

Why do you say that?

Because I sense a sourness in the air as if a deep melancholy of past times drenches the land. I fear a great evil may be lurking.

A chill crawled along Abby's spine. *Great, glad to hear it. You would be good at telling creepy bedtime stories, you know.*

Finlay bumped Abby's backside once again. *Onward, child. Let us not keep our companions waiting.*

Abby scooped up one of Rory's hands and marched inside the stronghold.

The Scotsman grinned at Abby, squeezing her hand in response to the sudden stop of rumbling and grating.

The pair spun around to see the tree line meshed in a swirling mass once again.

"Cool." Abby turned back, absorbing their new environment. Trees of many species stretched into the sky. It seemed as if their branches wove together to create a canopy penetrable only by light.

Riffin fluffed his feathers before half hopping, half flying into a nearby tree. Gripping its lowest branch, the bird side-stepped to the enormous trunk and disappeared into a deep hole. With a whooo-winnie, Riffin hunkered down, leaving nothing but his eyes visible in the darkness of the cavity.

Abby giggled quietly at the bird. *Aw, Riffy-boy has his own tree. Have a nice nap, Riffin.*

The owl acknowledged Abby with a soft coo. *Pretty Amaray.*

Abby crinkled her face when the owl's final thought before closing his eyes wafted into her mind. *Pretty Amaray? Hey, wait a minute, that name sounds familiar! Riffin. Hey, Riffin?* She groaned, realizing the bird would not be answering her any time soon. Making a mental note of yet another mystery to solve, Abby returned to examining their immediate surroundings.

By Abby's estimate, there was not a single tree less than five feet in diameter. Many of their shallow roots zigzagged along the ground, creating an intricate pattern with the neighboring tree.

"You are enchanted by our home," Wren stated, walking back to the trio. "Come," she continued, "Emi will be pleased to see you. She takes great pride in weaving new creations, in your case, new clothing."

Rory examined the tunic and khakis borrowed from Abby's father. With a hint of a frown, he fidgeted with his scabbard and smoothed his shirt.

Abby brushed up against the Scotsman's side. "Hey, no need to worry. I know you were probably getting used to these new clothes," she said, tugging on his sleeve, "but I bet this Emi will make us something comfortable. Besides, we need to be willing to fit in here, so we should just roll with it. But I promise," she snickered with a devious grin, "no more dresses for you, unless maybe it accents your hair."

Rory made a funny face as he held back a laugh. "Ye are right, A-by," he sighed. "But I do no' want to dishonor yer faither and me kin for givin' me such kind gifts."

Abby smiled at the young man as they walked along behind Rowen and Wren. "You know, you are definitely one of a kind, Rory, and I mean that in a good way."

Rory stood a little taller as a giant grin stretched across his face. Abby was not certain but she thought she detected a hint of red in his cheeks. She breathed deeply, feeling a blush of her own developing, and looked away for anything to act as a distraction. She did not have to look far, for in the distance stood the biggest tree Abby had ever seen — one she never could have imagined.

"Whoooaaa!" Abby exclaimed, pointing ahead.

Rory followed the line of her finger. His jaw hung low and his eyes widened. "Is amazin', A-by. Do ye think it is real?" he asked after finding his voice.

"Why of course it is real," Wren sang with amusement. "Please, welcome to the Great Willow, largest and oldest tree in Shay."

Abby took in the sight, ignoring all else around her. *How is this even possible? That tree has got to be at least 50 feet across. And those roots, they're thicker than my body!*

"Come," Wren called, pulling Abby from her private reverie, "you may pay homage to the Great Willow if you like."

The group walked in silence to stand before the tree. Wren and Rowen both placed their hands upon its trunk and bowed their heads, whispering something Abby could not quite hear. Shrugging, she stepped up and mimicked their actions. The moment flesh and bark connected, Abby felt a rush of warmth swirl through her. She closed her eyes and cocked her head, thinking she had just heard a distant voice. Shutting out everything around her, Abby concentrated on the wispy sound. What was but only a whisper grew louder and louder until an ancient voice boomed in her mind.

"Complete his circle."

Abby jumped back from the tree, pulling her hands to her chest. "Did anyone else hear that? Please tell me you heard that!"

Wren and Rowen raised their heads abruptly and looked from one another to Abby with surprise. "Tell us what you heard, Abby," Wren prompted.

Abby composed herself, hoping she did not appear crazy to her new friends. "The tree, it...it talked to me."

Wren's expression remained collected as she glanced at Rowen. "Please, Abby, tell us what you heard."

"It said, 'complete his circle.' It was like the voice was all around me, yet in me, too."

The entire group exchanged silent looks until Wren cleared her throat and gestured toward the forest floor. "Come, let us sit. It is time for you to share how you came to be in Shay."

Doing as instructed, Abby and Rory lowered themselves into a seated position. Finlay curled up next to Abby as Wren and Rowen sat across from the trio.

Abby reached out to Finlay while Wren stared at her with expectant eyes. *What do you think? Is it safe to tell them?*

Finlay lifted his head and yawned. *Yes, child. We are wasting time without guidance and it is unwise for us to leave the Red King's body unattended any longer than necessary. It is clear to me now, as it should be to you, he was a Protector of Shay.* The dog paused, swinging his head toward Rowen. *Before you sits a Protector of Shay. He will know what to do.*

Abby nodded to herself and exhaled.

"I sense your uncertainty," Wren prodded gently, "but Finlay has assured you of our trustworthiness, has he not? Do not be afraid. You may tell us all."

Abby glanced at Rory who gave her an encouraging nod. "Well, okay then. No better place to start than at the beginning, right?"

For the next ten minutes, Wren and Rowen sat silent as Abby described in brief their incredible adventure, from Finlay's entrapment by Mavis and Tavis and solving the Prophecy of Myst, to finding the Book of Shay and saving her father, to ultimately discovering the Red King's body and opening the portal between worlds. "And so," she said after taking a deep breath, "we knew we had to bring his body home. But," Abby paused, studying her audience, "we had no idea what to do with him, so we hid him...in a log."

Rowen exhaled slowly and laid his hand over Wren's. "Could it be? Yes," he answered his own thought, "yes, it must be. It is Redwin they have brought home to Shay. And you," Rowen said, locking eyes with Rory, "are his successor."

Rory replied with a quick nod. "Aye, it is true. The Red King is me kin."

"This is most excellent, Brother," Rowen said, reaching out to clasp Rory's arm. "Sadly, not all Protectors survive to bear and raise a successor. But when a Talisman is passed on through a bloodline, it grows more and more powerful." Rowen smiled at Wren, squeezing her hand. "It is a wonder, though, you were able to find the Stone of Enlightenment. It was long ago when Redwin, first and only King of Shay, took it with him during the Great Crossing."

Abby tipped her head to one side. "You guys keep mentioning that. What exactly is the Great Crossing?"

Rowen gestured for Wren to explain. She stared up into the treetops for a moment, lost in thought, then brought her gaze back to Abby. "Over 800 years ago, an all-consuming evil crept into the peaceful lands of Shay.

You will learn more of this, in time," she said, bowing her head. "Our people, knowing no defense then, relied on the Protectors. For years, this dark power grew, taking the lives of many innocents among the Manta tribe until, one day, Redwin made a decision in hopes of saving our people. But there were those who saw it as drastic and reckless."

Abby glanced at Rory with a slight cringe. "What exactly did he do?"

With a solemn nod, Wren continued. "Using his Talisman, Redwin opened a portal to the Other and led those willing into the unknown. They were never seen nor heard from again. This would be known forever as the Great Crossing.

Abby gasped. "Just a sec," she said, holding up a finger and leaning toward Rory. "You remember all those women and girls in the cave? And all those people you saw in your memory at the hollow where we found the Rose?"

Rory nodded with a grunt. "Aye, A-by, but what..." he trailed off before lifting his brow.

Abby slapped a hand on his knee, seeing understanding fill the Scotsman's eyes. "Exactly. That was them, the Manta tribe! The younger ones all had golden curls, remember?"

Wren scooted forward and reached out to touch Abby's hand. "You saw our people from long ago? You are certain."

"Positive. I mean, it was in the past and all, in Rory's time, but yes, I'm certain."

"And they were well?"

"If you ignore the fact they were held captive in a cave for years by two crazy faerie brothers, yeah, they were well. Plus, Finlay did end up taking them home."

Wren leaned back and smiled at Rowen. "So, perhaps Redwin's choice was not misguided."

Rowen touched foreheads with Wren. "Perhaps not. And now," he turned to Abby and Rory, "his circle must be completed. The Great Willow commands it, we must do so tomorrow."

Abby's eyes grew wide. "So, the tree did talk to me!"

"Yes, Abby," Wren said, "though..."

"Though what, Wren? Is something wrong?"

"No, Abby, you need not worry. It is unusual though. In the past, the elder trees of Shay spoke only to one person, and she has been lost to us for countless years."

"Oh, uh, I see," Abby mumbled, unsure what to make of the statement.

"Come," Wren said, taking Rowen's hand and standing up. "Let us go to Emi, she will be happy to see new faces." Wren motioned for the group to follow as she rounded the Great Willow and continued deeper into the woods.

The trees and their root systems became more interesting and complex the farther they traveled into Willow Wood. Abby kept turning her head from side to side, not wanting to miss anything. "Wow," she whispered as they approached a mysterious weaving of roots reminding her of the structure that had held the Rose for safekeeping.

"It is for sleeping," Wren said, stopping once aware of Abby's curiosity.

Roots from the nearest tree networked together creating a cocoon-like structure stretching 15 feet into the air. A tall archway on one side allowed for access into the creation. Abby ran a hand along the outside, surprised by its smooth feel.

Wren stood next to Abby, sweeping an arm toward the opening. "You may inspect."

Abby peered inside. "Kinda dark in there."

Wren tossed her head back with a light laugh, "There are many things to learn yet, Abby. Please, explore."

Abby shrugged and grabbed Rory by the sleeve. "Come on, you can protect me."

With a goofy grin, Rory followed Abby to the opening, placing a hand on his hilt. The pair crossed the threshold in unison, amazed by what greeted them. In reaction to their presence, the interior of the structure glowed with an array of soothing colors from orange blending to a deep blue. Abby approached the wall of roots and stretched a finger out, hovering it inches from the glowing substance. The wall reacted to her movement, glowing with increased intensity.

"Cool. Check it out, Rory."

Abby waved her hand in front of the roots. They responded with a blazing orange, subsiding when her hand moved away. "Sort of reminds me of that fuzzy grass we saw."

Abby followed the curvature of the walls, creating a wave of various colors. Smiling at the effect, she moved to the center of the structure. "Wren said this is for sleeping, but there are no beds, no nothing for that matter." Shrugging in unison, they exited the odd room.

"Did you enjoy the Goldenglow?" Wren asked.

Abby wiggled her nose. "The what?"

"The Goldenglow. They live in harmony with the trees and help us see our way when we need light."

"Ah, yeah, the colors were really pretty. But where do you sleep?

"You will see in time. Come," Wren said, continuing on her original path.

"Hey, Wren," Abby said after the group had worked their way through the woods for about a half hour.

Wren slowed to match Abby's pace. "Please, what questions do you have?"

"Just how big is Willow Wood, exactly?"

"If you were to do so, you would find you could travel an entire day in any direction from the core of the woods before finding the protective barrier of the Mantara."

Abby nodded, mouthing the word 'wow' to herself. "So, where is the rest of the tribe? I thought we would have seen some other people by now."

Wren frowned. "There are not many of us left. We come together every fourth day at the Great Willow to tell of our doings and to gather Bria together."

"To gather Bria together? How come?"

"For reasons you will learn, the lifeblood of Shay is dying. It burdens the land to produce that which we need, so we must weigh our actions and not take more than required."

Abby stared ahead, feeling sad for the clear losses and struggle, yet appreciative of the tribe's philosophy. "So, tell me about Emi," she asked thoughtfully.

"Yes, Emi. You will meet her soon, her home is in the clearing ahead," Wren replied, pointing off to the right. "Emi, the Weaver, is an animal guide."

The group crossed out of the tree line into a small pasture filled with more fuzzy, orange grass. In the distance stood an enormous dome-shaped weaving of roots. To the left of the complex structure sat a large, deep brown figure.

Abby squinted with uncertainty. The figure seemed to be sitting back on its haunches, rocking side to side.

Rory leaned close to Abby's ear. "What do ye think it is, A-by?" he whispered.

"I'm not sure," she whispered back. "Emi, I hope."

Wren smiled at the pair's uncertainty. "You need not hope, Abby. Come, Emi awaits us. I believe you will find her gift most amazing."

***

Abby glanced at Finlay as they approached the weaver. Emi outdid the wolfhound's size with ease. *I wonder what she is*, Abby thought to herself. *Almost like a giant badger or something, except the color is off.* As the group came within a few feet of the strange creature, garbled sounds, which turned quickly into melodic words, floated through Abby's mind, bringing her to halt.

Weave, weave, stitch, stitch, la-la-la, fix, fix...

"Uh..." Abby stared wide eyed at Emi.

Emi stopped rocking herself and jerked her head up at the group as if surprised by their presence. She gazed at each person with large, yellow eyes, tilting her head upon reaching Rory, then shaking it rapidly back and forth as she shifted to Abby. *Tsk, tsk, no, no, this will not do. Weave, weave, stitch, stitch, fix new wares for you.*

Abby raised a hand, pointed at Emi, and tried to formulate her thoughts.

"Abby?" Wren asked, looking to the weaver and back, cutting her short. "You can hear Emi?"

Abby felt all eyes on her. "She's singing in rhyme," she said finally with a soft chuckle.

Wren stared at Rowen for several seconds before nodding with a smile. "I do not know this word, rhyme, but have no surprise to hear she sings." Wren approached the weaver and scratched her side. "She creates beautiful things from the sacrifices of the land. It fills my heart to know she is happy when doing so."

Emi rolled herself forward, placing all paws on the ground. She swung her elongated head toward the woven dome and chuffed before entering.

"Come, friends," Wren said, "Emi would like to show you her home."

The group watched as the weaver waddled into the dome. A soft, yellow glow emanated from inside the structure in response to Emi's movement.

Abby examined the walls of the dome as she followed Wren and Rowen through its opening. *Must be more of the Goldenglow, wish we had some of that back home!*

She then sensed a sudden slope. *Huh. She lives underground?*

In answer to her unspoken question, an immense cavern opened before Abby's eyes. Goldenglow covered the dirt walls and ceiling, casting plentiful, soft light into the near-barren chamber. To one side of the room, thick grasses created a large nest on the ground. Along the opposite wall, tips of tree roots poked through, acting as hangers to various pieces of animal hide.

Emi shuffled to the wall and inspected the remnants one by one, looking back at Rory and Abby in between each. She huffed and waved a paw at Abby before pulling a chunk of caramel colored hide from the wall. *This will do, fit you well, young one.*

Wren pulled Rowen alongside her near Emi's bed and motioned for Rory and Finlay to step back. "Stand there in the clearing, Abby," Wren indicated, pointing to the middle of the cavern. "Emi will need plenty of room to do her weaving."

Abby complied, moving to where Wren suggested. She glanced around nervously. "Um, where exactly am I supposed to change clothes? This is the only room; no way I'm going to undress in front of everyone."

Wren smiled warmly at Abby's concern. "Please, allow Emi to use her gift. There is no need to fill yourself with worry."

Abby released an uneasy breath, "Okay, this better be good."

Emi approached Abby, hide in paw. The weaver tilted her head side to side as she made a slow circle around her new subject.

Abby could hear Emi mumbling strange words to herself. The weaver continued circling around her, increasing speed with each revolution. With a whoosh, Emi became but a blur as she sped around Abby at an incredible rate. What felt like little tugs and pokes danced along her body. *Wild, this has got to be the weirdest thing all week.* Moments later, the blur slowed and the recognizable form of Emi, panting, stood before her again.

The weaver nodded with satisfaction. *Perfect as it always is.*

Abby held her arms out and examined herself. Her jaw dropped. Except for her hiking boots, new clothing adorned her body. Sleeves to the wrist covered her arms and 'just loose enough' pants tucked neatly inside her boot tops. She rubbed her hands along her thighs. "Wow, this is super soft." Spinning around, Abby tried to examine her backside, stopping when she sensed an unusual yet familiar presence behind her neck. She reached back, her fingers meeting soft folds of animal hide. "Hey, a hood!" she cried gleefully, pulling it over her head. Abby turned to the weaver, "Thanks, Emi. I love it." Flipping the hood back from her head, she realized she still felt the weight of her backpack. She released her right arm from the strap and swung it around front. Her eyes widened at the sight. "What the..." Abby stopped herself from being impolite and marveled at her new bag. Made from the same caramel hide, it consisted of two perfectly sized, simple straps and hide drawstrings at a solitary opening for cinching it closed. "This is great," she said after checking the contents and shouldering the new bag. "But what happened to my old clothes and stuff?" she asked, looking around the chamber.

Emi huffed and wiggled her front paws. *Gone. Use no more.*

Abby crinkled her nose, then shrugged, deciding it didn't matter. She sung playfully as she whirled around to point at the Scotsman. "Your turn, Rory," she finished with a mischievous smile.

Rory scowled playfully as he traded places with Abby. She watched in fascination while Emi waddled back to her stockpile, selecting a piece with a deep, copper hue. As she did with Abby, the weaver circled the Scotsman slowly, sizing him up.

"Just hold still, Rory, Emi will be done before you know it," Abby said encouragingly, noticing him fidget.

Rory settled and, in a matter of moments, Emi's blurred form traveled so fast, Abby could catch only small glimpses of her companion. The weaver slowed to a stop, revealing Rory's new attire. As with Abby, his original boots remained, along with the scabbard given to him by Mrs. MacTavish and the small pouch containing his Talisman. Rory checked himself over, adjusting his sword and dirk. He glanced at Abby with a silly smile, then placed a hand on his hip. "What do ye think, A-by?" he asked, swinging his chin toward the ceiling.

Abby snorted at his antics. "You look great, Rory, it really does go with your hair."

Rory pulled one of his long, fiery braids over his shoulder, brought a forearm to his chest and draped the braid over it. After a moment of contemplation, he grunted with a nod, then winked at Abby.

Abby turned away, feeling her cheeks warm. "What do you think?" she said, walking over to Finlay, who had taken the liberty of curling up in Emi's nest. "We look like part of the tribe now." *And,* she continued privately, *what are you doing, fuzzface? That bed belongs to someone else.*

Finlay stood, stretched, and stepped out of the woven ring of grass. *It was empty, and she did not seem to mind,* he replied with a deep yawn before peering over the top of

Abby's head. *The boy is watching you. I believe he appreciates your new clothing.*

Oh brother. Abby rolled her eyes at the dog and scratched him lovingly under his chin. *I think I like the serious Finlay better, can I have him back please?*

Ruffling Finlay's chest, Abby turned to Wren and Rowen. "Emi is amazing. I've never seen anything like that before!"

Wren nodded. "It pleases me to hear you say so." She motioned toward the tunnel, "Come. It will be nightfall soon. Let us leave Emi, and we will show you where you may sleep."

Abby grabbed Rory's arm and pulled him along with her into the passageway. "Thanks again, Emi!" she called out over her shoulder.

Stepping into the fresh air, Abby took a moment to appreciate how pure everything smelled. "So, now what?" she asked, watching as the others exited the dome.

"We sleep, Sister," Rowen replied, bowing. "At first light we must travel to the Forest of Souls. We must see Redwin's circle completed."

Wren touched her forehead briefly to Rowen's. "Come," she said pointing to the forest line cloaked in dim light just beyond Emi's dome, "let us show you where you may take rest."

As the group walked along, Abby became lost in thought, staring at the twinkling, orange lights of the disturbed grass. Excitement filled her at the prospect of learning what 'completing one's circle' might mean, though equal uncertainties ran in circles through her mind. Why did the Great Willow talk to her, and why was she the only one able to communicate with Finlay, Guido, Riffin, and Emi? She sighed. *Talking animals is one thing, but who ever heard of a talking tree? That cannot be right!* Abby's lip quivered as she further contemplated. *Maybe something is wrong with my brain! Like, like a tumor or something.*

The gentle voice of Wren pulled Abby back to present. "Here," she said upon entering the tree line, "you may sleep in peace here." Wren stopped next to a structure identical to the upright, cocoon-shaped oddity Abby and Rory inspected earlier. "There is room for all of you." She gestured for the trio to step inside.

Abby entered, feeling a sense of calm upon passing by Wren. She relaxed and glanced around at the empty space, pleased to see more Goldenglow. "But, where do we sleep?"

Wren smiled and bowed, whispering something Abby could not hear. Moments later, roots uncoiled from the ceiling. Whirling this way and that, three hammock-like root-beds formed several feet above the ground.

"Cool! Just like in the hollow back home, guys," Abby exclaimed as she plopped down on the center bed, placing her pack on the floor. Rory followed Abby's lead, and they both watched as Finlay navigated himself awkwardly into the last bed, flopping down on his side and tucking in his legs. Soft snores emanated from the dog's hammock just as Abby thought to poke fun at him. Laughing to herself, she turned her attention to their hosts. "See you tomorrow then?" she asked, laying her head back.

Rowen tipped his head in acknowledgment, "At first light, Sister. Until then."

4

Following behind Rory and Finlay, Abby strolled into the clearing, stretching her arms high, before reaching down to run the tips of her fingers through the fuzzy grass. "Where to, Rowen?" she asked, righting herself. "You mentioned something last night about a certain forest?"

"Yes, Sister, the Forest of Souls." Rowen draped an arm over Wren's shoulder as he spoke. "It is the sacred forest of the Protectors, where those fallen give of themselves back to the lifeblood of Shay."

Abby wrinkled her face. "What exactly do you mean by lifeblood?"

Rowen raised a brow in contemplation. "The essence inside you," he said, touching his chest, "is everywhere. In the trees and plants, in all the creatures, and even the land itself. By giving ourselves back to the land, as Redwin will do, we again become one with the lifeblood. It is the strength of Shay."

Abby nodded thoughtfully. "Is the Forest of Souls far from here?"

"No, Sister, but it will take most of the day for Wren to lead you there."

"For Wren? But what about you?"

Rowen lifted his head, whistling into the sky. "Riffin and I will fly ahead. I must tell Jovan and Javani of these new happenings and prepare for Redwin's arrival."

All eyes shifted to the sky when Riffin soared into view, circling lower and lower above the group. On silent wings, the owl glided to the ground, hopping over to Rowen with a whooo-winnie.

Rowen touched foreheads with Wren. "In life and in death," they whispered to each other before he broke free to pull himself onto Riffin's back. The bird took two lengthy hops away from everyone and, with a powerful stroke of his wings, launched into the morning sky.

Wren watched the pair depart. When they were but a dark, shrinking spot over the tree line, she turned back to the trio. "Where will we find Redwin? We must hasten if we want to arrive at the Forest of Souls before nightfall."

Abby glanced at Finlay and Rory, tapping a finger on her chin. "Well," she said, "you remember where we first met?" Abby waited for Wren's acknowledging nod before continuing. "We hid him at the top of that ridge overlooking the valley."

Concern washed over Wren's face. "We must cover more ground than I anticipated. Come, we must leave at once."

As Wren turned to go, Abby reached out and gave a gentle tug to her elbow. "Wren, hold on a minute. We have a faster way."

Wren paused, turning back to Abby with curious eyes. "Oh? Why yes," she said with a smile, "I have forgotten your guide's gift is quite useful. Can Finlay take us to Redwin?"

Abby swelled with pride. "You bet. It only works if he has seen the location, and you won't believe how quick it is. That should save us a lot of time, right?"

Wren bowed her head. "Yes. The Forest of Souls is not more than a half-day's walk from where we met. Please, ask Finlay to take us there now."

"Sure thing," Abby replied, entwining her fingers with those of the Scotsman. "Just take Rory's other hand and do not let go, no matter what. As soon as I touch Finlay, close your eyes. When you open them, we will be on top of the ridge.

Wren tilted her head in understanding and held a hand out for Rory.

Satisfied everyone was ready, Abby sunk her hand into Finlay's coat. *Okay my fuzzy guide, take us to the Red King!*

***

"There he is, just like we left him." Abby motioned for Rory to help her pull the Red King from the log. "Sure hope Guido's magic is still working, otherwise we will definitely have a problem."

The pair eased Rory's kin from the fallen tree and Abby could tell by touch Guido's magic remained intact. *Whew. Thank you, giant deer.*

Wren walked around the floating body several times. Kneeling down, she placed her hands upon one of Redwin's arms and whispered just loud enough for the others to hear. "Your circle will be completed. You will be one again with the Origin." After bowing her head in silence, Wren rose and pointed away from the original path Abby and Rory had taken when first entering the canopy of monstrous plants. "Come, let us waste no time. We must get Redwin safely to the Origin. Hidden dangers may seek him out."

Abby and Rory pushed the Red King in the indicated direction, stepping over plants and moving giant leaves aside with their arms. Abby glanced at Rory, wondering if he took note of the word Wren spoke.

"Wren? What is the Origin?" Abby asked without further hesitation.

"It is the core of the Forest of Souls and is what we call the ground from which a Protector rises, falls, and rises again."

Rory glanced sideways at Abby with wide eyes. "What do ye mean, rises again? Ye do no' mean to say me kin will rise again, do ye?"

"You will see, our essence lives on in many ways."

Rory looked to Abby again and shrugged, seemingly satisfied with the answer.

With Finlay forging ahead next to Wren, his ears alert and nose in the air, the group made their way out of the concealment of greenery and into a rocky clearing. The land dropped off to their right, a precipitous, unforgiving slope of jagged rocks and large boulders. To their left, a pathway no wider than six feet skirted along a steep rise of burnt orange dirt streaked with rocky veins.

Wren pointed toward the pathway, which curved to the left and out of sight. "Come, we must take extra care with our footfalls." Leading the way, she directed Abby and Rory to walk in single file with Redwin between them.

Abby opted to push the floating remains from behind. She peered carefully over the drop-off to her right and cringed. *A long way down.*

Bringing up the rear, Finlay used his muzzle to shift Abby to the left, closer to the safety of the wall. *Indeed, child. And you would be smart to keep your eyes and feet forward.*

Yeah, yeah. I was only taking a peek. I have no desire to add death by falling from a cliff to my plans today.

Finlay loomed over Abby's shoulder, snorting in her ear. *Focus, lass, that is all I ask.*

Abby shut out the wolfhound, knowing he was right. She moved her eyes from her feet, to the path, to Rory and back.

"Hold!" Wren cried after rounding a tight curve.

Rory released his grip on the Red King and stepped forward to peer around the bend. He turned back immediately to meet Abby's eyes, a frown on his face.

"What is it, Rory?"

Wren appeared by the Scotsman's side as he explained. "Rubble blocks part of the path beyond the bend, A-by. There is no' much room for safe travel," he said, with his hands raised to either side, showing a reduced walkway of one foot.

Wren nodded at Rory's description. "It appears a section of the wall has broken free and slid onto the path. The debris is too high to step over," she added, holding a hand at her waist to indicate the pile's height. "We must pass to its side."

Abby frowned, "Well do you think we can still get by?"

Wren considered the group before responding. "Yes. But all must move with true steps. Once past, we will soon find ourselves on a descent into the forest below."

"Okay then." Abby eased around the others to see the obstacle for herself, "We obviously need to go one by one."

"Come," Wren said, turning back and disappearing around the bend.

Abby waited for Rory to maneuver his kin, allowing him to take control of the body by the feet. She watched as he pushed the Red King around the curve, then followed close behind.

Wren stepped gracefully along the narrowed way, not once hesitating. After reaching safety, she stopped and turned around, motioning for Rory to send the body toward her.

Rory paused to examine their surroundings. With a grunt, he raised the Red King upward to clear the crumbled pile of dirt and rocks and eased his kin forward through the air.

Wren grabbed the body's shoulders and stepped slowly backward toward the safety of the wall. Once far enough away, she brought Redwin to a rest and gestured for the others to join her.

Rory craned his neck back at Abby. "I shall help ye across, A-by, once I find safe ground for meself."

Abby stopped herself from rolling her eyes at the young man's chivalry. Giving him a smile instead, she shooed Rory forward with her fingers.

With two long, sure strides, Rory cleared the impediment, stepped closer to the wall, and turned to lean against the pile. He stretched his left hand out, offering it as stability to Abby.

Ignoring Rory initially, she glanced to her right at the rough ledge, then to the narrowed path in front of her.

Finlay nudged Abby gently in the back. *Across with you, child. Hold your pride and take the boy's hand.*

Okay, okay, she groaned, reaching out with her left arm to accept Rory's assistance. Just as Abby's fingers brushed the Scotsman's and she placed a foot in the constricted lane, the upper rock face shook violently. Without warning, a second slab of burnt orange dirt dropped to the ground, landing atop the first, sending a spray of debris and rock chips into the air. The impact sent a rush of dirt flowing toward the escarpment.

Abby gasped, watching the debris stream straight at her. "Ahhh!" She flailed her hands at Rory, unable to clamp onto him in her frenzy.

"A-by!" Rory cried out when the dirt slammed into her legs and swept her from her feet.

No, no, no! Abby screamed inside as the flow sent her over the edge.

Finlay roared, crouching and snapping at her hood, teeth clamping on teeth as he missed his mark.

Abby grunted when her back scraped along the jagged rock face, sending a wave of pain through her body. She looked below, panicked to find less than ten steep feet between her and the unknown. She tensed her core muscles and flipped herself over. Clawing at the bluff, she scrambled to gain a hold of any kind. Her body slid to a momentary stop alongside a boulder. Draping her left arm over it and laying her cheek against the dirt, she let out a deep breath. In response to frantic shouts of her name, Abby looked up to see three sets of panicked eyes watching her. As she took notice of the burning throb along her spine, she flipped a hand in the air. "I, I think I am okay, guys. But hurry, pull me up, there's no way I can climb this."

Though Wren and Rory disappeared from view, Abby could hear animated voices debating possible solutions. Abby laid her cheek against the cool dirt again and readjusted her grasp on the large rock. She winced at the painful pulsation in her back. The soothing feeling of Finlay reaching out to her filled her mind.

Remain still, lass. We will find a way to bring you to safety.

Abby closed her eyes and concentrated on her connection with her guide. *I'd tell you to zap yourself down here so I could grab on to you, but seeing how you are now the size of a horse, that probably wouldn't be a good idea. It's way too steep. Don't need you sliding to your doom too.*

Finlay snorted from above. *Glad to see your spark remains even during dire times. Now give your attention to the boy and talk him from what crazy idea he seems to be brewing.*

With effort, Abby lifted her head again. Rory laid on the ground, hanging the upper half of his body over the ledge. He stretched his arm as low as possible as if testing the distance.

"Rory, what on earth are you doing? You can't reach me like that," Abby croaked.

Rory furrowed his brow, letting out a sigh as he shimmied back from the ledge and stood. "We have no rope, A-by. I do no' know what else to do."

"We may have no rope, but a fallen tree branch should offer the same solution, should it not?" Wren contemplated. "Come," she said to Rory, "let us descend quickly to the forest floor."

Indecision filled Rory's face. A low rumbling cut him short just as he replied.

"Not again," Abby cried, feeling the ridge vibrate. She gulped hard as the boulder to which she clung shifted. Moments later the shaking stopped and Abby exhaled with relief. Calming her nerves, she reexamined her predicament, estimating the distance from the rock to her companions. *Maybe if I get on top of the rock and stand on it while leaning against the slope, I might be close enough for Rory to reach me.* Abby nodded to herself, knowing she needed to be proactive. She scooted closer to the boulder, then turned her body so she could hook both arms around it.

"A-by, what are ye doin'?"

Abby grunted as she pulled herself up. "Getting on top so I can stand on it. I think you can reach me then."

Finlay paced along the ledge. *Child, this is not a wise decision. Please, lower yourself for a moment.* He paused and looked back in the direction they came from. *Perhaps I can find a fallen limb to use in place of a rope as our companion has suggested.*

Abby continued pushing herself into a standing position atop the rock while leaning against the ridge. *It will be fine, trust me.*

"Okay, Rory, see if you can reach me now," she hollered, stretching to her tiptoes.

The Scotsman scrambled to lower himself, motioning for Wren to grab his ankles as he scooted over the edge.

Abby raised both arms over her head as high as she could, turning her head to the side. "Am I high enough?" she groaned, unable to see Rory's position.

Rory wiggled himself even further over the edge. "Just a few more inches, A-by."

Abby relaxed her arms for a moment and with a second effort, stretched as high as she could. She sensed the warmth of Rory's fingers close to her own. *Just a little higher.* She grunted and stretched but to no avail. *Maybe I can jump and grab his hand.* With this thought, Abby lowered her feet, flexed her knees, and pushed off from the rock with all her might. When she still could not connect with Rory, she realized her error. The moment the tips of her boots landed back on the boulder, it began to wobble. Abby looked down in horror. Dirt around the base of the rock started skittering away. She gulped, turning herself around for a better view. *Not good! Not good!* Before she could consider her options, gravity decided for her. The rock eased away from the wall, sliding slowly toward the inevitable drop off. Abby balanced precariously, her heart pounding in her ears. As the rock continued to pick up speed, it slammed into another boulder of greater proportions, causing the smaller rock to stop abruptly, pitching Abby upward toward the edge. She landed on her back with a thud. Realizing she had not plummeted over the edge, she lifted her head and looked to either side. A small, level outcropping supported her body. She sighed, choking back hysterical laughter, when a sudden grating demanded her attention. She twisted her head in search of the source, her fear renewed upon finding it. A section of the second rock split off and tumbled toward her. "No!" she screamed, folding her arms over her head. The rogue fragment smashed down onto Abby's left leg with a sickening crunch and lodged there.

A blinding flash of pain consumed Abby, the roars and screams from above only distant whispers to her fading consciousness. She tried to open her eyes but instead succumbed to a wave of blackness.

***

"Amaray."

Abby twitched at the comforting sound.

"Amaray, free yourself. You must complete the circle."

Abby's eyes flickered open to a sea of white mist. "Wha, what?" she groaned. Taking in the smoggy void, Abby realized she felt no pain. She whirled around in recognition. "Hey, wait a minute," she drawled. "I am not seriously back here again, wherever here is."

"Amaray, free yourself," came the wispy voice again.

Abby spun around. "Hey! Who are you? Where are you?"

Silent moments ticked by causing Abby to fill with frustration.

"Amaray, use the power surrounding you."

Abby moved as if to stomp her foot, only then realizing she could feel no ground. "Why do you keep calling me Amaray? My name is Abby. Abby Fletcher."

The voice responded with more urgency.

"Amaray. You must free yourself. Use the power within you."

Abby continued to whirl around in search of the owner of the mysterious voice. She sighed when all remained silent. "Great. Alone again with no way out. And what the heck did she mean to use the power within me?" Abby snorted at herself. "This girl is no magician!"

Turning full circle again, she could see nothing through the mist. *Finlay!* She screamed mentally as loud as possible. "Rory! Wren! Where are you guys?"

Holding back a whimper, Abby drew a slow breath in, releasing it just the same. *Okay, get a grip, Abby and calm down.* Feeling herself relax, she contemplated the words of the unknown voice. *She said I have to free myself using the power around and within me. Makes no sense, but maybe I can will myself back into my body somehow.*

Abby slowed her breathing even more. *In through the nose, out through the mouth.* She repeated the mantra over and over while imagining herself laid out on the rocky outcrop once again. As the vision dominated her mind, a familiar voice called out to her.

"A-by! A-by!"

Abby focused solely on Rory's voice. When pain erupted in her leg, she gasped at the sudden intrusion, only to feel a swift pull to her midsection. In that moment, everything went black.

***

"Ahhh!" Abby shrieked, opening her eyes to a blue sky. She lifted her head to examine her lower body, her view filled by the large rock pinning her leg. Thumping her head back with a whimper, she panted and tried to search out her companions.

Rory squatted atop the ledge, both hands tugging at his long braids. "A-by! I will come for ye and move the stone from yer leg."

Wren gave a gentle touch to his shoulder. "We will find a way, Rory, but you must stay where you are."

"But..." Rory disputed, stopping short when Wren squeezed his shoulder.

"Do you hear it?" Wren asked, focusing her attention to their left.

A distant, rhythmic thumping echoed along the ridge, gaining intensity with every passing moment. As the source drew near, the recognizable din of hooves pounding the dirt took shape.

Abby struggled to put a name to the noise. *Is that a horse?* She twisted her head to the side and back, straining to look upwards to her right over the ledge. To her surprise, the massive form of a deer slowed to a stop and peered at her with a snort.

"Guido?" Abby called out as she relaxed her neck, confused by his presence. She gasped, a sudden realization filling her mind. "Guido! Lift this rock off my leg," she pleaded. "Please, it's killing me."

Guido swayed his enormous antlers side to side. *I cannot.*

Abby scowled. "What do you mean you can't? Of course you can. Please, hurry," she cried as a wave of pain washed over her.

Guido lowered his head and stared at Abby. *Must touch. I cannot.*

"You have to touch the stupid rock?" Abby groaned, trying to focus. "Well, of course, that figures." She propped herself up on her elbows, wincing at the reminder of the wounds along her back. She glared at the rock. Frustration boiled in her veins. Pushing herself into a seated position, she cried out at the movement as she leaned forward and pounded both hands on the heavy stone. "Get off me!" she screamed, tears welling in her eyes. Abby placed her palms on the rock and shoved with what little energy remained in her beaten body. Realizing her efforts were useless, she bowed her head and closed her eyes, willing herself not to break down into a sobbing mess. As she concentrated on her respiration, a strange tingling danced along her fingertips. Abby snapped her head up and opened her eyes. "What the..." she whispered, not believing the sight before her.

A whirling, yellow glow surrounded the stone. Abby pulled her hands away as it lifted into the air. "Guido? How did you do that! You said you had to touch it," she questioned, staring up at the deer in disbelief.

Not me. You.

Abby snorted, suppressing a deep laugh. "What? That's crazy. Of course you did it," she challenged.

Guido replied with a silent stare and tilt of the head.

Abby turned back to the hovering stone, thinking about what the mysterious voice had insisted. *The power within me?* Abby shook her head. *No, that can't be true, can it? How could I have Guido's power?*

Rory's voice disrupted Abby's contemplation. "A-by. Move the stone from yer leg."

Abby nodded in response. *Don't care how this thing started floating, better take advantage in case whoever did this changes their mind.* With a gentle push, the stone bobbed away through the air, releasing Abby from her prison.

"Can ye move yer leg, A-by?"

"I'm not sure, let me try." Abby grimaced as she inspected it. "I think I'm going to be sick. Pretty sure I see bone sticking out." Feeling nauseous, she lowered herself back once more. "I, I can't. Just give me a minute here." Abby laid in silence for several minutes, focusing on her breathing, pushing the frenzied whispers from above into the background. She opened her eyes when a cheerful singing pushed its way into her mind.

Weave, weave, stitch, stitch, la-la-la, fix, fix...

"Emi?" Abby whispered, wondering how she could hear the Weaver.

Because I brought her here, child.

Abby wrinkled her brow as she lifted her head enough to see Finlay and Emi filling the path overhead. *What? Why did you do that, fuzzface?*

Wren insisted I bring the Weaver here at once. She believes Emi can be of assistance, though how, I know not.

Abby closed her eyes again. *Well she better assist away, I feel like I might pass out.*

"Abby," Wren called out in a soothing voice, "Emi will bring you back to us, but please, do your best to hold still."

"I really don't see how..." Abby quit talking when she heard a strange noise coming from beyond the drop off. She rolled her head to the left, uncertain of the sound. She glanced quickly back to the top of the ridge, disquiet in her eyes. Emi sat on the ledge, rolled back on her haunches. The Weaver moved her forepaws back and forth in the air, akin to an orchestra conductor. Abby could hear her humming a tune.

A soft scratching pulled Abby's attention back to the cliff's edge. She quivered as a mass of vines appeared, slithering into the air from some unknown place, hovering over her. Realizing she lacked the ability to escape, Abby stiffened her body in response. *Oh man, what now?*

Emi's singing streamed into Abby's mind. *Weave, weave, stitch, stitch, gentle plant please fix, fix.*

Tension released from Abby's core. *Okay, not going to freak out. The creepy vines are here to help. Just hold still and see what happens.*

One by one, individual processes slipped free from the undulating tangle of growth. The tip of each thick vine prodded Abby randomly with a gentle touch. Lifting back into the air, the vines seemed to nod at one another as if connected by collective thought. Abby flinched when two by two they wriggled underneath her body, only to pop out the other side and wrap themselves over her, creating a swaddle-like structure.

Abby shifted her eyes to find Emi. The Weaver lifted her forepaws into the air once the vines secured their creation. Following Emi's silent directive, the plants rose from the outcropping, lifting Abby high above the slope. Placing her gently on the ground near the Red King, the vines unraveled themselves from Abby's body and slithered away out of sight.

Rory rushed to her side. "Oh, A-by," he said, staring in horror at her leg. "It must pain ye so."

Abby let out a misery-laced laugh. "I've definitely had better days." She closed her eyes and gulped down the grotesque feeling in her stomach. "Heal me, Rory, use your sword. Please, I can't take this much longer."

Rory jumped to his feet, determination in his eyes. Stepping back, he unsheathed his sword. "I will no' see ye in such pain!" he exclaimed valiantly.

To Abby's surprise, the instant the blade pulled free, the stone secured in the hilt pulsed a blazing yellow, brighter than she could ever recall. A swath of light blasted from its center and encompassed Abby's prone form. She shielded her eyes and noticed a warmth wrapping around her. As the glow increased, the pain assaulting her body lessened until it became only fragments of a bad memory. The healing shroud around her blocked out all but a single sound. Abby furrowed her brow and lifted her head.

"Amaray."

Abby's eyes lit up in recognition. "Please, tell me who you are."

"Amaray, you must break my binding chains."

"Your binding chains? Has someone kidnapped you?"

"Free me, Amaray..." said the ethereal voice as it trailed to silence.

"How can I free you if I don't even know who you are?"

Abby sighed when no further response met her ears. Sitting herself up, she watched as the yellow radiance dissipated, fading its way back to the amulet. Abby whipped her head toward Rory. "Rory! I..." she stopped short, running her hands all along her body. "You...you did it!" She jumped up, putting full pressure on her once crushed leg.

Rory smiled as he returned his sword to its scabbard. "Are ye sure, A-by? Yer pain is no more?"

Abby hopped up and down, then twisted her midsection side to side. "Good as new," she replied, walking toward the Scotsman. "I don't know how you do it, Rory, but," she paused, wrapping her arms around him impulsively, "you are one amazing Mr. Medieval, as my sister, Sage, would say." Releasing her arms, she stretched to kiss his cheek. "My hero," she said with an exaggerated flutter of her eyelashes.

Rory's face flushed a bright red upon the touch of Abby's lips to his skin. "Is nothin'," he replied, clearing his throat. "No need to thank me, A-by. Ye know I will always do me best to see no harm comes to ye," he finished, breaking into a sheepish smile and staring at the ground.

Abby stepped back and smoothed her hair, not knowing how to respond. Her stomach fluttered as Rory stared at her with strange intensity. "Thanks," she managed to choke out.

"And thanks to you," she continued quickly, throwing herself on her dog, "for bringing Emi here to save me."

Finlay nuzzled into Abby's side. *It seemed the only reasonable option. I too, child, want no harm to come to you. And I could not fulfill that want myself this time.*

Abby straightened up and gazed into the wolfhound's eyes. *It wasn't your fault, Finlay. I'm the klutz that didn't pay attention and take the situation seriously enough. You're always telling me to think before I speak. Now I know I need to think before I move too. I could have died...*

You are destined for great things, lass. It will take far greater forces to bring you to your end. Now, he continued, licking Abby's cheek, *do not be a rude young one...thank the Weaver for keeping you from an ill fate.*

Abby sighed at herself, realizing Emi should have been the first she thanked. Giving Finlay one last stroke to his coat, she turned around to search for the Weaver. "Hey," she called out, surprised, "where'd Emi go? I need to thank her."

"Emi has already returned for Willow Wood," Wren said with a slight bow.

"Oh," Abby replied with a frown, "well, guess I'll thank her later. How did she do that anyway, the thing with the vines?"

"Emi has a deep connection with the land. Not only does she have the gift to create from that which has completed its circle, she is also connected to the living. The plants do freely as she asks of them."

"Huh, cool. Well, thanks then, Wren, for sending Finlay to get her," Abby said with a genuine smile. "I don't want to think about what would have happened otherwise."

Wren bowed again. "You are one with the Manta tribe. We go to great lengths to help our own." She stared at the hilt of Rory's sword, a deep contemplation in her eyes. "Come, we must lose no more time in completing Redwin's circle. Let us hasten our journey to the Forest of Souls. The others await us."

5

Abby stood in awe. Everything about the land of Shay seemed so foreign, yet so beautiful. The Forest of Souls, or what she assumed to see in the distance as the group maneuvered their way out from under dense cover, was no exception. The ground sloped downward and, on either side ahead of them, a body of water pressed in, creating a narrow isthmus leading to the Forest. From her vantage, Abby guessed their destination centered itself on a broad peninsula jutting into either an ocean or large lake.

"Rowen." Wren's face lit up as she looked to the sky, tracking a dark figure circling above. "Come, we are nearly there. Let us quicken our pace, there may be Thraxen about."

Abby glanced at Rory with wide eyes, mouthing the word 'Thraxen' to him.

Rory raised his hands and shrugged in response.

"Uh, Wren," Abby offered, "if you're still worried about the Red King's safety, now that we see where we're going, Finlay could always take us there."

Wren nodded to Abby. "Yes, of course. Your guide's ability is a new presence to us. I must do better to remember his gift when we are in need."

Abby intertwined her fingers with Rory's. "You guys each put a hand on the Red King. And Wren, you put your other hand on Guido," she directed, looking around with confusion. "Where'd that deer go to now?" Not seeing the stag, she snorted. "Always with the disappearing."

Wren tossed her head back with a light laugh. "Yes, that seems to be his way. As his name says, he is a forest guide. He saw us through, so I imagine he felt his duty completed."

Abby shook her head with a smile. "Okay then, guess we don't really need his help anymore," she said, sinking her hand into Finlay's coat. "Everybody hold tight." Abby massaged Finlay's skin with her fingers. *Whenever you're ready.*

The group stood at the outskirts of the Forest of Souls. A whooo-winnie sounded behind them and they turned to see Riffin glide to a hopping stop. Rowen dismounted, ruffled the feathers on the owl's chest, and pointed to the sky. "Patrol," he said with a stern voice and curt nod. "Brothers, Sister," he continued, opening his arms wide as he approached. He slowed to a stop in front of the floating body, inspecting it from head to toe. "You have brought Redwin home to us." His voice softened when he spoke again. "The Manta will be forever grateful." The Protector kneeled next to the body and bowed his head. "My King, may your completion help heal the land," he whispered.

Wren took Rowen's hand as he rose, their eyes sharing secret thoughts. "Come," she motioned into the forest, "we must begin the ceremony."

Abby watched as their new friends walked hand in hand into the forest. *Not as many trees as I was expecting, and not much of a forest really. But these are the coolest trees I've ever seen.* A sparse number of trees speckled the way ahead, connected into a random framework by more of the strange, orange grass. Though few, the trees filled Abby with a sense of awe as she looked from tree to tree; their shape and size reminded her of most any other tree back home. The colors, however, did not. "Whoa," Abby whispered as they passed one with deep, blue bark and equally blue leaves. In the distance to the right stretched a tree of bright orange, with leaves of similar hue and, to the left, one looking as if it were made of crystal. But then Abby's eyes crossed a spot in the landscape which gave her pause. A gnarled shape, black as a starless night, bent low to the ground.

"Um, guys," Abby said, pointing, "what happened to that one? That is a tree, isn't it?"

Wren and Rowen shared a frown.

"Yes, Sister, you are correct," Rowen replied, his expression somber. "It belonged to the predecessor of Pixius."

"Oh," Abby said, feeling a bit ignorant. "Sooo, what happened to it? Was there a fire or something?"

Rowen shook his head. "No, Sister, the Thraxen destroyed it."

"Well I don't know what the Thraxen are, but I bet Pixius was pretty mad, huh?"

Rowen's head tipped forward with a deep sigh. "That I wish I could say yes to."

Abby scrunched her brow. "I don't get it."

Wren stepped forward and wrapped an arm around Rowen's waist, giving him a gentle squeeze. "Abby, when a tree dies in the Forest of Souls, so falls the Protector that is one with it."

"Wait, so you mean Pixius died when the tree died?"

Wren replied with a nod.

"I'm sorry," Abby said, imagining herself removing her foot from her mouth. "What do you mean by a Protector being one with the tree?"

Wren smiled at Abby's inquisitive nature. "This is something you will come to understand soon enough when Redwin's circle is completed."

"Oh, well, can I ask though," Abby paused with uncertainty, "what exactly is a Thraxen?"

Abby studied Wren's face when she delayed her response. "What's the matter, Wren?"

Wren squeezed Rowen's waist again and stole a deep breath as she composed her thoughts. "There is much to teach you all, Abby, but for now know the Thraxen are evil creatures, which have infested our land since the time of Redwin. Their sole purpose seems to be destroying the Manta tribe."

Abby glanced at Rory, noting the anger in his eyes and the veins bulging in his arm as he gripped the hilt of his sword.

"Show me where these creatures hide. I shall help ye be rid of them!" Rory exclaimed, readjusting the grip on his sword.

Rowen clapped a hand on Rory's shoulder. "In due time, Brother, we will fight side by side to do as you say.

But for now," he nodded his head toward Rory's kin, "we must complete Redwin's circle. Only then will we have the strength."

A rumble of thundering hooves broke through the conversation. Rory whirled around to locate the source of the noise and, with his left arm, pushed Abby behind him while he drew his sword with his right. Finlay crouched low with a growl when two dark forms appeared from deeper into the forest.

"Brothers, please," Rowen said, motioning for Rory to lower his sword, "do not be alarmed, the Protectors of the Forest come to join us for Redwin's final journey."

Abby watched as Finlay stretched to his full height and paced. She could feel uncertainty flow through him. *Relax, Finlay. Rowen says there's nothing to worry about. I think by now we can trust him.*

Finlay continued to pace but with a slower stride. *This may be so, young one, but my gut tells me something is amiss. There is an unease in my bones, but from what I cannot say. Just stay alert.*

Abby nudged Rory in the side as he sheathed his sword. "Hey," she whispered, "Finlay says something doesn't feel right to him. We need to keep our eyes open."

Rory tightened his brow and nodded with a grunt.

The speedy forms of two colossal horses with riders sitting tall came into focus. As they neared the group, the horses slowed to a trot. Abby exchanged looks with Rory, both their mouths agape. She shifted her gaze back to the approaching strangers, finding herself filled with wonder. The horses stopped several yards away, stamping their feet and snorting as the riders pulled back on their reins. Large, defined muscles rippled beneath their black, iridescent coats. Their manes and tails flowed in such a manner, Abby wanted to reach out and run her fingers through them. *They don't make horses like this back home.*

Shifting her attention from the animals, she examined their handlers. A man and woman of equal height both dismounted their steeds, jumping to the ground from what Abby estimated to be an easy eight feet from the horses' withers. Strange, earth-colored armor similar to Rowen's covered their clothing, which Abby understood now must be typical of the Manta tribe. *Wonder if Emi made theirs too.*

The riders turned in unison as Rowen stepped forward to clasp forearms with each of them. "Jovan, Javani, meet our new sister and brothers, Abby, Rory, and Finlay."

The newcomers bowed. "Welcome," they said in unison.

Abby smiled in return, then studied the forest Protectors' features. *They must be twins. Same thick, copper hair and, hey, she has a golden curl too!* She backed away from the Red King to make room when they both approached his remains from either side.

Jovan gazed at the body. "It is true then."

"Redwin has come home," Javani finished.

A soft nickering floated through Abby's mind. *Redwin has returned,* said a husky voice. *Hurry, hurry, complete his circle, Thraxen are near,* insisted a second.

Abby gasped, drawing all eyes to her.

Wren tilted her head. "Abby?" She followed Abby's line of sight to the horses. "Abby, have Tiffa and Daylo spoken to you?" she asked knowingly.

Abby darted her eyes from horse to horse, then scanned over both her shoulders. "Thraxen. One of them said the Thraxen are here."

Movement flashed all around Abby as the Protectors drew their weapons.

Rowen sounded a piercing whistle as he looked to the sky.

Rory turned his back to the Red King and pushed Abby behind him. Her body tensed as she watched everyone position themselves in a protective barrier around Rory's kin.

Finlay squatted to Rory's right, working the air with his nose.

Abby called out to her white warrior. *Hey! You picking up on anything?*

Besides our natural surroundings, I smell nothing other than humans and horse-stink, he grumbled back. *Perhaps the beasts are mistaken, lass.*

Abby thought she detected a hint of jealousy in her dog's words toward Tiffa and Daylo. "Wren," she whispered, taking a step to her left and leaning in. "Finlay says he doesn't smell anything weird, and I don't see anything. What do the Thraxen look like?"

"Most are tall and slender with strange, glimmering bodies. They remind us of giant, human-like insects, but you are unlikely to see them until the moment they attack."

"How come? Are they like ninjas or something?"

Wren frowned at her friend, confusion in her eyes. "I do not know this word, Abby, but they possess magic. They can control the air around them, making themselves unseen or tricking you into seeing a falsehood."

Abby groaned to herself. *Oh great! Magical insects. What next? Flying pigs that spew fire?*

Wren glanced around the group. "Let us all be silent and become one with the Forest. If the Thraxen are here, they will come for Redwin. We must protect him at all costs."

The forest fell quiet as everyone heeded Wren's words. Abby strained her ears, hoping the horses were wrong and no cries of attack would sound. She could see Riffin soaring quietly overhead in circles.

Wren sidestepped toward Rowen, tapped his shoulder, and pointed toward a purple tree off to the right, thirty feet away. "Arrow," she whispered.

Rowen nodded and notched an arrow, taking his time to aim.

Abby peered at the tree, unable to see anything. "Hey, Wren, what's he doing? Can you see something?"

"Rowen is keeper of the Stone of Illusion. An arrow fired near any magical presence will reveal its true form."

"Cool," Abby murmured to herself as Rowen let loose the arrow.

The missile cut through the air and sank into the ground near the base of the tree.

For several moments nothing appeared to happen, but then Abby saw it. "Whoa, what's going on?"

The air, the ground, the tree — anything near the arrow — wavered slowly until a crouched shape took form.

Without warning, the creature hissed and sprang into the air, flipping gracefully in a tucked ball before landing ten feet from the group. Abby's knees locked, though instinctively she wanted nothing more than to put as much distance as possible between her and the unthinkable 'thing' staring back at them. Its sinewy, human-like body shimmered, covered by an opal, form-fitting material Abby could not identify. It tipped its head up, directing several strange and intense clicking noises into the air. Lowering its gaze again, it locked its multiple eyes on Abby. She cringed as the creature blinked one set, then a second, each pair shifting between random colors.

Finlay's ominous growl rumbled next to Abby, triggering the Thraxen to draw a weapon from seemingly nowhere. In that moment, a shock of realization slapped Abby in the face. Its claw-like hand gripped the handle of a sickle-shaped blade. A blade not unfamiliar to Abby. "I don't believe it," she blurted, "Mallena is a Thraxen?"

The creature tilted its head. "Mallena," it buzzed with adoration, "our leader will reward me well when I sing to her the glory of my doing this day. The day Redwin meets his final death."

Rory pointed his sword at the Thraxen, "Ye shall do no harm to me kin, no' on this day or any to follow."

The insectoid sprang forward, twirling its blade in front of it. "Death to all Manta filth!"

As it landed, Rowen and Wren fired several arrows in quick succession. The Thraxen jumped back and to its right, dodging the assault narrowly. With a hissing screech, it whirled its blade, tossing it from hand to hand in dramatic show, oblivious to the enormous horse somehow creeping up behind it.

With her long strides, Tiffa covered the distance quickly. When in range, she turned her backside toward the Thraxen and delivered a powerful, bone-crushing kick, sending the creature face first into the ground.

Jovan and Javani capitalized on the Thraxen's compromised position. They leaped forward in unison, driving the tips of their broadswords deep into the insect's torso. A shrill and surprised scream filled the forest, then the Thraxen went silent. Pulling their blades free with a wet tug, the twins wiped the accompanying blue goo off using the creature's body suit.

Jovan sneered at the body with disgust as he sheathed his sword. "I will remove this beast from our sacred ground," he said, picking up the limp remains and throwing them over a shoulder. He motioned for Tiffa. "Well done, girl," he said, stroking her muzzle. She bowed, bending the knee of one leg to afford Jovan an easier mount with the extra weight he carried. Sliding onto her back, he sat tall, the Thraxen now laid across his lap. "I have no doubt more Thraxen lurk near the Forest. Make haste and complete Redwin's circle. Do not wait for me." With a nod to Javani, he patted Tiffa's side. She neighed and took off into a purposeful gallop.

"Come," Wren tipped her head at Rory, "you must choose Redwin's final resting place."

Rory sheathed his sword with a frown. "Is a great honor ye bestow on me, but..." he trailed off.

"But what? What is your worry, Rory?"

The Scotsman glanced uneasily at Wren. "What if I do no' choose correctly? How shall I know where me kin should rest?"

Wren smiled, her eyes filled with warmth. "You will know. The land will guide you. Come, we should waste no more time."

Rory straightened as he looked to Abby. "Help me push, A-by?"

"You betcha. Where to?"

Rory scanned the trees in the distance, spotting one with rosy leaves, "That way," he said, bucking his head toward it as his lips formed into a confident smile.

Hopping on Daylo's back, Javani nodded. "We will scout ahead," she said before urging the horse into a trot.

Finlay trailed behind as Rory and Abby pushed the Red King toward the rosy tree.

Wren stepped in line next to Abby, touching her elbow. "Abby, how do you know Mallena? Did she cross into the Other?"

Abby wrinkled her nose. "Guess I didn't mention her name when recounting our story to you and Rowen, did I? She's the one who kidnapped my dad and then stole the Book of Shay. She and that dirty rat Aillig came through the portal with it."

Wren stared ahead, lost in thought.

Abby tried catching her attention with her eyes. "Is it bad that Mallena has the book? It doesn't have some magical secrets or something, does it? I mean, all we could see in it was a bunch of pictures of different plants and animals. We tried reading it but it was in some weird language."

Wren pulled her gaze from the nearest tree to look at Abby. "It is said the book contains all the secrets of the land, but no one knows for sure. So long as Mallena does not destroy it, the book's contents will remain safe."

Abby squinted at her companion. "I don't get it. How can the secrets remain safe if Mallena has it?"

"Because there is only one person in Shay who can read it. Its creator."

"Oh. Well, shouldn't we get the book back and give it to them then?"

Wren stared at the ground for several paces before answering. "The book's creator is gone. She disappeared mysteriously long ago. It remains a great loss. Without her, the land continues to weaken.

Abby tightened her lips. "But shouldn't we try to find her then if it would help the land?"

Wren glanced at Redwin's remains. "I am afraid she has suffered the same fate as he."

"Oh, you mean she probably died hundreds of years ago? I see. So, what was her name?"

"The Manta revere her as the Keeper of the Land, but she is also known as the Red Queen."

***

Abby's stomach lurched, and she was certain she felt her eyes pop from their sockets. "The Red Queen?" she whispered back.

Abby watched as Wren remained quiet, staring off into the distance. She groaned to herself, a million questions running through her mind, but she opted for silence. *Concentrate on the task at hand, Abby, there will be time for questions later.* Nodding to herself, Abby focused her thoughts back to pushing the Red King's body.

When they neared their destination after several minutes, Rory paused.

Abby glanced sideways at him. "Something wrong?"

The Scotsman shook his head as he surveyed the forest. "There." He pointed to a barren area fifty yards beyond the rosy tree. "Me kin should be there."

"Well done, Rory," Wren said, "come, let us begin."

The group trekked to the spot of choice, their feet causing the orange grass to put on a glowing display with each step.

Rory eased the Red King to a stop. "What shall ye have me do, Wren?"

Wren studied the floating body with a frown. "We must dispatch of Guido's magic before we can complete Redwin's circle. I should have considered this sooner."

Abby rolled her eyes with a moan. "Great. No telling where that deer is. He's probably miles away from here."

Wren dipped her head. "True. But there may be another way."

Abby eyed her new friend. "What you got in mind?"

"Rory, Javani," Wren directed, "push Redwin's body down until it touches the ground. Be gentle, but make sure he stays there." Wren circled the body while Rory and his fellow Protector squatted, doing as she asked. "Good. Now, Abby, please join them and place your hands on Redwin's chest."

Abby raised an eyebrow but did as asked, curious as to where Wren's plan would lead.

"Excellent. Now Abby, I want you to imagine reaching out to Guido and making a connection with him."

Abby snorted disbelief. "Uh, okay, how's that supposed to help anything?"

Finlay's voice rumbled through Abby's mind. *Do as she asks, child, she knows more of this land and its magic than either of us. It is unwise for us to waste any further time. Open your mind. And please, lass, think before you speak.*

Abby sighed as she glanced up at Wren. "Sorry, didn't mean to be rude."

Wren nodded, her expression hiding all emotion. "Close your eyes and concentrate. Hear his voice in your mind. Feel his magic flowing around Redwin. Then imagine removing it."

Abby attempted a serious face before closing her eyes. *Remove Guido's magic? I can't do that, why is she even asking me to try? She should tell Rory to do it, he has the magical stones, after all.* Abby peeked to her left at Rory, surprised to find him staring at her with a slight smile. The intensity in his eyes caused a rapid flush of heat to roll across her cheeks. She clamped her eye shut again and tipped her head toward the body. *Okay, get a grip, ignore the cute boy. Wren is counting on you, you could at least try.*

Taking in a deep breath, Abby fixated on the feel of the ancient remains brushing against her hands. She imagined the sound of the deer's voice in her head. She cringed, recalling how the first time he communicated with her she thought her brain would explode from the pain. *But when he talked to me here in Shay, it didn't hurt at all, it was just like talking to Finlay. Huh...*

Next, she shifted her thoughts to watching his magic materialize for the first time; the swirl of yellow spinning faster and faster. *Uh, what's that?* A tingling sensation danced along her fingertips. *No way. Is, is that his magic I'm feeling? That's impossible!* Abby focused on the feeling, allowing it to consume her hands. *Okay, that's definitely his floaty magic, it's got to be, but how am I supposed to turn it off? I don't even know how he makes it.*

A new thought came to Abby. *Hmm, when Rory uses the golden drop to heal, the magic gets sucked back into the stone when he's done. Maybe I can suck the magic up through my hands and send it back to Guido with my mind.* Abby snorted at herself. *That's got to be one of the dumbest ideas I've come up with yet. But...I've got to try something, I can feel everyone staring at me!*

Abby exhaled slowly then beckoned the magic supporting the Red King into her hands. She squeezed her face tight from the effort and found herself gasping when the tingling in her fingers moved into her arms before flooding her entire body. She pictured the deer in her mind, willing his magic back to him. A wave of dizziness washed over her and she fell back with surprise, landing on her bottom. Abby continued to keep her eyes closed as she tried to work out what had just happened.

"A-by, ye did it, ye did it!"

Abby jumped at the sound of Rory's voice, flicking her eyes open. "No way," she whispered to herself when she saw no yellow glow surrounding the body of the Red King. She stood and raised her hands in front of her, stunned at the possibility. "I don't believe it! Did I really just do magic?"

"Every Manta bears a unique gift, perhaps this is yours Abby," Wren said warmly, "but let us think on this later. Because of you, we may now complete Redwin's journey." She turned full circle, searching the trees nearby. "I sense no immediate danger, but this could change at any moment. Come, Rory, the time is now."

Rory squared his shoulders. "Aye, tell me what to do."

"A Protector must create a circle in the ground around Redwin's body. How you do so is of your free will."

The Scotsman considered the task. Drawing his sword, he worked it into the grass and tried to carve a line. After several feet, he stopped to examine his progress. Abby squatted with him and helped part the grass.

"I don't think you're pushing hard enough, Rory, I can't see anything."

Rory stood, staring from his blade to the grass and back.

"Uh, if you're thinking fire, I wouldn't even try it. You don't want to be remembered as the Protector who burned down the Forest of Souls."

Rory frowned, "Yer right, A-by," he replied, sheathing his sword.

"Maybe use your dirk? I bet you'll get better leverage."

Rory grunted and drew his knife. Getting down on all fours, he stabbed the tip into the dirt and pulled toward himself. Working meticulously, he rounded the Red King's head with Abby following behind to check his progress.

"It's working, Rory, keep doing what you're doing."

Rory gazed at the ground before him, scooting backward, dragging the knife along without lifting it from the soil.

As he neared his starting point, Abby ran back around and parted the grass. "Here," she said, "I'll keep the grass out of the way for you, just don't slice my fingers off!"

The Scotsman nodded, paused, and turned his body to face his kin. He dragged the knife from left to right in front of himself, aiming for the initial gouge in the ground visible between Abby's hands. He slowed as he approached Abby's fingers, then grunted and flicked his head to the side as if to say she should shift her hands. Picking up on his meaning, Abby moved away to watch him finish.

Rory rose with a sober smile. "Will this do?"

Wren circled the body. "Yes, this will do. Come," she continued, motioning Rory toward her, "now you must stand over Redwin and sacrifice three drops of your blood to his body. As you do, say the words 'one with the land you are whole again, your circle is complete.'"

Rory stared down at the body of the Red King, his emotions unreadable. He wiped both sides of his dirk against a pant leg, then raised his hands in the air. Holding the blade in his right hand, he ran the tip across his left palm. As soon as a thin, red line appeared, he balled his hand into a fist and squeezed. He hovered his hand over his kin's chest, watching as the first drop of blood fell to its mark, creating a bright stain. He sucked in a deep breath and exhaled slowly. "One with the land ye are whole again, yer circle is complete," he intoned, squeezing his fist again to send the second and third drops of blood on their way.

When the final drop of blood soaked into the weathered body of the Red King, the ground began to rumble. Wren, Rowen, Javani, and Daylo stepped back several feet instinctively. Abby shot her hands out from her sides for balance, startled by the shaking. Seeing the reaction of those native to the land, she, Rory, and Finlay followed suit and joined them.

Abby's jaw dropped when the grass surrounding the body stretched into the air and wrapped around it. Soon only the shape of the Red King was visible under the fuzzy, orange mat. The rumbling stopped abruptly, and Rory's kin seemed to dissolve into the mound of grass.

"Where'd he go? That's not it, is it?" Abby asked, glancing at Wren.

"Just wait," she replied, a twinkle in her eyes.

Abby turned back, her mouth opening wide again. The grass where the body once lay shifted as if controlled by the land. Small mounds of dirt bubbled up, making way for what appeared to be three thick, red shoots. The trio snaked into the air, growing thicker and thicker with every inch they rose. Higher and higher they went until their purpose revealed itself. One shoot expanded into a six-foot-wide trunk, the second slithered around the trunk, up and up, forming sturdy branches, and the third whirled rapidly in and around each branch leaving fiery, red foliage in its wake.

Rory stepped forward, pulled his sword, sinking its tip into the ground and kneeled. "Me King. May ye live on as one with Shay," he whispered.

Wren bowed next to the Scotsman. "Come, Rory. Redwin's journey is not yet complete. He has one last sacrifice to make." She motioned for him to follow her to the grand tree.

Rory stood and accompanied Wren, sheathing his sword when they approached its base.

"Place your hands on the tree of your ancestor and repeat my words. 'I give of myself and accept your gift. In life and in death I am one with Shay.'"

Rory gulped, turning to find Abby's eyes.

Seeing his uncertainty, Abby ran to his side and stood on her tiptoes to whisper in his ear. "It's okay, you're meant to do this." She stepped back and smiled. "I believe in you."

The tips of Rory's ears shifted from pink to red. Abby giggled quietly when he pivoted to stare at the tree while rubbing the back of his neck. Shaking his hands out in front of him, he glanced one last time at Abby and placed his palms on the massive trunk. "I give of meself and accept yer gift. In life and in death I am one with Shay."

Rory fidgeted as he leaned in on his palms when nothing happened. Just as he released a long sigh, a soft crackling grabbed everyone's attention. Next to both of Rory's hands, the bark split open and a fiery shoot wrapped around each wrist.

Seeing his panic, Wren placed a gentle hand on his back. "Do not be afraid."

Rory nodded rapidly, his arms tensing.

The shoots circled faster and faster around his arms, soon covering his entire body. In the next moment, Rory stepped free from the tree and turned toward Abby.

"Whooaa, cool, Rory! You have armor now just like the other Protectors!"

Rory held his arms out to examine them, then attempted looking at his backside. Abby and Wren laughed at his antics. He halted and reached his right arm awkwardly behind his back. "Is that..." His words trailed to silence as his hand wrapped around the grip of a bow. Pulling the weapon in front of him, Rory ran a hand along the finely crafted wood, stopping at a strange indent above the grip. "Is amazin'."

"It will bear your Talisman." Wren nodded to the spot Rory's fingers caressed.

Rory tilted his head, recognition filling his eyes. Pulling the Rose from its pouch, he held it experimentally over the indentation. Pink sparks sizzled around the stone and, moments later, a dull click filled the air. The Scotsman grunted, turning the bow for everyone to see. The Talisman nestled seamlessly in the weapon's shaft.

"Brilliant, Brother," Rowen clapped a hand on Rory's shoulder. "You are now one with the Land and will be forever connected to your kin through the Talisman."

Rory ran his hand over the stone, standing tall. Abby watched in awe as Rory slipped the bow behind his back and the quiver, with no straps in sight, seemed to latch onto the weapon, magically holding it in place. Looking satisfied, Rory stared up at the grand tree again. Abby imagined what thoughts he must be sharing with his long-gone kin and found herself filled with pride and admiration for the young Scotsman.

"We did it, guys. We really did it," she said, first running a hand along Finlay's chest before jogging over to Rory. After giving him an awkward hug, Abby turned to Wren. "That's it, right? The Red King's circle is complete?"

Wren bowed. "It is. Because of your selfless bravery, Shay will feel his healing presence once again. But," she paused with a frown, "there is more to do if we ever hope to be free of the evil pressing upon us."

Abby thought to question what Wren meant, but instead found herself staring back toward the entrance to the forest. "Do you guys hear that?"

The sound of pounding hooves grew steadily until the massive form of Tiffa barreled into view, Jovan crouched low to her neck. "Thraxen!" he yelled, once within range. He urged his steed to cover the remaining distance. "Three, not far behind," he said when Tiffa slowed to a stop in front of the group. "They revealed themselves to me when I disposed of the last monstrosity." Tiffa stamped her feet and neighed, causing Jovan to pat her shoulder in reassurance. "Let them meet a similar fate."

The twins nodded at each other and, in one fluid movement, Javani sprang onto Daylo's back. "For Redwin, for Shay," they yelled in unison as they galloped off.

Rory drew his sword, looking at Rowen and Wren. "Should we no' help."

Rowen whistled twice, waving an arm in the air at Riffin. "I will help drive them off, Brother." He locked eyes with Finlay. "Please, do me the service of seeing Wren back to Willow Wood."

Riffin landed silently and chirruped, hopping toward his Protector. Rowen touched his forehead briefly to Wren's before hefting himself onto the bird's back, "Be swift. I will follow shortly."

The owl shot into the air, creating a sudden draft on the ground as he flapped his enormous wings. Abby smoothed her hair and glanced around the group, wondering if she were the only one feeling uncertain. "Will they be okay, Wren?"

"Do not fill yourself with worry. When few, the Thraxen pose no threat to a Protector. It is when they swarm in large numbers their power is formidable."

Abby shivered at the idea of an army of Thraxen, picturing their creepy eyes blinking one after another in rapid succession. "Should we go then? Back to Willow Wood? Rowen seemed pretty serious about it."

Wren nodded. "Yes, it is best we leave, if your guide would be gracious enough to transport us. But we will not go back to Willow Wood quite yet."

"Oh?" Abby asked, confused. "Where are we going?"

"There is something else I wish to show you."

6

"Where to now?" Abby asked, scanning the clearing where she, Rory, and Finlay initially arrived in Shay.

Wren pointed in the opposite direction from where the Red King's body was hidden previously. "This way. It is not far." She led the group through a maze of giant, rhubarb-like plants. Red stalks and floppy, over-sized leaves acted as shade from the afternoon sun.

Lost in her own thoughts, Abby wondered what was next for them. *We fulfilled our duty in completing the Red King's circle, and it's super cool Rory is a full-fledged Protector now, but it would be nice if we could go home.* She sighed, picturing her family, wishing she had a way to tell them she and Rory were okay. *But what about the Book of Shay? I promised Dad we'd get it back.* Abby studied Wren as she trailed behind her new friend. *Even if we get it back, that'd be pretty low to just up and leave.*

The book belongs here. And those Thraxen! The Manta could definitely use our help fighting those gross bugs.

Abby shielded her face, feeling the hot sun beating on her forehead. They now stood in an expanse of the orange grass. Along the horizon to their right, a towering, rocky outcrop broke the monotony of the fuzzy plain.

Wren pointed to the stony feature. "There is where we must go."

"It's still a bit of a walk. Anybody want to do it the fast way?" Abby asked, gesturing to Finlay.

Before any response came, Abby tilted her head and raised a finger. "Do you guys hear it?" she whispered.

Rory and Wren shook their heads.

"There it is again!" she exclaimed, staring back into the hodgepodge of 'rhubarb' plants. "You seriously can't hear that? Someone's coming, and it sounds like they're in a rush."

A streak of white bounded over the group's head, causing them to crouch. Abby tracked the motion with her entire body, turning back toward their intended destination. Her jaw dropped when the white form hopped to a thudding stop.

Before them hunched a massive hare, its overly-large ears standing tall. Abby shook her head in disbelief. *Holy jackrabbit, that's a big one.*

The hare propped itself onto its hind legs, thumping a long foot rapidly. *Oh good, there you are. I worried I would not find you.*

Abby scrunched her face in surprise, turning to glance at Wren. "In case you're going to ask again. Yes, the giant rabbit is talking to me."

Wren smiled at the hare. "Please, ask its name. I do not know this splendid creature."

"So, what's your name?" Abby asked, looking back to the hare. "And why did you say you were looking for us?"

The animal twitched its nose. *My name is Cody, young Manta, and I am a hare, not a rabbit. I was answering the call, of course.*

A mischievous smile spread across Abby's face. "Wait. Did you say your name is Colby? And you're a jackrabbit. Colby Jack? Get it?" she said with a snort turned giggle. Her laugh trailed to silence and then embarrassment upon realizing no one in her company would understand the cheese joke. She groaned to herself, imagining Finlay's common lecture. *Think before you speak, Abby.* Feeling awkward, she glanced around the group, fully expecting to see blank stares. When her eyes fell upon Rory, she was surprised to see him staring at Cody, his mouth hanging low. "Uh, Rory, what is it? Surprised to see a giant rabbit? You know you can't eat him, right?"

Rory shook his head slowly. "Nae, Lass, I would no' dream of eatin' him," he struggled to say. "And his name is Co-dy."

Taking a moment to register what the Scotsman had said, Abby waved her hands in front of her. "Whoa, hold on! You can hear him?"

Rory nodded, his eyes full of shock. "Aye, A-by. But how could this be?"

In answer, Cody hopped toward Rory, standing on his hind legs to meet Rory's eyes. The hare sniffed inquisitively at Rory's hair and armor, then stretched around the boy's back to inspect his bow. *Ah, yes,* he remarked to those who would listen, *there it is, the Stone of Enlightenment. I knew I heard its call. And any good guide knows you always answer the call.*

Rory continued to stare at Cody, speechless as the hare sat down on all fours in front of him.

Abby ran to Rory's side. "Don't you get it?" she asked. "You're a Protector now, so that means a guide will bind to you. He's your animal guide, Rory. Just like Finlay and me, or Rowen and Riffin." Abby clapped her hands enthusiastically. "This is so cool. Rory gets to talk to a rabbit in his head." She glanced at Cody, clearing her throat, "Oh, sorry, I meant hare." Abby pulled Rory in toward her, fake-whispering in his ear, "Remember, no eating him." She stepped back, suppressing a giggle, knowing she was not acting her age.

Cody trembled at the statement. *Why would the boy desire to eat me? This is a most unheard-of start to a sacred binding.*

Abby straightened up and turned serious. "Sorry, Cody. It's just a private joke we have. Rory absolutely will not eat you. I swear. You're a hare after all, not a rabbit."

Finlay nudged Abby with his muzzle. *Enough with the jesting, child. Give them some space and let the boy sort it out on his own.*

Abby sighed. *I know, I know. You're right. But you have to admit it's ironic his guide is a rabbit, I mean hare. You can't make that stuff up.*

Finlay rumbled a gruff laugh and sighed, his serious demeanor faltering for a moment. *Aye, child, it is coincidental,* he replied, giving in to Abby's humor with a final chuckle.

Wren passed between the guides and their humans and set off toward the rocky feature in the distance. "Come, let us walk a bit and allow Rory and Cody to acquaint themselves with one another. They have much to discuss," she said, looking over her shoulder at the new pairing.

The group walked on in relative silence. Abby stole frequent glances at Rory, wondering what conversation he might be having with his guide. Contemplating what Cody said about the stone calling out for a guide, a burning question rose in her core. Confused, she reached out to Finlay. *How are we bound together?*

The dog swung his muzzle toward Abby. *I am not sure I understand your question.*

Well, I don't have a Talisman, or know any magic for that matter. And I'm not a Protector. Haven't you ever wondered why and how we're connected?

Finlay strode on without answering.

Well? You don't know, do you? I mean, not that it really matters, just seems weird it's even possible, that's all.

It is true, lass. I have no answer to this, and until this point, had not considered it unusual. Perhaps it is something best left unquestioned.

Abby shrugged, gazing ahead at the approaching rock formation. "Almost there. Guess it was worth the walk instead of you zapping us over," she said, running her fingers through Finlay's coat. "Hey," she paused, a thought coming to mind as she turned to Rory and his guide, "what's your special gift, Cody?"

Rory grinned, nodding at the hare. "He is amazin'. Co-dy is what they call a green-speaker."

Abby wrinkled her nose, "A green-speaker? What on earth is that?"

"He can talk to plants, A-by. Can ye imagine it?"

"Okay, wait. Plants are sentient, and," she said pointedly, "they can talk? That's almost too ridiculous to believe." Abby tapped the tip of her boot into the fuzzy pasture, "So what's this grass say then?"

Rory stared at Cody momentarily. "Is called Day-glow, and it wishes ye would no' kick it so, A-by," he replied with a sheepish grin.

Abby stopped tapping her boot immediately. "Oh, ah, okay, sorry about that little grassies," she said, looking at their fluffy tops. She eyed the hare. "Green-speaker, huh? Pretty cool then."

Wren waved for the group to continue on. "I have heard of this green-speaking. It is a rare and useful gift. One which I believe may see us to healing our land."

Rory grinned, nodding to his guide, his pride clear to Abby. "Do ye hear that, Co-dy? Yer goin' to heal all of Shay."

Wren smiled at the Scotsman. "Let us hope this is so," she said as they approached the massive rocks.

Not far beyond the structure, the plain dropped off into a deep valley with no visible end. "Follow me." Wren pointed around the right of the rocks and stopped in front of a cave entrance, allowing everyone to gather near her.

Though the sun warmed her skin, Abby shivered.

"This," Wren motioned to the opening, "is a place of great meaning to the Manta tribe. When we are feeling lost and defeated, it is a place that pulls our hopes back from even the darkest of shadows."

"Um, Wren," Abby interrupted, "you guys keep mentioning things about evil and darkness, and we've seen how nasty those Thraxen obviously are, but what's happened to Shay? From all I've seen so far, things seem fine on the surface. Is there something more to it?"

"Indeed there is, Abby, and this is why I have brought you here. Before we enter, though, I wish to answer any questions you all may have."

"Well, what's up with the Thraxen?" Abby asked without pause. "Are there lots of them? I mean, I know you can't always see them, but we've only run into a few. Where do they live, anyway?"

Wren hesitated, considering her answer. "The Thraxen are a mysterious creature. We believe they hide and thrive in Darktree Hollow. No one knows for sure, but their life cycle is not like anything else in Shay. They are not one with the land as we are and have no circle to complete. It is said they devour the insides of trees, using their essence to sleep for many years, only to wake refreshed and hungry for the destruction of more Manta."

Abby nodded slowly. *Hmm, sorta sounds like cicadas or something that hibernate in the ground for a long time.*

"So, why not just go to Darktree Hollow and kill them while they sleep?"

"If it were only so easy, Abby. The answer is twofold. At present, they are in a period of wake and will remain so for years to come. But no one knows the location of Darktree."

Abby creased her brow. "No one knows where it is? Really?"

"I regret this is so. Long ago, a powerful mystic cast a spell on the hollow, keeping it from the eyes of the Manta. Some even say he bears the ability to move it from place to place, though I have my doubts."

"Well, has anyone gone searching for it? If the magician can move it around, that'd explain why no one can find it," Abby said with a shrug.

"You have a point. It pains me to say many brave Manta, determined to bring an end to the mystic's ways, went in search of the hollow, never to return or complete their circles."

"Oh, sorry." Abby frowned. "What's this guy's name? This 'mystic'."

"Shaeron," Wren replied, her composure cool.

Abby glanced at Rory, noting the recognition in his eyes. "Uh, like as in the Rose of Shaeron? At least, that's how we first came to know Rory's Talisman," she said, motioning toward his new bow.

"Yes, they are one and the same," Wren nodded. "He is its creator."

"What? Really?" Abby raised a brow. "Shaeron made Rory's stone? But this guy sounds completely evil. Why would he make something so opposite?"

Wren stared out into the valley for a moment before motioning toward the ground. "Please, let us sit. There is much to explain."

Abby nodded at Rory, plopping down next to him once he found a comfortable spot. Finlay and Cody curled up next to their respective humans, each keeping an alert ear.

"Ages ago," Wren began softly, "before the time of Redwin, two brothers — mystics as we called them for their great abilities — newly made their home in Shay. For many years, the Manta tribe lived in peace and, with guidance from the mystics, learned to nurture and strengthen their inner gifts. The land and people flourished until, one day, Shaeron's brother had a terrible vision. He prophesied the coming of a great evil to the land, one that would demolish everything pure. And so," she said, gesturing toward Rory's talisman, "the brothers set to work, determined to create thirteen magical stones capable of protecting our home. Made from the very essence of the land, these stones, or Talismans as we now call them, grew in power when entrusted into the care of those destined to be Protectors of Shay."

"Thirteen stones?" Abby interjected when Wren paused for a breath. "We've seen what, four, if you count Rory's, Rowen's, Jovan's, and Javani's. Where are the rest?"

"Seven of the stones have faded away becoming one again with the Brana, the essence of Shay." Seeing the confusion on Abby's face, Wren explained further. "When a Protector dies, if there is no living blood line to assume care of the Talisman, it is summoned back to the Brana. And so, the stones of fire, wisdom, light, clarity, thought, regeneration, and balance have been lost to us." She glanced at Rory. "This should help you understand the importance of your Talisman returning to Shay. It gives us great hope."

"Okay, wait." Abby counted off the stone names on her fingers. "That accounts for eleven, what about stones twelve and thirteen."

Wren hinted a sigh. "The final Talisman was never created."

"Oh, well, why not?"

"Because Shaeron's brother abandoned our land, our people."

Abby raised a brow. "Why did he do that?"

"It is complicated, Abby. It is said during the creation of the stones, a darkness crept into Shaeron's heart. He grew to despise the Protectors one by one as they took the Talismans into their care, his immense jealousy and hatred evident. Disgusted, his brother refused to help make the last stone, fearful Shaeron would try taking it for himself. And so, he left, somehow opening a portal to the Other, taking his daughter with him."

Abby narrowed her eyes, a suspicious thought in her head. "Wren, how come you keep saying 'Shaeron's brother' instead of his name? Who was he?"

Wren drew her lips tight before answering. "As much as I find difficulty giving life to the name Shaeron, he who perpetuates the surrounding darkness, I take even less pleasure in saying his brother's, he who left Shay behind." She exhaled heavily. "His name was Sylvan."

***

Abby's chest squeezed as she shared an intense stare with Rory. "Sylvan. Sylvan Myst," she whispered, frowning. "But that doesn't make any sense. Sylvan was good, wasn't he? I mean, he was basically responsible for protecting our home, the Other, from the faeries when he summoned the Red King." Abby frowned further. "But I guess that made things even worse in Shay too, with the Red King leaving."

Wren sighed, relaxing her shoulders. "In truth, yes, Sylvan was pure of soul. Though his intentions may have been good, the Manta have long held him responsible for the disappearance of our Queen."

Doubt consumed Abby. *Here I thought Sylvan Myst was this great magician or whatever. If it weren't for that sword he made for the Red King, we never would've rescued my mom and locked up those nasty faerie brothers. And now it looks like he was just a selfish old man, maybe a coward even. How could he run away from Shay like that?*

Sensing her disappointment, Wren rose. "Come. It is time I show you."

Rory helped Abby to her feet, giving her hand a comforting squeeze. "Do no' worry yerself, A-by."

She quirked a brow at the Scotsman.

"I can see it in yer eyes, Lass. We can no' control what happened in the past. It is done, as horrible as it may have been. But we can control our choices for the future. We shall do right by Shay."

Returning the Scotsman's smile, Abby glowed inside, admiring his maturity and wisdom. "You're right. We'll do everything we can to help what's left of the Manta tribe."

Hearing their exchange, Wren waved them toward the cave opening with a knowing nod. "Please, follow me closely. The way is tight for a short bit."

Abby glanced at Finlay and Cody. "How tight? Can they come with us?" she asked, pointing to the animal guides.

Wren halted abruptly and turned to face the group. "Again, something I did not yet consider. Thank you, Abby," she replied, contemplating the animals' considerable size. She bowed to each. "Finlay? Cody? May I ask that you stay behind and guard the entrance? I am afraid you will not fit through the passage. Be assured, though, our journey will be short and safe."

Cody hopped forward, bowing dramatically to Wren. *At your service, my dear, I always answer the call,* Abby could hear him say as she giggled at his theatrical flair.

He really is the perfect guide for Rory.

Finlay stretched, sticking his nose into the air. After sniffing deeply to the left, then to the right, the dog marched to the cave entrance, plopping onto his haunches to one side of the opening. *I detect no danger, child. The giant rabbit may join me as I stand guard.*

Abby snorted. *You are so weird sometimes, you know that?* Scratching Finlay's chin, she followed Wren into the cave with Rory in tow.

True to Wren's word, the entryway narrowed after only a few feet, forcing the trio to walk in single file. Realizing darkness did not cloak their path, Abby glanced up to see a fissure of sorts mirroring the course of the passageway. The sun filtered through, creating enough light for Wren to guide them. After a handful of steps, the rocky walls gave way to a large chamber. The fissure flowed into an even larger opening in the middle of the cave's ceiling. Wren stood in a halo of light and gestured to the surrounding walls.

Abby and Rory joined Wren in the middle of the cavern. "Whoa!" Abby blurted, "there are drawings all over the walls."

Wren nodded. "Sylvan was not the only one to foretell of future happenings. Once a favorite place of contemplation for her, our Queen and Keeper of the Land left behind her own visions. Please, take your time," she said, motioning toward the drawings.

Abby peered all around with amazement, pulling Rory with her to the left of the chamber's opening. The pair inched along, studying each depiction. "Kinda looks like they were drawn with white chalk or something." Strange symbols accompanied each picture, stirring Abby's memory. "Hey, Rory? Don't those symbols remind you of the Book of Shay?"

The Scotsman simply nodded in response as he stared at the cave wall.

Abby slowed to a stop in front of a crude picture of a forest. "I think that's the Forest of Souls, don't you?"

"Aye, A-by, me eyes see the same. But," he paused with a frown, "the trees, they do no' look well."

"I agree. They remind me of the one that was black and toppled to the ground." Abby studied the picture further. "Either the Queen's vision was wrong, or this hasn't happened yet."

Rory's face hardened. "Dead trees in the Forest of Souls means dead Protectors. We can no' let this happen."

"Come on," Abby squeezed his hand, "let's keep looking."

The duo worked their way along. Abby shivered when they approached a drawing of what could only be an army of Thraxen. "They're hideous, even as little better than stick people on a wall." Abby cringed, "There's so many of them. How could we ever kill them all?"

"Kill the creator, kill the beast," Wren answered. "Or so is the hope of our people."

Abby turned around to face her fellow Manta. "Wait. Kill the creator?" Her eyes grew large at a forming thought. "You mean Shaeron is still alive? How is that even possible? He'd be like a thousand years old or something!"

"The twelfth stone."

Abby scrunched her face, confused. "The twelfth stone? What does that have to do with Shaeron?"

"The twelfth Talisman is the Stone of Longevity. It slows the bearer's growth and is the driving force as to why Sylvan refused to create the thirteenth and final stone."

Abby and Rory both stood dumbfounded, motioning in unison for Wren to continue, but as she began to speak, Abby found her voice.

"Hold on," she said, piecing together her thoughts. "Did Shaeron steal the twelfth stone?"

"That he did, and in doing so, he murdered a Protector."

"But, I thought only those of the Origin could touch the stones? At least, I remember what happened to that rat Aillig when he tried to touch Rory's."

Wren tipped her head. "Yes, this is true. But Shaeron is a powerful mystic and somehow harnessed the stone, bending it to his will."

"Who did he murder?" Rory asked, gripping his hilt, his knuckles turning white.

Wren sighed. "Aster. He murdered Aster, my kin."

Abby gasped. "Oh Wren, I'm so sorry. I can only imagine how that makes you feel. I bet there isn't a moment you don't think about finding Darktree Hollow so you can teach him a lesson and take back what's rightfully yours."

"My bloodline has never lost hope that one day Shaeron would be defeated. The Queen tells us it will be," she said, turning to point at the last drawing Abby and Rory had yet to examine.

Abby stared beyond Wren at the cave wall. "What the..."

Tugging Rory with her, she passed Wren hurriedly, stopping several feet from the artwork. "That can't be," she managed to whisper.

Three figures, side by side, loomed over a fourth body at their feet. Though drawn with imperfect strokes, certainty filled Abby's mind; she could never mistake the three images capturing her gaze. She pulled on Rory's sleeve. "You see it, right? You know who that is?"

"It can no' be, A-by! How can this be?"

"The Queen. She...she had a vision of us." Abby gulped. "And that must be Shaeron lying below us, dead."

Abby glanced over her shoulder to see Wren approaching. She turned back to the drawing, her eye caught by four lines of indecipherable writing next to it. "What does it say?" she asked, pointing to the scrawls.

"This," Wren swooped an arm past the markings, "has fueled the hearts of the Manta tribe for hundreds of years. I have shown you this so you would understand why I believe it to be fate our paths have crossed, but I do not want the meaning of the Queen's vision to weigh heavily upon you."

"Don't worry about us, Wren," Abby said, meeting Rory's eyes, "please, tell us what it says."

With a brief nod, Wren read the lines, a lyrical quality to her voice.

"A salvation foretold

With hair of fire

A Protector to free all

From sickness so dire."

Rory turned to Abby. "With hair of fire," he whispered, disbelief in his eyes. "It can no' mean me."

"Of course it's talking about you. It makes perfect sense, Rory," she said, taking his hand again. "With everything you've done so far to help others, you're a real hero. And don't forget the fact you're a Protector now and have a fancy, new bow and a green-speaking animal guide. I bet you'll have Shaeron shaking when he sees your flaming sword," she finished with a grin.

Rory turned back to the drawing. "Shaeron. Defeat the beast to free the land."

"Exactly, we just have to figure out how to..." Abby trailed off, pulling free from Rory and walking to the center of the cavern. "Do you guys hear her?"

Wren and Rory looked to one another, confused.

A familiar, ethereal voice called out to Abby. "Amaray. You must break my binding chains."

Abby whipped around, searching for the source of the voice. "Where are you? Who are you?"

"Find my tree to find your way."

"Find your tree? What tree? There are thousands in Shay." Abby groaned when all fell silent. "Hello?" she called into the air. "She always does that," she huffed, turning back to her attentive audience, seeing their bewildered expressions. "What? You couldn't hear her?"

"Hear who, A-by?"

Wren stepped forward and took Abby's hand. "Yes, Abby, who? Please, it is important you tell me everything."

Abby sighed, willing the building frustration to roll off her back. "There's this mysterious sounding woman, she's talked to me like four times now, the first was when we were back home. I thought I was dreaming then, but now I think it was something else."

"Something else? Please, tell me, Abby." Seeing uncertainty in Abby's eyes, Wren tilted her head with a warm smile. "Do not be afraid."

"Well, it might sound crazy, but I think I've been having out-of-body experiences. You know, like if your soul or whatever separates from your body, and you can float around and see yourself but you aren't actually dead." Abby relaxed her shoulders when no change came to Wren's demeanor. "Anyway, that's how I heard her the first time." Abby paused, replaying the encounters in her mind. "And now that I think about it, I've heard her two other times here; the first time was when that stupid rock smashed me." She reached down to rub her leg in memory. "But this, just a second ago, is the only time I've heard her when everything is normal."

Wren nodded as if nothing were unusual. "And of what does she speak? I must know."

Abby lifted her chin toward the cave ceiling and squinted. "Hmm, well I think the first time she told me I needed to find my way home or all would be lost. When the rock trapped me, she said I needed to use the power within and around me to free myself. Oh yeah, and she keeps talking about me freeing her, breaking her chains, whatever that means."

"And what of the tree, Abby? Moments ago you called out to her about finding a tree?"

"Right. I'm confused by it, but she said to find her tree to find my way. Don't know how I'm supposed to do that though, Shay is full of trees."

"You need not worry, my friend. I believe I can take you there."

"What? You can? But...how could you possibly know what she's talking about?"

"Though I am perhaps somewhat doubtful, please, trust in me. We shall travel there tomorrow, but first we must return to Willow Wood. Come," Wren headed toward the passageway, "it will be nightfall soon and I do not wish to alarm Rowen with our extended absence. If you would, Abby, perhaps your talented guide will take us there?"

Abby and Rory exchanged shrugs and followed Wren out of the cave.

"No prob, one lightning fast trip to Willow Wood coming up."

7

The group gathered outside Emi's home under a cloudless sky. During an animated retelling of the events inside the cave, Abby noted long stares and quick nods exchanged between Wren and Rowen. As Rory described the many drawings in the cavern, Abby drifted into her own thoughts. *What is with those two? This isn't the first time I've seen them pass secret looks to each other. I'm thinking there are other things they aren't telling us.* She shrugged to herself, decided it was not worth troubling over right then, and concentrated on the discussion.

Once finished, all parties agreed to retire for the night. Abby, Rory, Finlay, and Cody stood before the odd cocoon-house.

"Um," Abby eyed both animal guides, "no way we're all going to fit in there."

Rory nodded at Cody. "He says he prefers to burrow. He'll meet us here in the mornin'."

Twitching an ear in response to the Scotsman's salute, the hare bounded off into the forest.

Abby scratched her head. "Huh. Okay. That was easy."

Turning back to the house, she stepped inside, filling with delight when she saw the Goldenglow. "Don't think I'll ever get over how cool this stuff is." She waved her hand over the curious life form, watching as it displayed an array of color. "So pretty."

At the sound of her voice, a mass of roots flopped down from the ceiling. In moments, three inviting hammocks formed, swaying gently as if calling out for tired occupants.

Rory bowed in front of Abby, a silly smile on his face. "Good night, me lady."

She snorted a laugh. "Good night, yourself," she smiled, falling into her hammock. "Here's to some good sleep, though all I can think about is Wren taking us to this mystery tree." As much as her mind raced, Abby could not contain a deep yawn. "Good night then, Rory, Finlay." Giving in to her body's exhaustion, Abby drifted into a deep sleep.

***

Abby flicked her eyes open, finding herself engulfed by darkness. She twisted her head around. *Wha...where'd all the glowies go?* She squeezed her eyes shut again for several seconds. *I must be dreaming. Just clear your mind and go back to sleep, you have a busy day tomorrow.* As she tried to shut out all thoughts from her mind, a strange scratching sounded from some unknown place.

She opened her eyes again to find the same darkness. *What the heck was that?*

The scratching continued, intermingled with soft clicking. *Uhh...hey, Finlay? Do you hear those weird sounds too?*

When the dog did not respond, Abby attempted to sit up in the hammock, only to recognize a familiar floating sensation. She gasped, reaching down to feel for a body that was not there.

No! Not again. Pleading with herself not to panic, Abby whirled around, squinting into a black void. *Where am I?*

As the strange sounds grew louder, a blue haze in the distance commanded Abby's attention. *Am I seeing things?* She wished her eyes would adapt to the gloom. *No, there's definitely a blue light out there.* She imagined herself floating toward the source. *Hey, it's actually working, the light is getting brighter!*

She glanced to her left, thinking she sensed movement. Nothing. Narrowing her eyes, she focused on the blue aura again. As she drew closer, large, dark shapes formed all around her. She slowed to a stop and blinked. *Are...are those trees?* She forced her eyes wide open, centering in on one of the objects. *I knew it! It is a tree. But I think something is wrong with it.*

A gnarled tree tipped low, its branches bent at unnatural angles to form a tangle of wood, the blue light creating a creepy aura around them. A flash of movement caused Abby to flinch. *I'm not imagining it, there's something else here.* She gulped, moving away from the tree. Scanning the area, shivers crept along her spine. Realizing it unwise to call out, Abby clamped her mouth tight. *Don't freak out, don't freak out. Whatever it is, it can't hurt you, you aren't really here.*

She moved even closer to the blue light. More dead trees took shape, accompanied by further streaks of movement. Abby bit back a rise of nausea after a form passed through her, skittering off to her right. *Okay, not cool! Any time you want to wake up would be great, Abby!*

She meditated for several minutes, bringing herself back to a state of calm. *I must be here for a reason. And I bet whatever is making that blue glow is it.* She steeled her nerves and floated head-on toward the light. As she gained speed, a hunched form holding something in its hands materialized before her. Abby slowed to a stop, hovering not ten feet from a man as gnarled as the surrounding trees. He squatted atop a rotted chunk of wood, leaning forward in tattered robes. An egg-shaped stone hung from a chain around his neck. Its blue radiance stretched beyond Abby, illuminating everything in front of the old man.

Movement again in all directions caused Abby to flinch first one way, then another. In that moment, she realized she must have been tuning out the clicking and scratching noises. Distorted insect sounds threatened to drive her crazy. *Thraxen,* she hissed to herself. There would be no mistaking their calls. Panic swept through her body. *No, no, no! I know where I am. And I know who that is.* She whirled around full circle, hoping her presence remained undetected. *This is Darktree Hollow, and that's Shaeron!*

Abby's stomach fluttered. *Get a grip! Breathe. They can't see you. He can't see you.*

Just as the thought rolled through her mind, the old man looked up as if to lock eyes with her, but returned his gaze seconds later to the object tucked close to his belly.

"Foolish I was to trust Mallena!" he spat with a grizzled voice at the Thraxen nearest him. He held his hands out in front of the glowing stone. "Complete subjugation of Shay will be impossible without the book."

Motion behind Shaeron stole Abby's attention. Something as black as the forest with icy, blue eyes lurked. When a Thraxen leaned in too close to the old man, an ominous growl rumbled through the forest. "What have I told you?" Shaeron barked at the intruding insectoid as it skittered away.

Abby shivered at his cold and harsh tone. *This guy is crazy!* She leaned in, trying to determine what lay on the magician's palms. *He's got a wooden box with fancy markings. Maybe a tree carved on top.* Bravery seeped back into her bones, convincing her to float closer. *Wow, yeah, it is a tree on top. Kinda reminds me of the Great Willow. Wonder what's in it...*

With crooked fingers, Shaeron worked the lid of the box. "Blast it!" he cried when the lid refused to give. He slipped the box into a large pouch hanging at his side. "I must have the book," he said, lashing out at the nearest Thraxen, knocking it back several feet. "Find her. Find the book." He jabbed a contorted finger at the Thraxen's eyes, "And don't come back until you have both."

A group of Thraxen scuttled into a loose formation and bowed, before leaping into the unknown beyond the stone's luminous reach.

Abby floated backwards faster and faster. *I've got to get back. Have to tell them I've found Darktree Hollow. We can save my people and all of Shay!* Surprising herself, she slowed her speed. *My people?* She contemplated the weight of those two, simple words. *Yes, I am part of the Manta tribe. I haven't met many of them, but yeah, they're my people.* She smiled at her revelation. *But...just because I'm here doesn't mean I know where I am. I'd never be able to lead the Protectors here; this place could be anywhere.* She groaned. *Great. Just great. At least I know what the old creep looks like. That long, stringy hair and clothing that probably hasn't been washed in two centuries. Hey, and that stone around his neck. Yeah! I bet that's the Stone of Longevity. I can't believe it's kept him alive all this time. We have to get it back. It belongs to Wren. She should be a Protector, after all.*

Abby focused to slow her pounding heart. *All right, now I have to figure out how to get back. How did I do it the last time?* Abby thought back to the boulder smashing her leg. *Right, concentrate on my breathing and maybe picture where I need to be.* Satisfied with her plan, Abby drew a slow, deep lungful of air, all the while picturing her comfy hammock. *In, two, three. Out, two, three. Feel yourself stretched out in the bed of roots, dreaming of pizza.* Abby repeated her chant over and over, tuning out all else. Her world silenced and before she could prepare, a quick tug to the midsection pulled her backward into the black void.

***

Abby cracked an eye open. Goldenglow shimmered all around her. She raised her head to meet the morning sun inching its way into their sleeping quarters. She wiped a hand across her groggy face and smacked her lips. "Ugh."

Swinging her legs from the hammock, she realized the other two hung empty. "Hey guys," she called, standing and stretching, "did you have weird dreams too?" When no answer came, she approached the threshold of the cocoon and peeked outside. A still forest welcomed her. *They must be in the clearing already,* she decided. Taking advantage of the privacy, Abby found a patch of bushes and crouched between the plants, obeying the protest of her bladder. Stretching tall again, she headed toward the clearing. Emerging from the tree line, she could see everyone milling around several stone's throw away, watching as Rory danced about with Cody, showing off his swordsmanship.

"Morning all," she called out, waving an arm as she broke into a jog. Slowing to a stop when she reached

Finlay, she bent over, hands on knees. "Geesh, why am I so exhausted?"

"Did ye no' sleep well, A-by?"

Abby straightened up, turning to the Scotsman. "Guess not. I'm feeling pretty low on energy. I had a scary dream, but I can't quite remember about what." She lifted both shoulders. "Probably a good thing, eh? Really wiped me out though."

"Let us restore your spirit, Abby," Wren said. "Come, we shall find a Bria for whoever is in need."

Abby's mood perked. "That sounds great. Hey! Will you teach me how to find them?"

Wren bowed. "Yes, of course. You and Rory both need to learn this skill."

Leading Abby and Rory back into the tree line, Wren paused for a moment before heading to the right. She walked slowly, running a casual hand along the bark of each tree they passed. "Here," she said, stopping in front of a three-foot wide hardwood.

"So how do you know where to look? Is there something special about the tree you pick?" Abby asked, her brow askew.

"I sense their presence," she said, squatting in front of the tree. "One day, you too will feel the energy of the land, with patience and practice." Wren gestured toward the ground. "Here, join me."

The pair did as directed, kneeling on either side of Wren in front of the tree.

"Let us raise our hands in silence, and when you feel the energy of Shay coursing through you, sink your fingers deep into that which supports all life and thank it for its offering."

Keeping her doubt to herself, Abby followed suit, closing her eyes and raising her hands. She tried to clear her mind and calm her nerves. *I don't know about this but I'd better figure it out if I want to eat.* Not feeling anything out of the ordinary, Abby stole a quick glance at the others, finding both with relaxed expressions and closed eyes. She groaned in her mind, shutting her eyes again. *Get in the game, Abby.* Imagining the sensation of sinking her hands into the dirt, Abby tried to clear her mind and focus on her senses. Within moments, she felt a tingling of dull pins and needles travel along her legs and into her knees. *That must be it.* For fear of breaking her concentration or of being wrong, Abby threw herself into thanking the land. *Dear Shay, your trees and animals are amazing. I've never been anywhere as beautiful. I know I'm new here, but if you could spare any Bria for me, I'd be extremely grateful. We have to go find a special tree today and will need plenty of energy, so your help is appreciated. So, um, thanks.* She groaned at herself, certain she delivered a ridiculous thanks, but reached down and pushed her hands into the dirt nonetheless. Ignoring the soil packing under her fingernails, Abby continued to burrow her hands until suddenly, she felt something smooth. She opened her eyes to find Rory and Wren equally dug in. "I think I feel one," she exclaimed, wrapping her fingers around a circular object. "Thank you, Shay," she whispered, extracting her hands.

Rory smiled at Abby with delight and held his palms out for her inspection. Three pulsing orbs rested on his hands.

"Awesome, Rory!" Abby beamed, looking down upon her own cache for the first time. One giant Bria twinkled at her and she could feel the warm flow of energy emanating from within. "Look Wren, I almost can't believe I did it," she said, glancing at her friend who clutched four spheres to her chest. Abby's smile weakened. The Bria vibrated in her hand, its warmth dissipating. "What the..." she muttered, watching as the blue ball shifted to black before disintegrating to nothing.

The trio shared a moment of shock. Abby flicked her hands, then wiped them along her pant legs as she stood. "What the heck just happened? Did I do something wrong?"

Wren shook her head. "No, Abby, you have done nothing wrong. It is as I have long feared," she sighed, standing up to inspect the tree. "The sickness Shaeron cast upon the land has made its way into our beloved sanctuary. Though this is the first I have seen of it here, all of Shay will succumb to his evil."

Abby eyed the other's Bria. "Well what about those, are they safe to eat?"

"Yes, I believe they are. Their essence is strong, I can feel it course through me," Wren replied.

Abby wiped her fingers again, making sure no remnants of Shaeron's evil remained. "Good then, at least everyone else will get something to eat, just my luck I find an infected one," she said, casting a frustrated glance at her empty hands.

"A-by, do no' speak so. Yer need comes before mine. I shall always give freely to ye." Rory held his Bria in front of him. "Take what ye need."

Abby struggled not to blush. "Thanks, Rory, I think I only need one though." She hesitated, "But we need eight and only found seven, someone else will go hungry if I take one."

Wren smiled at Abby's unselfish words. "Emi prefers to bore for her own. Please, do not feel guilt in taking one."

"Well, okay, if you're sure," Abby conceded, popping a Bria into her mouth. "Mmph," she mumbled through chews, "it's so good." She stood a little straighter upon her final swallow. "It's downright amazing, Wren. I seriously feel better already." She hopped up and down, a surge of energy streaming through her. "All right, I'm ready, let's go find this mystery tree."

Wren suppressed a giggle. "Come, let us share our find with the others, then we will be off."

8

Abby, Rory, Finlay, Cody, and Wren trekked into early afternoon. Fragrant fields and lush valleys enhanced their travel as Rowen and Riffin soared overhead, circling back often to check on the group before disappearing again beyond the horizon to scout for dangers.

"It is not much farther," Wren pointed to the top of the gorge in which they all sat resting. "Just there, perhaps a minute's walk beyond."

Abby hung her legs over the flat top of the large boulder on which she and Rory perched. She tapped the heels of her boots rhythmically against the rock. Leaning back, she considered the steep climb ahead. "All in favor of a quick trip to the top?" she asked, raising her hand as she stared at Finlay. Seeing all heads nod, she hopped to the ground, soon followed by Rory.

"If everyone's rested up, you know the routine. Well, oh," she remarked, looking at Cody, "I guess you don't, but Rory can fill you in, just let him grab hold of a paw or something." Abby joined hands with Wren and then meshed her fingers with Rory's as she tipped her head back to eye their destination. "Oops, wait, I have to grab hold..."

In the next startling moment, the group stood atop the cliff. "...of Finlay," Abby finished in a bewildered whisper. She glanced around frantically, confusion flooding her mind. "Uh, what just happened?" she asked, looking at her dog. "How did you do that? I wasn't even touching you!" She raised a suspicious brow. "Your doggie powers getting stronger or something?"

Finlay peered over the edge to where the group had just stood, then swung back to look at Abby. *I do not feel this was my doing, young one. I am as confused as you.* The dog shook his body. *I felt our minds become one as you took the boy's hand, and then, we were here. I was, however, concentrating on where we needed to be, but I do not recall initiating the move.*

Abby bit the corner of her lip. *Hmm. I think your powers are growing and you just don't know it, fuzzface. Otherwise, how else could we have gotten here? There's magic everywhere in Shay, and this is where you're from, so it only makes sense you'd be able to do 'your thing' with more ease.*

Finlay pawed at the ground. *Perhaps you are correct, child.*

Wren tilted her head, watching the obvious exchange with curiosity. "Have you come to an acceptable answer? If so, please, let us continue on, it is not far, just over the hill in the distance."

"Yeah, sure," Abby replied, lifting a shoulder, "we're good." She glanced at Rory and Cody. "Ready?"

The Scotsman turned to the hare, then grunted with a nod.

Abby motioned with her hands for Wren to lead the way. *Hope this mysterious tree lives up to the expectation I'm feeling,* she thought to herself. *Sure could use some answers to all the weirdness. Wonder if that invisible lady will be there...*

The group marched along, Abby keeping stride with her dog and Cody showing off to Rory just how high he could jump. The hare landed with a loud thud each time, shaking the ground around him and throwing the Scotsman into a fit of laughter.

It warmed Abby's heart to see the obvious joy consuming Rory. *So glad he gets to experience a bond like I have with Finlay.*

As they trudged up the hill, Riffin's piercing screech overhead brought Abby back from her thoughts. She watched as the owl disappeared from sight beyond the crest. Pumping her arms with anticipation, Abby doubled her pace, eager to see the tree. When she stood atop the hill, she froze. *Well, I wasn't expecting that. It's almost like Berry Brae Circle!*

The five travelers lined the ridge, watching as Riffin soared to a graceful landing inside an enormous stone circle. Thirteen stones, creating a ring fifty feet across, encircled a lone tree. A tree, in Abby's eyes, that wished for better days. Its limbs, devoid of leaves, drooped low and at odd angles, its bark hinting a tinge of black.

"So, what's this place called? I wasn't expecting a stone circle." Abby asked, turning to Wren.

"The Manta know it only as Amaray's tree."

Abby's stomach flipped. *Did she say Amaray? This is getting weirder and weirder. That lady and Riffin keep calling me Amaray, and now there's a tree with that name?* Confusion filled Abby, but she did her best to hide it. "That's a pretty name, what's it mean?"

Wren smiled and bowed. "It is the Queen's tree. Amaray means Keeper of the Land."

"But what of the stones, Wren?" Rory asked. "The por-tal through which we arrived in Shay was in a similar circle," he paused, raising a hand to count the thirteen stones, "though, one stone laid on its side."

"Thirteen stones for thirteen Protectors. All standing tall to guard the Queen's tree."

"So...what happened to the tree?" Abby asked. "It doesn't look so hot."

Wren nodded, "Before the Great Crossing, our Queen vanished. It is believed she was last seen here, her favorite place in Shay, but no one knows what became of her. As hundreds of years have passed, it is only logical to assume she died at the time of her disappearance." Wren gestured toward the stone circle. "Come, let us reunite with Rowen."

Abby led the way across the clearing and entered the ring. "Wren, I don't get it. Why do you think this is the tree that strange voice told me to find?"

Wren embraced Rowen, touching her forehead to his before responding. "Though I am not certain," she said, looking back at Abby, "I believe it is the Queen speaking to you."

Abby stared at Wren for several quiet moments. "Seriously? You think a thousand-year-old ghost is following me around and talking to me?"

"I do."

"But," Abby spoke, then closed her mouth for a moment. "It doesn't make sense. I mean, why me? Abby Fletcher from the Other? Why would she be talking to me?"

"Every Manta has a unique role and place in Shay. Do you not see, Abby? You are one of us. Perhaps this is where your duty falls."

Abby fingered her golden curl. "You're right. Shay is in my blood." She glanced sideways at the tree, pushing away her doubt. "What do you think she meant by me breaking her chains? Like, is she trapped somewhere? Or maybe someone is holding her prisoner? But that doesn't make much sense if she's dead."

"Is too bad we can no' go back into the past to see what happened to her," Rory remarked.

Abby's eyes lit up. "Rory!" she exclaimed, causing the Scotsman to jump. "That's it! You're a genius." After receiving a blank stare, she paced around the tree. "Don't you get it? Your stone, and what happened in the hollow back home? That's exactly what you can do!"

A slow realization rolled across Rory's face. "Aye, Lass. I believe yer right once again. But," he paused, scrunching his brow, "we do no' know if we stand where the Queen met her own demise."

"Well," Abby motioned toward Rory's bow, "only one way to find out!"

The boy nodded, pulling his bow from his back. He stared at the stone embedded in the wooden shaft and ran his fingers across the Talisman, then covered it with his hand and closed his eyes. It seemed a lifetime to

Abby before anything appeared to happen, but then Rory's body jolted, and the Scotsman wheezed. His eyes shot open and he stumbled backward, stabilizing himself against the tree. He stood silent and shaking, rage filling his eyes.

Abby rushed to his side. "Rory. What is it? What's wrong?"

"I do no' believe it, A-by."

"Believe what, Rory? Tell us, what did you see?"

"It was them. Those devilish brothers."

Abby shook her head, confused. "Them who?"

The next words to pass the Scotsman's lips shook Abby to her core.

"Mavis and Tavis."

***

Abby placed a hand against the Queen's tree to brace herself. Anger boiled inside her, and her knees quivered from the memories that resurfaced upon hearing the faeries' names. She watched as Rory stomped back and forth muttering unpleasantries. "I...I don't understand," she whispered. "How can that be?" she voiced louder. "Are you sure about what you saw, Rory?"

He stopped pacing and whirled to meet Abby's eyes. "There be no mistakin' it, Lass. Was those dirty pigs, as ye'd say. They murdered her and stole the Book of Shay!"

A hush fell over the circle as everyone contemplated the seriousness of Rory's words. "Please," Wren said, approaching the new Protector and placing a gentle hand on his arm, "you must tell us everything you saw in your vision." She waved a hand toward the ground when he nodded agreement. "Let us sit then."

Rowen and Wren sat across from Abby and Rory while their animal guides stood guard with alert ears. Rory inhaled deeply and placed his trembling hands on his thighs. Abby intertwined her fingers with his. "It's okay," she said, feeling the tension leave his body upon her touch. She smiled at the reaction. "Whenever you're ready."

Rory nodded and swallowed hard. "She was there," he twisted his torso to point at the tree behind him, "sittin' peacefully, curled up against her tree. She is nearly the most beautiful woman me eyes have ever beheld," he said, clearing his throat and casting a sideways glance at Abby. "Her hair," he continued, taking up one of his own braids, "outdid the red of even me own. I have niver seen such a thing." He paused for a moment to survey their immediate surroundings. "Many colorful flowers filled the circle, and the tree, well, its branches bore leaves of every shade of red. Was an amazin' sight to see." Rory glanced back at the tree again. "There she sat, a large book opened in her lap."

Abby squeezed his hand, "I bet it was the Book of Shay, right?"

Rory nodded, "Aye, Lass, I am most certain of this. And she was most peaceful. She was writin', or maybe drawin' somethin' in the book." He lowered his head mournfully. "Would be her last entry."

A hint of tears appeared to glisten in Wren's eyes. "Please, continue, as difficult as it may be."

The Scotsman drew another deep breath. "She heard somethin' and so closed the book in her lap. There were voices arguin'. I could hear them too. It was them," he said, looking to Abby, "Mavis and Tavis. They came from that way," he continued, pointing beyond the circle between Wren's and Rowen's shoulders. "But when they saw the Queen sittin' defenseless against the tree holding a beautiful tome, they went silent. The Queen, I think she sensed their malevolence, for she tucked the book behind her back, I think in hopes of hidin' it. But it was too late. The brothers had already seen her treasure." Rory paused with a distraught look.

Rowen reached across and clapped a hand on Rory's shoulder. "I am sorry, Brother, that you now have these visions in your head. But it is the price we must pay in protecting our land."

Rory nodded an understanding before resuming his vision. "An argument broke out between the Queen and the faeries. They demanded to see the book and, when she refused, they concluded it must be somethin' filled with powerful magic. This drove them to near madness when the Queen continued to hide it from them. Mavis, ye know, the crazy one," he said, tipping his head at Abby, "started jugglin' several green orbs in front of him, taunting the Queen with his magic. Why she remained seated with the faeries towerin' over her, I do no' know, but she did no' lose her resolve. Tavis asked her one last time to see the book. She refused and closed her eyes, had a most peaceful look about her. Tavis nodded to his brother. It happened so fast. Mavis flung three orbs at the Queen, all of which slammed into her chest."

Abby choked back a sob. "And so they left her there like that and stole the book? Those pigs," she seethed through clenched teeth.

"Nae, Lass, they thought it wise to dispose of her body."

Wren gasped at this revelation. "Have you seen where they placed her, Rory?"

"Aye, well, I have seen it, but I regret I do no' know where in relation to the circle."

Wren leaned in, "Please, go on, perhaps one of us will know."

Rory dipped his head. "Tavis stood upon a ledge, the Queen draped over a shoulder. Mavis paced next to him, clutchin' the book to his chest. And no' far below them I could see somethin' murky, perhaps a thick bog, but I can no' be sure." He looked at Wren with expectant eyes.

Wren sighed in response. She turned to Rowen who simply shook his head.

"I am afraid we do not know of this place."

Abby lifted herself up and walked to the tree, kicking at a pebble. "This is so messed up. I can't believe Mavis and Tavis killed her. But how did they even get here in the first place?"

The others stood with blank stares as if trying to find an answer.

Wren raised her brow, turning to Rowen. "The Queen disappeared not long after Sylvan deserted our great land. Could it be Sylvan failed to close his portal, allowing these murderers access to and from Shay?"

Rowen nodded slowly. "Yes, this seems a reasonable explanation, but it does not answer the burning question of where our beloved Queen may be."

Abby walked around the tree, frowning at its decrepit state. *Now would be a good time to talk to me, Your Majesty, if that's who you are.* She sighed when no response came and continued to circle the tree. A strange depression in the trunk caught Abby's attention, beckoning her to lean in closer. When she placed her hands against the tree, a tingling sensation rolled through her body, and images of a murky bog filled her mind.

"Amaray. You must break my binding chains."

Abby gasped and jumped back from the tree, shaking her hands.

Rory ran to her side. "A-by, are ye okay? Did somethin' happen?"

"I'm good, I'm good. But you're right, Wren," she said, turning to her friend, "it's the Queen that's been talking to me. She just told me again I have to break her binding chains. And you guys won't believe this, but I know where to find her!"

A buzz filled the circle as the rest of the group voiced their excitement.

"Ye've seen it then, A-by, the bog I envisioned?"

"Yep, it's just as you described, Rory. I even saw the path those creeps took to get there. So maybe that's what she means by her binding chains; her body being trapped, or dumped in the bog? Hey," she questioned, turning to Wren again as a thought occurred to her, "could the Queen's body being put somewhere like that keep her from completing her circle?"

Wren cupped the side of her face, lost in thought. "I believe it is possible. If no magic were placed upon her body as Sylvan did with Redwin, perhaps the unusual environment has acted to preserve her, stopping the completion process. In fact, I do not know how she could communicate with you otherwise." Wren fell quiet again and tapped her chin.

"What is it?" Abby prodded.

"Rory mentioned the Queen closed her eyes and appeared peaceful just before Mavis struck her down. Abby," she said, "the Queen was known for her ability to separate herself from her physical being, just as you can. What if," she paused, shaking a finger in the air, "she sensed inevitable death looming and moments before, removed herself from her body?"

Abby nodded. "And...and she's been trapped, like with invisible chains, with no body to return to. Yeah, that's got to be it. Her binding chains!" She shuddered at the thought of becoming trapped outside her body. Floating around with no way back. *A thousand years like that. I can't even imagine...*

"We must find her then and return our Queen to her tree," Rowen said, crossing an arm over his heart.

Wren bowed her head. "To complete her circle so she may be one again with Shay."

Abby blew out a deep breath. "All right, let's do it. Let's go get her. Follow me."

***

One by one, the eager group stepped cautiously up to the edge of a short drop off. A quick, five-minute jog across the clearing and through a short stretch of woodland had brought them to their destination. Abby peered down at the moss-covered bog. A thick matting of deep reds, greens, and browns allowed no view into the swamp's depths. The sounds of chirring insects and tiny, croaking frogs filled the air. "This is a problem. How are we supposed to know where she is?" Abby asked, glancing to Wren and Rory on either side of her. "Can't see a single thing through that mossy stuff."

Silly girl, silly girl.

Abby turned with a start to find Cody looming behind the Scotsman and herself.

When the hare is near, there will be no problems to bear.

Abby rolled her eyes at Rory's strange guide as he wedged his way in between them and peered over the edge.

Yes, you are correct, we seek the Queen. Cody twitched his nose rapidly. *Oh, yes, why thank you, you have been most helpful.*

Abby narrowed her eyes at the giant-eared herbivore. "Uh, Cody. What are you doing? Having a conversation with yourself?"

Rory laughed but composed himself with a serious face immediately after Cody turned to him with a confused look. "Do you no' see, A-by?" he asked, clearing his throat and pointing to the bog with a proud smile, "Co-dy is talkin' to the plants."

An embarrassed understanding washed across Abby's face. "Oh, ah, sorry about that Cody. Guess I forgot about your cool power. So," she stammered, "what did the plants tell you?"

The Gillybloom, to be precise, young Manta, agreed to lead us to the Queen. Though I must say they are quite the arrogant bunch.

Abby filed yet another odd plant name. She stared at the hare, thinking to herself the flora wasn't the only creature before her practiced at self-importance. "That's kind of the Gillybloom, Cody, but exactly how are we supposed to get to her, let alone get her out? We don't even know how deep it is. Plus, what if there are giant snakes or something in there?"

Rory stepped to the side and pulled his sword. "I shall use me blade to test the depth. Co-dy will guide me." He locked eyes with his hare and nodded. "Ye need no' worry, no threatenin' creatures call these waters home." Before anyone replied, the Scotsman removed the rest of his weapons, followed by his boots, and laid everything out on the ground. He grunted at himself and pushed his pant legs up as high as the material would allow.

Abby caught herself staring at Rory's calves. Feeling heat rise on her cheeks, she turned to Wren and Rowen. "What do you guys think? Sound like a plan?"

The pair exchanged whispers with Rowen nodding at his love. "It seems a reasonable approach," Wren said. "Please take great care, Rory. We cannot know for sure in what state we will find the Queen's body."

Rory sidestepped carefully down a gradual slope off to the right of the overhang, jumping the last bit to stand level with the marsh, the hardened soles of his bare feet knowing no different. "I shall do me best to preserve her honor."

Cody bounded from the ledge, landing next to Rory with a thud. His head tipped and ears rotated outward. His nose twitched so fast, Abby thought for sure he might hurt himself. She cleared her mind and focused on the hare but decided he must have blocked her from his thoughts.

"Aye." Rory gave a quick nod to his guide and eased his feet into the water. The Gillybloom parted as if creating a path for the Scotsman. He stretched his arm forward and prodded with his sword, smiling when the blade sank only a foot and a half.

Abby watched curiously as Cody's ears bent and pointed to the right. Rory put himself on the same course, inching his way along and testing each step with his blade as the Gillybloom floated apart, allowing uninhibited movement. This slow pattern went on for several minutes until Cody's ears stood at attention, stopping Rory in his tracks.

The Scotsman watched as the Gillybloom in front of him pushed farther and farther away, revealing a large, arced area free from plant life. He peered into the water, pulling his sword from its shallow depths. "The Queen, ye're certain she is here?" he asked, twisting around to look at the hare.

Cody nodded and clicked his teeth. Thumping a foot, he motioned the boy forward with his ears.

With a serious expression, Rory sheathed his sword and turned back to the open water before him. He leaned forward, staring. "I am unable to see anythin'. I shall have to feel with me hands."

"Maybe you can find her with your feet first, if you slide them along the bottom," Abby hollered.

Rory grunted affirmatively, moving his left leg forward without lifting his foot. He repeated the action every few inches, switching from leg to leg. After traversing several feet, surprise danced across his face, and he came to an abrupt stop.

Abby lifted up onto her toes with an excited hop. "What is it? Do you feel her?"

Rory bobbed his head, then looked back and forth at the water's surface. "Somethin' is happenin'," he whispered.

A hush fell over the marsh.

Moments later tiny bubbles floated up from below, popping upon reaching the surface. Over and over they appeared, increasing until a thick froth surrounded Rory. The bubbling then subsided as quickly as it started and a large mass of Gillybloom pushed out of the water. One by one the mossy stalks unraveled, slinking back into the marsh, revealing the petite form of the Queen.

Rory squatted and scooped his arms under her body when it was evident she would not stay afloat for long. The last of the Gillybloom pulled free as the Scotsman stood tall, the Queen cradled gently against his chest. He glanced up at Abby with a nervous smile and turned full circle to retrace his path to dry ground.

Rowen scrambled to the edge of the marsh, holding his arms out to relieve Rory of his burden. With compassion in his eyes, Rory transferred the Queen to his fellow Protector and wiped as much wetness from his legs as possible before slipping his boots back on.

The group traveled in silent homage back to Amaray's tree. Abby stared sadly at the peaceful yet lifeless form in Rowen's arms. "So, what do we do with her?" she whispered, "same as with the Red King, except here?"

Rowen and Wren dipped their heads in unison, stepping up to the tree. With great care, the Protector laid the Queen onto the barren ground, letting her feet touch first, followed slowly by the rest of her body. Wren crouched and arranged the Queen's arms across her chest.

Abby marveled at the pristine state of the woman before her. Wild, red curls, somehow dry after hundreds of years submerged in the bog, framed a beautiful face; one Abby imagined in life to be full of character and kindness. Upon closer inspection, she noticed it — one brilliant, golden curl nestled amid the red. *I bet she was an amazing queen.* She held back her anger at the grievous actions of Mavis and Tavis with a frustrated sigh. *At least I helped deliver what those creeps deserved.*

I can't believe they'd kill her for a book they knew nothing about. They really must have been crazy.

Rory squeezed Abby's hand and pointed to his dirk. She nodded and stepped back, understanding his intentions. With cautious steps, Rory bent over and worked his way around the Queen, carving a shallow circle in the dirt. Once finished, he scooted away.

"Now what?" Abby asked when nothing happened.

Wren smiled. "Do you not remember? A descendant must sacrifice three drops of blood while speaking the rite of completion."

Abby gestured at the group. "Well, that's going to be a bit hard, isn't it? I mean, I don't think anyone here is related to her, right?"

Wren bowed. "Yes. We find ourselves with unusual circumstances. In light of the situation, I feel it best if you," she touched Abby's arm, "complete the Queen's circle. Of all here, you have the closest connection."

Abby considered Wren's words for a moment. "You're right. She's been talking to me, so if you think it will work, I'll do it." Abby moved closer to the body, considering how she might draw blood from herself. She raised a hand in front of her and rubbed the tip of her index finger. "Can I..." she turned to Rory, gesturing at his dirk.

The Scotsman strode forward and wiped his short blade repeatedly along the underside of his sleeve. "Do ye wish for me to cut yer finger, A-by? I do no' wish to cause ye pain, but sometimes is best no' to do it yerself," he said, hesitating to hand over the dirk.

"That's sweet, Rory, but it's okay, I can do it myself. I'm a big girl." Abby smiled coaxingly as she reached out, working her fingers in between his and the hilt.

Rory returned her smile and released his hold.

Turning back to the Queen, Abby held the dirk eye level with its blade point-down. She raised her left hand, and with a crinkling of her nose, pricked the tip of her finger before she could change her mind. Keeping an eye on her digit, she passed the blade back to Rory. She squeezed below the tiny wound, persuading a blob of blood to pool.

"Do you remember the words, Sister?"

Abby glanced back at Rowen. "Uh, yeah, pretty sure I do." Holding her hand over the Queen, Abby watched as the first droplet of blood fell. "One with the land you are whole again, your circle is complete." As she put more pressure on her finger, the last two drops fell in rapid succession.

Abby sucked on her finger as she moved away from the body. Tense moments passed; she expected the ground to rumble, but to Abby's surprise, dainty flowers sprung from the dirt all around the Queen. Blooms of every color imaginable surrounded the body, stretching ever higher to encircle her. As if in response to a mysterious, warm breeze flowing through the stone circle, the flowers swayed in a synchronized dance, stroking their petals back and forth along the Queen's lifeless form.

The flowers multiplied, bending in on the body, leaving no visible trace of the Queen. As with the Red King, her body seemed to dissolve into the ground until only random petals littered the area where she once lay.

Abby wondered what magical thing might happen next. In moments, she had her answer. Amaray's tree creaked and groaned, its branches twisting and turning. A burning red materialized on the bark, drowning out the sickening black. Soon the entire tree morphed into a blazing beacon within the circle. Giant leaves sprouted along its limbs, giving way to an explosion of flower buds. Abby emptied her lungs finally. "Wow..." she muttered, mesmerized by the tree. Deep red flowers unfurled their petals in a dazzling show. "It's so beautiful," Abby choked, turning to Wren with wide eyes.

"Yes, indeed," she replied.

Abby sensed Wren also grasping for words amid such a display.

The warm breeze picked up, lifting Abby's hair from her shoulders. As it did, a wispy voice met the ears of all who would listen.

"Complete Aster's circle and return the Book of Shay to its rightful owner."

Figuring she was the only one to hear the mysterious words, Abby's jaw dropped when she met the stunned faces of the group. "Uh. Wait. You guys could hear that?"

Abby's own eyes grew large when receiving a chorus of acknowledgment.

Wren grabbed Rowen's arm as her legs turned weak. "Complete Aster's circle? But how could we do such a thing? Shaeron murdered him so long ago. How would we ever find his body?"

An urgent whisper seemed to emanate from the tree. "To the Howling Mountains with haste."

"Howling Mountains?" Abby scrunched her face. "That sounds ominous."

Wren grasped both of Rowen's forearms. "Of course!" she exclaimed, releasing her hold and circling the tree slowly. She studied its grand branches, deep in thought. "Shaeron must have cast a spell upon Aster's body, much like Sylvan did to Redwin, keeping his body whole. It would be the only way Shaeron could steal the Talisman of Longevity, for were Aster's body to become one with Shay again, the stone would have found its way to the next of his blood."

Excitement rolled through Abby. "So, if we complete Aster's circle, the Talisman should be drawn to Wren, its rightful bearer! Shacron won't have control over it anymore. And maybe he'll finally die naturally without it," she finished with a wicked smile.

Rowen frowned, running a hand through his hair. "Yes, Sister, what you say sounds possible, but the Howling Mountains are a dangerous place and many a day's travel by foot. The added uncertainty of even finding his body does not lift my spirits."

Finlay nudged Abby's side with his muzzle. *Our friend is forgetting my ability. I will make a short task of the travel as long as I can see where we need to go.*

Abby scratched under Finlay's chin. *I have the smartest doggie in Shay. It'll be like playing a game of leap-frog. We'll just keep zapping from spot to spot, all the way to the creepy sounding mountains. We'll be there in a snap.*

"You guys," Abby grinned, "getting to the mountains fast won't be a problem. Finlay can take us. We'll just have to do it in small hops so he can see where he's going."

"Yes, of course. This is an excellent idea," Wren said. "But what of finding his body? The mountain range, as

Rowen has indicated, is a dangerous place. Travel will be difficult, even more so when one does not know where to go."

The group stood silent. Abby tapped a finger on her chin, her eyes roaming. She gazed at Cody, then shifted her focus to Rory. "Easy!" she blurted. "I've got it!" Abby pointed at Rory's bow. "Rory can see into the past with his Talisman, right? So, when we get to the mountains, maybe he'll be able to see what Shaeron did with Aster's body. And," she continued after pausing for air, "are there trees growing there? Cause if there are, well, then can't Cody talk to them? Of course, it will only do us good if they were alive back then. But, it could work, couldn't it?" she finished, looking at her companions one by one.

"Aye, A-by. Co-dy says ye speak wisely." Rory glanced back at his guide and grunted. "Though he says most trees are stubborn and difficult to communicate with. But he is certain of his ability. He will get us the information we need."

Rowen stepped forward to pat Abby's shoulder. "Well done, Sister. Your clever thinking may see us through."

Abby swelled at the praise. "But," she paused, "what about the book? We're supposed to find it and return it to its rightful owner, which is obviously the Queen. Not sure what we do with it though, since, you know," she finished, nodding her head at the spot they had laid her on the ground.

"Come. Let us first place our focus on completing my kin's circle. If, as you guess, removing Shaeron's power over the Talisman will weaken him, this will aid us in retrieving the Book of Shay."

Abby nodded thoughtfully. "You're right, Wren, one thing at a time. And who knows," she shrugged, "maybe it will make it easier to fight the Thraxen, since it seems they're tied to him."

"Very well then," Rowen motioned to Riffin who perched atop the nearest stone. "We will scout ahead and warn of any dangers. Finlay," he said, bowing to the dog, "if you would follow in my general direction, I will show you the most agreeable route of travel.

Wren rushed to Rowen, touching his forehead with her own. After exchanging hushed words meant only for each other, Rowen mounted his guide. Riffin sprang into the air and with several powerful beats of his wings, they soared into the distance.

"Okay then," Abby looked at the remaining group members, "you all know the drill. Let's do this."

9

The journey to the Howling Mountains took far less time than Abby expected. A dozen well-placed transports brought the group to the base of a rocky range in less than an hour. Riffin floated overhead in slow circles, descending with each round. Upon touching ground at the base of the range, Rowen remained seated and beckoned the others to him. "Good travels my brothers and sister," he said, with an added wink at Wren. "I fear the path ahead of us will not be so kind. I will continue to scout above. If you hear Riffin screech, ready your best defense. There are dark tales of what lies in wait for the unsuspecting. We must keep our senses about us at all times."

"Yes," Wren agreed. "I have no doubt Shaeron has instructed the Thraxen, or worse, to guard Aster's body. He would not wish it discovered."

"Over this ridge," Rowen motioned to the right, "is a narrow pass between those two peaks. From what I can tell, it leads to an open area with a scattering of trees. Perhaps we can put Cody to work there?"

Abby followed Rowen's line of sight. Relief flooded through her upon seeing the small size of the mountain peaks. *Must be kinda like back home. The 'mountains' there are more like huge hills. Fine by me.*

With that, Riffin chirruped and took off into the air, propelling himself over the ridge.

"Come, let us keep our voices low and move with a swift yet sure step." Wren led the way up the ridge. Red and yellow grasses of varying height interspersed themselves among bushes and the occasional boulder, giving everyone with hands something to grab onto if needed. After several minutes of silent hiking, the group crested the ridge with relative ease.

Chills ran along Abby's spine as she surveyed the jagged cut, devoid of any plant life, between the two mountains. Slopes tinged with black appeared on either side of the travelers. *Great. The evil maniac has definitely left his mark here too.*

Wren signaled for all to follow her. She walked with bow in hand and arrow notched. Seeing her defensive gait, Rory pulled his sword.

A moment of envy passed through Abby's mind. *Why don't I have a weapon? Well, besides my pepper spray.* She thought back to her encounter with Beefy and Stinky in the Black Forest and smirked, but frowned when thinking of Mallena, her curved knife, and her freaky acrobatic skills. *Pepper spray won't cut it with the Thraxen, let alone Shaeron. Maybe I should ask Rory if he'd let me carry his dirk for a while. At least I'd have something.*

Just as Abby convinced herself to ask the Scotsman, the sound of rocks sliding down the left slope ahead broke the silence. Without hesitation, Wren whirled toward the mountainside, pulling the arrow to its anchor point against her cheek. She held the string at full draw and scrutinized the area. When no further noise or movement came, she relaxed her arms. "Come," she whispered, heading into the pass.

They walked single file at a brisk pace. Abby cast nervous glances from slope to slope. Though in the company of enormous, magical guides, a Protector, and a Manta warrior, an eerie sensation left Abby feeling vulnerable. She quickened her pace, eager to place herself under whatever cover the trees Rowen described might provide.

"There." Wren pointed to a small grove of trees in the distance as they stepped free from the oppressive pass.

Abby turned in a slow circle. To her surprise, they stood at the opening of a giant, bowl-like plain. A curved ridge of smaller hills connected both peaks. When she came to a stop, a sudden and fierce wind whipped through the pass. A piercing howl followed it, intensifying before trailing to silence.

"Uh," Abby's eyes darted around the ridge, "what in the world was that?" She eased up against Rory. "No way the Wolf's ghost followed us here, right?" she whispered.

"Do no' worry yerself, A-by. I do no' see it bein' possible, but whatever the beast, I shall protect ye."

"Please, do not be startled by the noise. As unnerving as it is, what you have just heard is why these mountains are called as they are, howling."

Abby held a hand to her chest upon Wren's reply. "Good to know. Just the wind."

"Come," Wren waved them to her. "Finlay, if you will, please take us to find shelter among those trees."

Abby nodded to her guide as everyone gathered around, making a physical connection with one another. In moments, they walked under the ancient canopy.

Wren ran her fingertips along a giant, sycamore-like specimen. "Rory," she smiled, "would you ask your guide to attempt using his gift? I do not expect we will find anything useful, but we must waste no talent in our search."

Rory agreed and turned to the hare.

Cody bent the tips of his ears, then hopped from tree to tree, staring intently and twitching his nose as he went. After his seventh attempt to communicate, he stopped and thumped a foot, gazing up at a broad trunk. For several minutes, the hare bobbed his head and appeared to be in deep conversation.

Abby tried to listen in on his thoughts to no avail, realizing she must wait like everyone else. Staying close to the others, she wandered among the trees, craning her head up to study their leaves. A flash of movement caught her eye. She turned back to see Rory and Cody eye to eye. The Scotsman grunted periodically in response to what Abby assumed to be an in-depth discussion. Finally, Rory nodded and turned to meet the eager eyes of Wren, Abby, and Finlay.

"Well?" Abby tipped her head. "Get anything good?"

Rory stared up at the tree. "Is an amazin' thing. This tree is Shadowbark," he said, placing a hand on its trunk. "He was just a saplin' when the veins of sickness began branchin' their way from Darktree Hollow."

"He must have seen if Shaeron brought Aster here, right?" Abby scrunched her brow at her own question. "But trees don't have eyes though, so how would they actually 'see' anything?"

Rory turned to his guide and after a moment wore an impressed expression. "Ye're correct, A-by. They have no eyes, but also have no need. They draw knowledge from the surrounding land. Their roots take in the experiences of the soil around them. Though I do no' understand it, I accept it as so."

"Huh. Cool, I agree. But did he say anything that can help us?"

"No' much other than to confirm our suspicions. Shaeron came to the Howlin' Mountains long ago carryin' a body, but Shadowbark can no' say where we may find Aster."

Wren touched a hand to Rory's elbow. "Please, then we must look to your gift to show us the way."

Rory hesitated before swinging his bow from his shoulder.

Abby sensed his momentary lack of self-confidence and nodded encouragingly. "Go on, Rory, I know you can do it. See if your Talisman will show you anything."

The Scotsman smiled at her words, studying his new weapon. Walking to the fringe of the tree line, Rory gazed out at the craggy, barren ridge. Grasping his bow, he wrapped his fingers over the stone. His body stiffened immediately and after several moments, he gasped, stumbling backwards to lean against a tree.

"Rory!" Abby ran to his side and grabbed one of his arms. "Are you okay?" She scrutinized his complexion. "You're looking a little pale. Well, more pale than normal. What happened? Did you see him?"

"Aye, Lass," Rory replied, the tension in his shoulders receding after seeing the concern in Abby's eyes. He straightened himself and stepped back into the clearing. "He came this way," he said, indicating with his bow from left to right, "with a body draped over his shoulder. I do no' know how he managed. He appeared old even then, usin' a staff to aid his movements." Rory shuddered as he continued. "And then he stood in a cave." The Scotsman scanned the ridge and pointed. "Up there, perhaps. He dumped Aster's body in the back of the cavern and waved his hand in the air. Then I could no' see our fallen Protector any longer."

"Sounds like he cast an invisibility spell or whatever," Abby said, rubbing her chin. "Would make sense. It'd make it harder for anyone to find him."

Rory nodded agreement. "Aye, but there is more," he said, glancing at Finlay. "He was no' alone."

"What, like there were a bunch of Thraxen there or something?"

Rory shook his head. "No' in this vision. A grand beast lurked in the cave, hidin' in the shadows. I sensed its hatred toward Shaeron. It growled when the old man approached."

"What kind of creature?" Wren asked, knitting her brow.

"Was a dog just as white that challenged his size," the Scotsman said, casting a glance at Finlay. "Shaeron raised a hand to it, sayin' it would bend to his will or die. The beast lunged at him, then crumpled to the ground with a howl. Shaeron placed a hand on the dog's chest. I could see its breath comin' fast, like it was fightin' somethin' unseen."

Abby listened intently but detected an uneasy sensation coming from her guide. Keeping one eye on Finlay, she motioned for Rory to continue.

"Before me eyes, a black mist rolled from Shaeron's fingers and swirled around the dog. It worked its way into the beast's fur and suddenly, no white remained. The old man stepped back as the dog rose. Its coat was so black, I almost could no' see it anymore in the darkness of the cave. But I could hear its heavy breathin' and see its eyes that turned a crystal blue."

Pinpricks danced along Abby's body. *Why does that sound so familiar?* She turned to Finlay, surprised to find him with haunches down, trembling. When about to question him, she noticed Wren staring at her guide. "What? What is it, Wren?

"I believe the dog Rory speaks of was Aster's guide."

Abby nodded, realizing it made sense his guide would not roam far from him, especially after Shaeron took his life. He had probably wanted to exact revenge for the murder of the Protector. "What was his name? Aster's guide?"

"Her name," Wren emphasized, "was Eirwen."

As soon as Wren spoke her name, Finlay howled, his body shaking uncontrollably.

Abby ran to him, throwing herself to her knees. "Finlay!" she cried, placing her arms around him and stroking his lush coat. "Finlay, please, tell me what's wrong."

She continued running her hands along Finlay's muscular frame for several minutes until his trembling subsided. Pulling back, she locked eyes with him. "Want to tell me what that was about?"

Finlay stood and shook out the tension in his body as Abby jumped to her feet. A sense of deep sadness washed through her mind. She reached out to her dog, hoping to break his unusual silence. *Please, tell me what's wrong.*

He swung his muzzle toward her, rubbing it along her cheek. Two words reached Abby's innermost awareness.

My mother.

***

Abby staggered back, shocked. "Your mother?" She turned wildly to Wren and Rory.

Wren sighed, looking at the dog with compassion. "It is as I feared. I am very sorry, Finlay."

Abby whispered Finlay's words again to herself. "But that doesn't make any sense. How could Eirwen be your mother? It was so long ago." As soon as she made the statement, Abby realized her error. "Duh, Abby, your dog can time travel. Doesn't matter that Eirwen was alive a thousand years ago," she shrugged. "Guess I never thought about the fact you had a mother."

"Have, not 'had'," Wren corrected. "Eirwen is alive."

"Wait, what?"

"I believe Finlay will sense the connection but, most assuredly, Eirwen is alive. Once Aster's guide, she is now bound to Shaeron."

"Is true," Rory nodded, "from what me visions revealed, she left the Howlin' Mountains side by side with Shaeron. She did so freely from what I could see, A-by."

Abby replayed Rory's description of his vision in her head, her eyes growing wide. "Okay, wait. It's just like what Mavis and Tavis did to Finlay! I bet you anything Shaeron cast some vicious spell on her, binding her to do his bidding. But," she continued, pacing around the group, "how could she still be alive too? That's a really long time, especially for a dog."

"Yes, indeed," Wren said. "The Stone of Longevity, this must be why. Perhaps its effect transfers to Eirwen because she is bound unnaturally to Shaeron."

Finlay pawed at the ground. *We must free her. And I will personally rip Shaeron's throat from his body to do so.*

Abby cringed at the thought, surprised by the intensity of her dog's emotions. "He says we have to free her," she said, jutting her thumb at Finlay. "Surely it's been torture for her to be tied to that creep for all these years."

Wren frowned. "While I do not doubt her turmoil, there have long been tales of a giant, black beast crushing the life from Manta who strayed too far from Willow Wood. I fear she has succumbed to the power of the sickness plaguing our land and freely follows a path of darkness."

Abby flung her arms around Finlay's neck and burrowed her face into his fur. *I'm so sorry. We'll make it right somehow, I promise, but first we've got to find Aster.*

Finlay plopped back onto his haunches again. *Hmm. Aster. Yes, child. This may be the solution to many problems.*

Abby smiled at him curiously. *The solution to many problems? How so?*

By completing Aster's circle, it stands to reason Wren will find the Stone of Longevity returned to her hands.

When this happens, it is possible it will free my mother from Shaeron's magic, assuming he has grown weak over the centuries. If nothing else, it may be enough for me to pull her from the darkness consuming her.

And, Abby pointed at the dog in agreement, *taking the Talisman away from him might be enough to stop, or even reverse, his ghoulish spell on the land. Maybe we wouldn't even have to fight him. It's brilliant, really, Finlay. Complete Aster's circle and we save your mom and Shay, and Wren gets to be a Protector.*

Abby whirled around and relayed their conversation to the others.

After digesting the information, Wren smiled. "Yes, it could be possible. Let us start by finding my kin, though. Without Aster, none of your revelations may come to pass."

"Right, of course," Abby agreed, "let's not get ahead of ourselves." She turned to Rory. "Where did you say you thought that cave was at?"

The Scotsman walked into the clearing and surveyed the ridge. "Hidden beyond our sight there," he answered, indicating a spot high on the ridge near the highest peak opposite them.

"Okay," Abby said, following the line of his finger, "so we need to figure out how to get up there as quickly as possible, preferably without being seen. No telling what's hanging around up in those hills."

Wren contemplated Abby's words. "It will be easiest for Rowen to search the area, but we must rely on ourselves to climb with quiet caution once he shows us where to go. It would be wise for Finlay to take us across the clearing; from there we must be swift. My unease for the mountains grows. I fear our presence is already known by those willing to do harm."

Tension squeezed Abby's gut at hearing Wren's nervousness. "Okay, that's easy enough for Finlay to zap us over there, but how are we going to tell Rowen we need him to search?"

"Perhaps ye could talk to his guide, A-by."

"Yes, Abby," Wren nodded, "do you think you can connect with Riffin?"

Abby frowned, searching the sky. "I don't know about that, guys. I can't even see him right now. Besides, half the time when I'm standing right next to a guide, they easily block me from their thoughts. I don't think I'm very good at it."

"Ye must have faith in yerself, A-by. Ye always accomplish what ye set out to do. I know this from seein' it with me own eyes many a time."

Abby's insides warmed from Rory's confidence in her. "Okay, sure. I can at least try." She stood at the edge of the tree line and gazed into the sky. Picturing the giant owl, she called out in her mind. *Hey Riffy-boy! Can you hear me? We need your help.* She continued watching the sky, sighing when no immediate response sounded in her head.

Moments later, Riffin and Rowen soared over the ridge to the group's right. A tickle brushed Abby's mind and then she heard him.

Pretty Amaray.

Frustration filled Abby momentarily. *Riffin! Good grief. Quit calling me that. You know we just completed her circle.* She shook her head at the bird and sighed. *Oh, just never mind. We need you to fly across to the other side, where I'm pointing, and see if you can find a cave back in there. We're pretty sure that's where Shaeron hid Aster's body. And tell this to Rowen while you're at it.*

The owl squawked and floated off in the direction Abby indicated. Not long thereafter, she could see the bird circling lower and lower over the area of peaks in question. He disappeared from view and after several seconds called out to Abby. *Cave. Here.*

"Sweet, guys. They found a cave, just like you said, Rory."

Another thought came to Abby as she studied the terrain in the distance. She reached out to the owl again with more confidence in her ability. *Hey Riffy? Are there any flat, open areas going up those hills that Finlay could take us to? But remember, he'd have to see them to use his magic.*

Riffin flew into view again, drifting low across the jagged landscape. He swooped back and forth several times before returning to the copse of trees. *No. Not safe,* he projected as he descended to the ground in front of his companions.

Rowen slid from his guide's back to embrace Wren. "Brothers, Sister," he said cheerily, "there is indeed a cave hidden from sight." He glanced over his shoulder at the ridge. "It is set back into a deep cut just over the second rise. Though it should be accessible by a steady pair of feet, I am uncertain how Finlay and Cody will maneuver their way up the face."

Abby glanced from the guides to the ridge and back. "Hmm. Yeah, maybe if you were a pair of mountain goats it'd be no problem. You're not holding back any shape-shifting abilities, are you?" she joked heartedly. "No, but seriously you guys, think you can manage?"

Finlay rumbled in response. *I will make my way without fault, little one. The ability of the one with the floppy ears, however, remains in question.*

Abby snorted at the distaste in her dog's voice. *Funny. We'll keep that between you and me.*

Do not forget, you will need me present in the cave to transport everyone along with the fallen Protector back to the Forest of Souls.

Abby tapped a finger in the air at her dog. *Right. Of course, didn't think of that.*

"Everyone needs to go," Abby said, turning back to the group. "Makes most sense if Finlay takes us back to the Forest of Souls straight from the cave. We don't have any time to waste with an extra trip trying to carrying Aster down the ridge just to meet up with Finlay and Cody. I'm sure they'll get on just fine climbing the rocks. Besides, the more eyes and ears watching for bad guys, the better off we'll be."

"Wisely spoken, Sister. Let us be off then," Rowen said as he jumped onto Riffin's back. "I will watch your path from overhead and guide you to the cave."

"Sounds good. Everybody grab hold," Abby directed, sinking a hand into Finlay's hide.

***

Abby stared up at the rocky face. "That doesn't look so bad I guess."

"Everyone remain as quiet and focused as possible," Wren whispered as she led the climb. "If Thraxen are about, we may not see them until it is too late. This will be difficult terrain to defend ourselves on, the advantage will be all theirs."

The group exchanged silent nods and began their climb. As Abby followed directly behind Wren, she glanced back to see Rory watching her climb with perhaps a bit too much interest. When her cheeks flushed, the Scotsman directed his attention to his foot placement, an embarrassed smile stretching across his face.

Finlay stepped in front of Cody, trailing closely after Rory. *Do not worry about the boy, young one. Concentrate on not breaking a leg.*

Ha ha, funny, but yeah, there will be no breaking of any bones. Mine or anyone else's.

Abby flinched when a sudden rush of air swept past her. She tipped her head back to view the steep embankment, surprised and confused to see Cody standing an easy twenty feet above them. "What the…"

Rory laughed aloud, hushing himself quickly when Wren looked coolly back at him. "No one can jump better than Co-dy," he whispered.

The hare twitched his nose, scanned the rock face, and exploded into another jump, landing half way up the first rise.

Abby shook her head, reaching out to Finlay. *What was that you were saying about the ability of the one with the floppy ears? I think he can manage better than the rest of us, short of your teleporting, that is.*

She giggled to herself and continued on when Finlay did not respond, hoisting her frame over the next rock. Upon clearing the first rise after ten minutes of climbing, everyone stopped for a brief break. Abby leaned against the rock-face next to Wren. "This is going far too well," she whispered. "My gut tells me something is watching us."

Wren scanned the ridge and nodded. "I believe your senses are in tune with our surroundings," she replied softly. "I, too, feel hidden eyes lying in wait. We must be vigilant. Come," she finished, waving for everyone to move on.

Cody launched himself up and to the right of the group, landing perfectly with a dull thump on a flat-topped boulder. Abby glanced up to watch his giant ears rotate, when a strange movement beyond the hare caught her attention. She squinted and leaned to the side, trying to focus on the rocks behind him. When she thought she could see something moving again, she reached back and wiggled her fingers at Rory. "Hey," she whispered, pointing toward the hare, "look up there past Cody. I swear I saw something move."

Rory pulled himself up next to Abby and followed the line of her finger. After several moments of searching, the Scotsman shook his head. "I do no'..."

Abby's breath caught at the same time Rory grunted surprise. She latched onto his arm with fright. "What in the name of Shay is that!" she exclaimed as a large section of the wall behind Cody came alive.

A dull grating of rock on rock accompanied the unnatural movement as Abby watched with wide eyes. A large, craggy chunk of the cliff face popped out and away, landing near the hare. Without pause, sections of it shifted simultaneously in different directions. It reminded Abby vaguely of an armadillo uncurling from a tight, defensive ball. She gasped as it took form, with four stubby appendages and a thick, concave head. Hundreds of pointed, rocky teeth filled what Abby assumed to be its mouth. The creature flopped onto its legs, turned toward Cody, and let out an ear-piercing roar. The instant the rock creature went silent, two more hunks separated from the ridge, but below and to either side of Finlay.

Abby slapped her hands over her ears as the three rock creatures roared in unison. She looked frantically to Wren. "What are they?" she tried to ask over the overwhelming sound.

"Stone Eaters," Wren replied with a frown once the noise tapered off. "Beings of legend. Many Manta, including myself, did not believe in their existence. It appears I was wrong."

"And do your old tales say how to fight these things?" Abby asked nervously when the Stone Eaters crept closer to the group, their misshapen heads swaying from side to side.

"No. And I fear my arrows will do little against their advance."

Abby gulped, fighting the fear rising in her stomach. "Fire," she whispered. "Rory! Your sword. Maybe you can cook these creepy things into piles of molten goo."

Rory wrinkled his brow, appearing confused, yet pulled his sword free from its scabbard all the same. Calling up its flames, he sliced the blade through the air, pointing it at the creature crawling up the ridge to his right. A blaze of fire blasted the Stone Eater, instigating a ferocious howl.

"Awesome, Rory! It definitely doesn't like that. Can you make it hotter?"

Rory grunted, the veins in his forehead bulging as he concentrated. Moments later, the flames morphed to a blazing white and the creature screamed out in pain.

"It's working!" Abby fist-pumped but lost her excitement quickly when she turned her attention to the other beasts.

Cody thumped his foot as a Stone Eater drew within striking distance. Abby bit her lip, wondering what the hare could do to defend himself. The rocky brute growled and swung a stubby leg forward. To Abby's surprise, spiny rock claws extended several inches from the end of its limb, taking aim at Cody's hind leg as the hare kicked out with force. Claws and foot connected brutally. Cody squealed when the creature's razor-like barbs sunk into his leg. The hare dropped to his back, shaking his leg violently until the Stone Eater relinquished its hold. Wasting no time, Cody thrust out with his other hind leg, connecting squarely with the rocky form. The creature rocketed backward and smashed into the jagged ridge face. Abby's jaw dropped when the Stone Eater burst into hundreds of tiny pebbles.

"Well. I guess that's one way to do it," she said, glancing back at Rory.

The Scotsman advanced on the Stone Eater, taking careful steps down the ridge. The beast stumbled farther and farther backwards, its rocky shape deteriorating with every movement.

Finlay leaped in front of Abby just as their third adversary readied for a strike. She gasped, realizing her lack of focus could have proved deadly. Her guide crouched low with an intimidating growl. *Stay behind me, child.*

Abby backed up against the ridge. *Don't have to tell me twice! But be careful, fuzzface. These things have some nasty claws.*

Just as Finlay prepared to pounce on the Stone Eater, a screech sounded from above. Abby startled when Riffin streaked toward the group, talons extended. Finlay stepped back to meet her against the wall, and seconds later, Abby recognized what was about to happen.

Riffin latched onto the Stone Eater and, with several powerful beats of his wings, rose into the sky. The creature's legs flailed as the owl rose higher and higher until they were but a dark spot. And then the dark spot became two. Abby smirked when she comprehended Riffin's intent.

The Stone Eater plummeted to the ground, crashing into the clearing below. Its body exploded, small bits flying haphazardly.

Rory let out a yell of triumph as he called the flames back to his sword. Remnants of the final creature lay still in a gooey pile. Abby patted the Scotsman on the back while he sheathed his sword. "Totally cool, Rory." She glanced up at Wren, who had climbed to stand next to Cody. "Now you can add to the legend," she said slyly, "death to Stone Eaters by smashing, crashing, or flaming."

Wren smiled back at her friend but motioned for Rory to join her. "Come, please. Your guide has sustained a terrible injury."

Elation of defeating the beast washed from the Scotsman's face, replaced with deep concern. He clambered over every boulder in his way to get to his guide. Kneeling at his side, Rory stared at the hare's hind leg. Wasting no time, Abby watched in awe as the boy pulled his sword free. Healing light wrapped around the hare until it was all she could see.

Feeling a strange urgency, Abby sunk her hand into Finlay's coat. *Zap us up there, would ya?*

In reply, Abby blinked to find herself standing behind Rory at the top of the first rise. "Wow," she said, turning to find her dog, "didn't even feel it that time. Your powers are definitely growing the longer we're here."

Finlay grumbled quietly. *Perhaps, child.* He peered all along the ridge. *Let us focus on finding our way to the cave as quickly as possible. I do not wish to encounter any further surprises.*

Abby nodded. *Can't argue with that. I think Rory's almost done fixing his bunny.* She turned around to gaze up at the second ridge awaiting them. *At least this one isn't high or steep. Shouldn't take but a few minutes to climb.*

When Abby spun back around, Cody hopped on his freshly healed leg. "Perfect. Let's not waste any time guys," she whispered, glancing around with suspicious eyes, "I'm sure we can all agree we don't want to run into any more of those stone-heads. Let's make this a quick and quiet climb."

Everyone nodded agreement, spurring Abby to take the lead. She chose her path deftly, making short work of cresting their second obstacle. As she waited for everyone to join her, she examined the rough environment to her left. Just as Rowen described, she could see a distant spot where two rock faces rose up within a few feet opposite each other, leaving the impression of a deep cut. "Guys," she said, looking back to see everyone accounted for. "Over there. I think that's what Rowen was talking about."

As if in response, Riffin floated overhead in the direction Abby pointed. He descended in a slow circle.

"Come," Wren said, "he awaits us. Let us find my kin and be gone from this dark place."

A howling wind ripped through the mountain ring after Wren set off toward Rowen.

Abby shook herself when the unsettling noise died down. "That makes my skin crawl," she mumbled to herself, taking off after Wren.

They hurried between the narrow passage formed by the two rocky walls. Abby ran her fingers along the cold surface, then recalled the stone creatures popping out from their camouflaged spots and cringed, jerking her hand away. The pass soon opened into a small, level clearing ringed on all sides by tall, uneven rises. As everyone gathered in the middle, Riffin spiraled to a silent landing.

Rowen slid from the owl's back and scooped Wren into his arms. He nodded knowingly to the others and pointed. "Brothers, Sister, the cave is on the far side…"

"What's wrong, Rowen?" Abby asked, seeing confusion on his face as he lowered his arm.

Rowen tilted his head. "This is most unusual. We could clearly see a cavern when in flight, but now," he paused, "perhaps I was mistaken."

Abby scrunched her face and scanned the rock face. "I don't think you were wrong. Think about it. Shaeron wouldn't want people stumbling on his secret. He probably cast a spell or something so we can't see the cave, and maybe you got lucky and could see it from up above." Abby's eyes brightened when she glanced at his bow. "Hey! Do that thing with your arrows, they'll show us if something is really there, right?"

"This is wise thinking, Sister. My Talisman will show us the truth. I can even save my arrows here," he said, walking toward the far wall, swinging his bow from his back, "the stone only need be close to dispel any falsehood."

Rowen stood close to the rock face, holding his bow at chest height. He inched his way along the wall, pausing after several feet. Directly in front of him, the deep gray of the granite wavered. "Here," he whispered when a five-foot wide, blackened crevice stretching ten feet high appeared.

"Now we're talking," Abby grinned, "bet it's going to be dark in there. We'll need some light. I seriously doubt we'll get lucky and find Goldenglow helping us out," she finished, nodding at Rory.

The Scotsman winked at her and unsheathed his sword. "A little fire for me lady?"

Wren smiled after noticing Abby's gentle blush. "Come, let our master of flames lead the way."

Rory stood tall and gave Wren an official tip of the head. Calling up a low level of fire, he stepped cautiously into the opening. After several paces, he signaled for the others to follow.

Abby recognized the need for more light once Cody, Wren, Rowen, and Riffin disappeared into the cavern. *Can't even see Rory's sword anymore.* After a moment of thought, she palmed her forehead. *Duh. You have flashlights, Abby. Wonder if there's any juice left in either of them?* She pulled her new pouch around to her front and dug out a light. *Shine bright for me one last time, baby.* Her shoulders relaxed when the welcome beam sliced into the dark opening. *Yes!* She grinned at Finlay. *Time to catch up with the others.*

After a handful of moments, Abby's light illuminated the massive backside of Riffin. She could hear soft chirrups as he waddled along through what she knew must be an unusual environment for him. For several minutes, the group made their way through the twisting tunnel. Just as Abby wondered how deep into the mountainside the cave could be, the owl vanished from her beam of light. Before she could consider where he went, flames burst to life in front of her, casting plentiful light throughout a modest cavern.

Stepping into the cave, Abby flicked the switch on her flashlight. "So now what? This cave's pretty small, and I don't see anything obvious. What about you guys?"

Rory held the sword above his head, finding just enough height to extend his arm. He commanded the flames to travel out in all directions along the rocky ceiling, providing sufficient light for all to see.

"I too see no signs of my kin." Wren sighed, turning full circle, "perhaps there is yet another spell of trickery hiding him from our sight."

Abby nodded at her friend. "I bet you're right. Maybe Rowen should try walking around the perimeter or wherever and use his Talisman?"

Rowen headed toward the left wall of the cave. "My thoughts exactly, Sister."

As the Protector took slow steps in his search, Abby motioned for Finlay to follow her as she wandered toward the opposite wall, thinking random thoughts. *Bet a week ago you'd never have guessed we'd be in a place called Shay, huh?*

That is so, little one. Our journey together has taken us down many unexpected paths. But I am a firm believer all things happen for a reason and you, lass, are right where you were meant to be.

Abby wrinkled her nose in reply. *I'm right where I'm meant to be? What do you mean by that?*

Is it not obvious yet that you have a powerful part to play in defeating Shaeron and restoring peace to Shay? Besides, he paused, rubbing his muzzle along her cheek, *I sense great things in store for you.*

A powerful part...

Abby halted when her foot bumped into something. She turned her light on and shined it straight down to find no clear obstacle. She swung her boot forward again with the same result. "Uh, guys," she called, glancing to the other side of the cave, "either I'm crazy or I think I found Aster."

Rowen rushed to stand next to Abby. He lowered his bow and within seconds, the solid form of Wren's kin materialized.

The group gathered around Aster's body in silence. Abby guessed, like her, everyone else waited for Wren to do something. As if on cue, her friend squatted and placed a hand on her fallen kin. "As with Redwin and Amaray, just as if he were sleeping," she whispered. "Your blood, my blood, I will see your way back to the land."

Wren stood and sighed. "Come, we must go immediately to the Forest of Souls. If the dark one is aware of what we are doing, every moment is crucial."

"Good point, Wren. Shaeron could have set some kind of alarm spell on his body." Abby signaled with her hands. "You guys know the routine. Let's get out of here!"

10

"There." Wren pointed beyond Redwin's tree. "My kin should be buried there."

Without delay, Finlay shifted the group to the desired spot.

Rowen removed his hand from Aster's body. "Thank you, Brother. This would not be possible without your incredible gift."

Finlay acknowledged the Protector by bending a front leg and kneeling to a deep bow.

Abby ruffled her dog's head as she took in the amazing colors in the Forest of Souls. "I still can't get over these trees. Dad would sure get a kick out of this."

Finlay nuzzled Abby's armpit. *And maybe one day he and the rest of your family will be as equally mesmerized.*

I don't know about that, she thought skeptically, *you really think things will work out that they'd be able to come here?*

Thundering hooves approaching at an alarming rate cut into any further thoughts of Abby's family. She whirled around to see Jovan and Javani spurring their guides forward with haste.

"Thraxen approach!" Jovan yelled.

"Fifteen, no less," Javani added.

Wren let out a frustrated sigh. "It is as I feared. Shaeron somehow knew of our doings. He has sent the Thraxen to retrieve Aster's body, or no doubt die trying." Her face hardened, "His circle must be completed. If we do not accomplish this today, I see no hope for our land."

Abby frowned, feeling the desperation in Wren's words. *We have to protect his body, Finlay, no matter what. I say if those creepy bugs get too close, you and I zap him to Willow Wood. At least then he'd be safe until they kill all the Thraxen.*

Finlay circled Aster's body. *A strategic suggestion, child, but you would be wise to alert the others of your plan. It would not do to add the sudden disappearance of his body to the chaos of battle.*

Yeah, you're right. Don't need to freak out Wren!

As the twins reined their guides to a sudden halt on either side of Aster, Abby turned to Wren and relayed her idea.

Wren nodded thoughtfully. "Yes, this sounds wise, but only if the urgency is dire. We need every Manta present to fight for our cause."

Abby nodded. "But," she replied quietly, scrunching her brow, "I have no weapon. Wouldn't even know how to use one if I did."

Wren projected an understanding warmth with her smile. "Then you will be our eyes," she said, pointing at a streak of movement in the distance. "There. They come. And it appears they feel no need to hide their attack."

Keeping her eyes on the approaching forms, Abby swung her bag around front and shoved an arm in. Moments later she snugged the bag to her back, pepper spray in hand. *It may not be much, but Stinky sure didn't like it. Hope it works on giant bugs.*

Everyone created a half-moon around Aster's body. With the twins on either flank and swords at ready, Tiffa and Daylo stamped their massive hooves. Abby glanced to her left to see Rowen and Wren side by side, arrows notched and pulled tight. She gulped and held her pepper spray nervously out in front of her, fidgeting until her thumb rested comfortably on the trigger. Abby darted her eyes to the right. Finlay crouched, ready to pounce, the growl from his deep chest so powerful, its vibrations rumbled in her gut. To her guide's right, Rory stood tall with sword drawn. Tiny red flames moved along its sharp edge. He nodded at Cody who hopped impatiently to his right.

After a brief mental inventory, Abby realized they were missing a party member. *Where'd Riffy-boy go?* A sudden gust of wind from behind startled Abby as the owl rose into the air. He gained impressive altitude in a short period and to Abby's surprise, dove sharply toward a tree twenty feet out and to their right. Sounding off with an alarming scree, Riffin plucked a Thraxen from the tree-top and surged straight up into the sky. Abby sneered, knowing what would come next. *Have a nice fall...*

Abby turned her thoughts back to the Thraxen ahead of them. "Be the eyes for everyone," she whispered to herself, trying to make a visual count. She scanned the area, watching as several of the enemy flipped dramatically from tree to tree. "There's five to the left," she said, loud enough for those around her to hear, "and I see eight to the right." Thinking back to Javani's warning, Abby whirled around several times. *She said fifteen. Riffin picked off one and I counted thirteen. Where's the last over-sized bug?*

Abby focused to her front. Her stomach tightened as the Thraxen drew near, hissing and clicking as they either jumped or sprinted from spot to spot. *Wonder if*

Mallena is here? Not sure how to tell though, they all look alike.

When but ten feet from the group, the Thraxen stopped, spreading out into a line. One by one, they each produced a crescent shaped blade. "Death to all Manta," they hissed in unison, "we will skin you from your hideous bones."

Abby pulled her head back in fearful disgust. "What a bunch of sadistic freaks!" While she continued to mumble disbelief to herself, a single Thraxen streaked forward.

"For the mighty Shaeron," the creature bellowed, running straight toward Wren.

Without pause, Rowen and Wren loosed several arrows in quick succession. Each met its mark with deadly accuracy. The Thraxen slowed with each step as arrow upon arrow sunk into its sinewy body. A multitude of colors flashed through its eyes before turning black. When it slumped to the ground, its brethren erupted into a chorus of hisses and shrieks. As one, they charged forward with a blinding hatred.

Abby stumbled back and bumped her heels against Aster, not knowing how to react to the flurry of action around her. Arrows and flames flew. Metal clanged against metal. Riffin screeched overhead and swooped low, plucking his second victim from the ground and lifting the hissing Thraxen high above. The sudden impact of its body hitting the ground moments later startled Abby. She jerked backward, tripping over Aster's body and losing her balance. She cried out in surprise as she landed on her backside and rolled to a stop after several feet.

Abby's exclamation caught Rory's ear. He turned around after striking down an opponent. "A-by! Are ye all right?"

"Ugh," she groaned, rubbing her lower back after pushing herself up to her knees. "Yup, I'm okay. Don't worry about me," she insisted, looking up at the Scotsman. "Behind you!" she screamed, pointing over his right shoulder.

Rory spun back to face a pair of Thraxen closing in on him. With a flick of his sword, he cast two streams of red-hot fire into their chests. The insectoids howled and crashed into each other, trying to use one another's body to squelch the flames. Rory took advantage of the moment, impaling both creatures in a single and powerful thrust of the sword.

Abby cringed as Rory pulled his weapon free and the bodies dropped to the ground. Just then, a soft clicking grabbed her attention. Though the cries of battle rang loud, her senses noticed the quiet sounds behind her. She pivoted on her knees away from the group to find what she knew must be the fifteenth Thraxen crawling along the ground toward her. Abby fumbled for her pepper spray, knowing she must have dropped it in her fall. *Where'd it go? Where'd it go?*

"All Manta must die," the Thraxen cackled.

Abby fell back onto her rump and scooted backward until she bumped into Aster's body. She searched the ground desperately for her only defense. Not finding it, she glanced up to see the Thraxen closing in on her. "Somebody?" she wailed.

Expecting Finlay or Rory to come to her rescue, shock rolled through Abby when Cody's giant form crashed down onto the Thraxen. Its body flattened with a sickening crunch in response to the hare's oppressive weight.

Cody! Abby called out with her mind.

The hare twitched his nose and winked. *Always at your service I am, young Manta.*

"A-by, oh A-by," Rory cried, rushing to her side as he sheathed his sword. He stretched out a hand to help bring her to her feet. "Are ye hurt?" he asked in a whisper, his eyes consumed by concern.

Abby paused before answering, aware of the sudden quiet throughout the forest. "I, I'm okay, thanks to Cody," she replied, squeezing the Scotsman's hand.

Rory smiled, nodding at his guide. "Well done. It pleases me to know ye too will see no harm come to me precious A-by."

Abby pulled her hand free and turned her head away, unsure how to respond to the devotion. She brushed stray blades of grass from her pants as she took in the many crumpled bodies. "Are they all dead?"

"Aye, A-by. Unless there are more hidin' somewhere," Rory said, glancing around cautiously.

Abby blew out a deep breath. "Nice job guys, sorry I couldn't be of any help."

Wren stepped close to Abby and placed a gentle hand on her back. "You may feel you are of no help, but trust me when I say the healing of Shay will not happen without you, my friend."

Abby lifted a brow. "Uh, what's that supposed to mean?"

Wren turned away as if she did not hear Abby's question. "Is anyone hurt?"

Both horses whinnied together, nodding their heads repeatedly. Tiffa raised her right front leg into the air, showing off several cuts. Daylo snorted, stamping her feet beside Tiffa, a deep gash evident from her left shoulder extending down across the chest. The twins whispered into their guides' ears as Rory rounded Aster's body to stand before them.

"If it pleases ye," he said to Jovan and Javani, "I shall heal their wounds with me sword."

Without speaking, the twins closed their eyes slowly while giving the briefest of nods to Rory.

The Scotsman looked from horse to horse, holding the gaze of each. "Do no' be afraid," he said, pulling his blade. Healing light shot from the amulet before Rory freed the sword from its sheath. For several moments, the yellow glow encapsulated both horses and their riders. As quickly as it began, the light retreated into the gem.

Tiffa and Daylo whinnied again and pranced around, showing off their injury free bodies.

Abby smiled at the horses' display. "Wow, Rory. Seems like it gets faster and faster each time you do it."

Rory grinned and returned his sword to his side.

Rowen slapped a hand on the Scotsman's back, "Well done, Brother."

"Yes, well done. Please, come," Wren motioned toward her kin, "let us lose no further time. I fear that will not be the last of the Thraxen on this day. We must complete Aster's circle now."

Rowen circled a finger in the air and whistled. "Riffin, patrol." Looking to the forest guardians, he bowed. "Brother, Sister, would you please guard our flank?"

The twins nodded and spurred the horses into a trot, each circling off in opposite directions.

Wren scanned the forest before staring down at her kin. "All is as it should be." She motioned at the ground, "Rory?"

Rory hurried over to Aster's body and drew his dirk, crouching down to carve the ritual circle in the ground. Once finished, he wiped the blade and handed it to Wren.

Holding her hands above Aster, Wren pricked the tip of a finger and handed the dirk back to Rory. Once a pool of blood formed, she allowed three drops to fall. "One with the land you are whole again, your circle is complete," she whispered.

As with Redwin's completion, the ground rumbled and the grass surrounding the body stretched into the air before wrapping it in an orange, fuzzy mat. The shaking seemed to go on much longer than the first time Abby witnessed a completion. *I wonder if it's taking longer because of the dark spell Shaeron cast on the body? I hope it doesn't make the forest sick.* Abby studied Wren's face but found no concern. She shrugged to herself when the body eventually sunk into the ground and the rumbling ceased.

Wren paused, causing Abby to study her again. *I bet she's nervous, probably excited too. Hard to tell since she's always so unreadable, but I'm sure that's how I'd feel. How cool to get to be a Protector!*

Movement in Abby's peripheral vision caught her attention. She shifted her gaze to see three thick, blue shoots zig zag into the air. She watched with wonder as a tree of the most beautiful blue formed rapidly before her. *Whoa. Watching that will never get old.*

When all movement ceased, everyone gathered around Aster's tree.

"Those are the biggest leaves I've ever seen," Abby commented, spreading her hand out in measurement.

"Yes," Wren agreed with a giant smile, "it is quite magnificent."

She stood close to the tree and placed both palms against its trunk. "I give of myself and accept your gift. In life and in death I am one with Shay."

A crackling split of the bark released two tiny, blue shoots to snake around each of Wren's wrists. They twirled faster and faster, mirroring Rory's experience, and in seconds, covered her entire body. When the process finished, and she eventually stepped back from the tree, Wren wore the armor of a Protector. She glanced down to examine herself.

She looked up with a proud smile to find Rowen, only to see him gesture toward her left hand. Wren followed his eyes and realized she gripped the strong shaft of a tall, wooden staff.

"Nice staff, Wren!" Abby said, running to her side. "Hey, look." Abby pointed to a deep indentation above the grip of the staff. "Bet that's where your Talisman goes."

"Yes, I am certain you are correct, though..."

Abby frowned, glancing around. "Right, can't put the Talisman in it if you don't have it. You completed Aster's circle. I thought that meant the Stone of Longevity would somehow magically appear in your hands or something."

Wren sighed, her brow creasing. "Yes, I too thought..."

"What? What is it?" Abby asked, tipping her head.

"Do you feel that?" Wren held her right arm out. "Look!" she exclaimed, pointing at the erect hairs on her forearm.

Abby wrinkled her nose as electricity buzzed in the air. A soft sizzling tickled the hairs around her ears. "What the..."

An abrupt crackling among the tree branches drew all eyes to the forest's new addition.

"There!" Abby pointed at the end of the lowest branch. "Do you see it?" She shielded her eyes when a bright, blue flash lit up the limb. Abby pulled her hand away from her face when the light dimmed sufficiently. A deep, black blotch grew from the center of the light, battling to overtake the blue haze. The darkness ebbed and flowed until Abby thought she could no longer see any blue. But with a sudden burst of light, the black pit pulled into its center-most point and disappeared with a sizzling pop.

"My Talisman!" Wren sang when the air stilled.

The source of the brilliant, blue light swung from the tree branch. A tarnished chain rocked slowly back and forth, an egg-shaped stone attached to its end with a crude, claw-like holder clamping its sides.

Wren ran to Aster's tree, reaching up almost hesitantly to remove the Stone of Longevity. Cupping it in her hands, she stared at the gem in silence. "My love?" she said, motioning to Rowen. "Please help me release the Talisman from this chain."

Rowen rushed to his binding's side. "Indeed. A chain which undoubtedly hung from an evil neck. Let us not touch it for too long."

Wren passed the Talisman to Rowen, a tinge of fear in her eyes. He lifted his arm above his head and dangled the stone in front of him by the chain. "Hmm." Lowering the chain, he grasped the gem firmly and with a thumb on each end, tried to pry the metal fingers outward away from its surface. He stopped with a grunt when success eluded him. "Brother," he said, glancing up at Rory, "may I use your short blade?"

Rory obliged, handing Rowen his dirk handle-first.

Rowen nodded his thanks, slipping the tip of the dirk under the first of six clamps. With gentle pressure, he wiggled the blade up and down under the metal until he found just the right leverage. Taking care not to scratch the stone, he lifted the edge, the clasp snapping and falling to the ground. Rowen smirked. "It seems you will not keep that which was not rightfully yours in your grasp any longer, Shaeron," he whispered as he moved quickly to free the stone from the remaining metal claws. When the last clasp relinquished its hold on the stone, Rowen cupped the Talisman in his hand and flung the chain into the grass.

To everyone's surprise, the grass parted, shifting away from where the chain landed. A handful of orange blades exploded to Abby's height, then dove toward the chain. Scooping it up, the giant grass whirled around it, choking out any recognizable form. For several moments, the weaving of blades swayed in the air. Abby thought she could hear a strange crunching and tensed with wonder. In one swift movement, the blades uncurled and shrunk to normal size, leaving only dust from the chain to float away on a timely breeze.

"Well. Okay," Abby said, "guess the forest didn't want any trace of Shaeron hanging around. Can't say I blame it." She studied the familiar stone as Rowen held it up toward the sun. *I feel like I've seen that before. Must've been one of my wacky dreams or something.*

Wren ran a hand across Rowen's cheek. "Thank you," she said, stretching up to touch her forehead to his. "Let us put the Stone of Longevity in its rightful place."

Rowen nodded, passing the gem to Wren.

Taking the stone in one hand, she rotated the staff until the deep groove above the grip faced her. After a brief pause, Wren armed her new weapon with the Talisman. She sighed slowly once the stone snugged into place. "We did it. I believe the beginning of the end has come for Shaeron..."

Before she could finish her thought, Wren doubled over, clutching her free hand to her side. "Ahh," she groaned. Just as quickly, she straightened, surprised.

"Wren! Are you okay? What happened?" Abby asked, stepping to her friend's side.

Wren stared at her staff before answering. "Yes, I am fine. It was an unusual cramp in my side, but it is gone now. Please, there is no need to worry."

Abby glanced at Rowen as he rubbed Wren's back, then shifted her attention to the Talisman. A fleeting swirl of movement caught her eye and she leaned in closer to the staff. *Was that a black splotch I just saw inside the stone?* She decided otherwise upon closer inspection when the deep blue of the gem shimmered back.

"Sooo, now what?" Abby asked, shifting her eyes back to Wren. "We've found Aster, completed his circle, you're a Protector now, which is super cool, by the way," Abby said with a head jerk at Wren, "and we got the stone back from that evil creep. That's a full day's work, right?"

Wren smiled. "Indeed, it is a full day. But we all know it is essential we now find the Book of Shay. It must hold the key to saving the land from Shaeron's darkness. I strongly feel we would not have been directed to otherwise."

Abby held her hands out, palm up. "But we can't even read it. How's it going to do us any good? I mean, I know the mysterious voice said to return it to its rightful owner, I just don't get how that will help us beat Shaeron."

"Please, let us not worry on this now but instead focus on finding our late Queen's treasured book. Things have a way of revealing themselves with time and patience," Wren said, gazing out above the treetops. "But perhaps we should regroup in Willow Wood and start fresh on the morrow," she added after watching Rory stretch and stifle a yawn.

Abby parroted the Scotsman's actions. "Sounds good to me. The sun's about to set anyway, searching in the dark probably isn't the smartest thing."

"Brothers, Sister, if we are all agreed, I will meet you in the safety of our sacred home," Rowcn said after parting ways with Wren. The group watched him climb effortlessly onto Riffin's back. "To Willow Wood," he called out as they gathered in a circle around Finlay.

Abby nodded when everyone joined hands and she sunk her fingers into Finlay's fur. "All right, a good night's sleep tonight and tomorrow we get that book!"

11

Abby strolled from their sleeping quarters after a fitful night's rest. She rubbed her stomach and licked her dry lips. *Ugh. I know Wren said the Bria should keep us from feeling hungry or thirsty for several days, but geez, I feel like I've had nothing to eat or drink in a week.* She shrugged as she walked along through the towering forest. *Maybe it's cause I didn't grow up here, just need to acclimate or something.* The snap of a branch in the distance caused her to jump. Peering around a grand trunk, she could see Rory practicing hand-to-rabbit foot combat moves with Cody. She giggled at the unlikely pair and jogged over to meet them. "Hey," she smiled with a quick wave as she approached.

Rory returned a wide grin upon seeing her. "Good mornin', A-by. Did ye sleep well?"

Abby rubbed the back of her neck. "I've had better nights. Weird dreams or something, I guess." She glanced around, "Have you seen Wren or Rowen? Seems kind of quiet this morning."

"Nae, Lass. No other soul besides Co-dy has met me eyes yet today," he paused, gazing beyond Abby for a moment. "And where might yer grand beast be hidin'?"

"Oh, Finlay? He's still sleeping. Was out cold when I left, must've been dreaming about chasing rabbits."

Cody's ears stood erect and his eyes widened.

Oops, Abby thought privately. "Don't worry, Cody, you're a hare after all, not a rabbit. Besides, he only chases them for play. It's not like he eats them," she said, holding back a snort, trying her best to sound convincing. "Speaking of eating," she continued, turning back to Rory, "you hungry by chance?"

Rory covered his mouth to conceal a laugh, then patted his belly, needing no time to consider the question. "Aye, A-by. Shall we test our hand at findin' some Bria?"

"Now you're talking. Let's go this way," she said, pointing deeper into the forest.

The pair walked hand in hand in silence for several minutes. Abby tried to focus on the land. She slowed her pace and approached the nearest tree to her left. Goldenglow grew along one side of the trunk, reminding Abby of moss on the north side of a tree back home. "This one, I think."

Rory nodded and knelt next to her before the massive trunk. They held their hands in the air and Abby relaxed her mind, searching for a connection with the land. As time slipped by, Abby felt a growing warmth enter her inner being. She took this as a sign and burrowed her hands as deep as she could into the dirt. She felt several round orbs instantly and dug them out. Opening her eyes, she found Rory smiling with the same success. They piled their stash together and counted eight Bria.

"We did it, Rory. We actually did it on our own!" Abby's elation soon turned to revulsion when all but two of the glowing orbs morphed into black globs before disintegrating into nothing.

"That," she stressed, "is not good." She grabbed up the remaining Bria and handed one to Rory. "This will have to do for now. I feel bad not having anything to share with the others, but at least we got something."

"Aye," Rory frowned, accepting the nourishment. "We best tell Wren. It seems the sickness in the forest grows greater with each day, A-by." Rory jumped to his feet, determination in his eyes. "We must find a way to stop it!"

Abby stood and brushed her knees clean. "We have to get the book back. I don't know how we'll read it, but it's got to have a clue in it. It's just got to. I don't know what we'll do otherwise."

Rory took up Abby's hand in his own. "Ye have great compassion in yer heart, A-by. We will save the land, together."

Abby blushed and turned back to their original path. "Come on, let's go wake up Finlay and find Wren. She'll know what to do."

***

The trio strolled into the clearing, with Cody bounding ahead. "Huh. Wonder where everyone's at," Abby said, scratching her head and exchanging looks with Rory and Finlay. "Let's go see if Emi is home. Maybe she's seen Wren. Zap us over there?" she asked, glancing at her dog.

In moments, they stood under the arch of Emi's woven root dome. "Hello," Abby hollered, "anybody here?"

After what seemed an extended period of silence, Abby could hear sounds of movement coming from Emi's tunnel. Shuffling steps and a soft thunk echoed repeatedly until, to Abby's great surprise, Wren appeared at the opening leaning on her staff.

"Wren?" Abby said with concern. "You don't look so good. You feeling okay?"

"Please," she waved a dismissive hand, stepping into the morning sun, "there is no need for worry. I am but feeling a bit tired is all."

Abby eyed Wren's pasty skin. "Are you sure? Not to be rude, but you look pale."

"I assure you, all is well."

"Okay, if you're sure," Abby murmured, unconvinced. "Hey," she whirled around and checked the sky, "where's Rowen and that awesome owl?"

Wren leaned against the dome's roots. "He went off several hours ago to search for the Book of Shay. I am not hopeful he will find anything on his own, but with Riffin's exceptional eyesight, they often surprise me."

Abby smiled and nodded slowly, sensing Finlay's presence in her mind.

The girl is ill, lass. Her scent is different today.

Well I'm not about to smell her, but I think you're right. Wren doesn't look good at all, she's not fooling anyone with the 'tired' act. Maybe the last Bria she ate was bad? I thought the ones we had yesterday seemed okay, but maybe she got one that was rotting from the sickness.

Perhaps, child, but I sense this is something more, though what I cannot say. We must watch her closely.

Agreed. Abby suppressed a frown. *But I don't know how we're supposed to help her if something really is wrong. Not like we can whisk her off to a hospital.*

Emi waddled to the tunnel opening, breaking Abby's concentration. "Oh hey, Emi," she greeted the giant badger, as she now deemed the creature, with a genuine smile. "What are you up to today?"

Abby picked up on Emi singing as usual. She watched curiously, and then with apprehension as the guide scooted next to Wren and sniffed intently.

Stitch, stitch, sick, sick, no good, no good, cannot fix, fix...

Abby stepped forward and raised a finger, ready to question Emi's disturbing rhyme, but flinched when a resounding screech, followed by screaming, filled the air. She walked into the clearing, shielding her eyes with a hand.

Riffin circled far overhead. As he made his descent, something did not look quite right to Abby. "Hey guys," she called over her shoulder, "do you see that?" She strained her eyes, then whipped back toward Wren. "Does he have something in his claws, like, a person?" she asked quizzically.

Wren leaned against her staff and joined Abby. She studied the floating form for a moment. "Yes, I believe you are correct. And a person showing great resistance at that. Unless I am mistaken, those are legs kicking."

Abby squinted into the air again and gasped. "No. Way. I don't believe it!" She ran to Rory and tugged on his arm. "Are you seeing what I'm seeing, or are my eyes playing tricks?"

Rory raised a puzzled brow before staring up at the owl. After several moments his face hardened, and he traded glances with Abby. He stepped to the side and drew his sword. "Yer eyes are no' playin' tricks on ye, A-by."

Finlay sprang to Abby's other side with a loud thump, landing in a crouch. *It appears we may have good fortune today, child.*

Riffin dove unexpectedly toward the ground, the screaming intensifying the faster he plummeted. At what seemed the last moment possible, he pulled his head up, pointed his rump down, and extended his wings in a powerful downstroke.

Abby's jaw dropped when the raptor somehow slowed his momentum and hovered five feet off the ground.

When Rowen patted his guide's side, Riffin released his talons and the now silent form flopped to the ground belly down, groaning on impact. With head hung low, the newcomer rose to hands and knees, spitting out a mouthful of grass.

Abby swore she heard a second, faint thud somewhere behind the owl but brushed it off and shifted her attention to the matter at hand.

Rowen slid from Riffin's back and motioned for everyone to encircle their would-be prisoner.

Following his gesture, Wren shifted to fill in the last gap but leaned hard against her staff, pain evident on her face.

Seeing her struggle, Abby made ready to run to her friend's side.

Wren looked up to see the concern in Abby's eyes but waved her off and stood up straight.

Having kept his sights on Riffin's catch, Rowen readied his bow. "Sister," he called out, glancing at Abby, "is this the thief from your courageous tale in the Other? Or shall I prepare an apology?"

Abby stomped forward. "No, Rowen, you got it right. The only person who should give out apologies is this dirty rat right here."

Abby watched as the old man got to his feet and whirled around nervously, clutching his satchel to his chest. "Why did you do it, Aillig? Don't you care that Mallena nearly killed Agatha?" Abby fumed, not waiting for a reply. "Give us back the book. If you have any decency left, you'll hand it over right now without a fight. I don't think you'll like the alternative."

Aillig reached a hand to his face and pushed his glasses snug to the bridge of his nose. He blinked several times and cleared his throat. "Ah, yes, yes. Apologies,

apologies. The old girl is okay then? I did not expect that putrid beast to take such harsh measures."

Abby slapped a hand to her hip. "Well," she paused, surprised by the sincerity in Aillig's voice, "yes, thanks to Rory, Agatha is just fine.

Finlay crept forward, prowling around the archaeologist in a wide arc.

Aillig cringed and shrunk back, stumbling. Losing his balance, he plopped onto his backside, landing just in front of Wren.

"Please," she said, stepping forward and extending a hand, "do not fear those around you. If you bear the Book of Shay, we ask respectfully for you to pass it into our care. Without it, the beauty all around you will die."

The old man craned his neck and peered back at Wren. Abby could see the bewilderment in his eyes. She too found herself impressed with Wren's compassionate tone.

Aillig accepted Wren's hand and pulled himself to his feet. Abby thought she noticed Wren wince when he tugged on her arm, but thought better of pointing out any weakness her friend might have.

"Well yes, the book, the book." Aillig turned full circle, his attention darting in every direction before stopping to face Wren once again. He lowered his satchel reluctantly and loosened the buckled straps. "I must warn you," he said, reaching inside, "that hideous creature will stop at nothing to take it back. She is delusional, I tell you."

"You're talking about Mallena, right?" Abby asked, stepping in closer, eager to see inside his bag.

"Of course, young lady, who else?"

Abby detected a hint of disdain in the old man's voice and scowled to herself. *I still don't trust this guy. Nothing but trouble.* Abby narrowed her eyes ever so slightly. "So, speaking of Mallena, where is she anyway? Did you ditch her or something? Can't imagine she'd let that book out of her sight."

Aillig considered the question, glancing at Abby with a slight smirk. Turning his attention back to Wren, he finished unbuckling his satchel as he answered. "You imagine correctly."

Abby glared at the old man, "What's that supposed to mean?"

Aillig pulled the Book of Shay from his bag, holding it tight to his chest. "A pity you do not recognize your own naivety." He paused, his eyes flashing around with dread. "The devil often hides in plain sight."

Ignoring what the man before her said, Wren nestled her staff into the nook of an armpit and stretched her arms out. "May I?" she asked, nodding at the book.

Abby watched as Aillig's knees appeared to quiver when he inched the book away from his chest and toward Wren. She tried to contemplate his last words but a soft clicking caught her attention. Abby whirled her head around, subconsciously recognizing the sound. *The devil hides in plain sight. Oh no! Why didn't I figure as much? Those nasty Thraxen can make themselves invisible.*

Abby gasped. "She's here! I don't know how, but Mallena is here!"

A devious cackle filled the air in response to Abby's declaration, startling all but Aillig who pulled the book back to his chest.

"It came from over there," Abby said, looking toward Emi's home. She scoured the area to no avail. "Where is she?" she muttered with frustration.

The familiar clicking started again, increasing until Abby knew where Mallena hid. "There." Abby pointed to the top of Emi's woven dome. "She's up there. I swear I saw movement."

Rory stepped forward, thrusting his sword into the air. "Show yerself, foul beast."

When all remained silent for several moments, Rowen released an arrow, sinking it into the upper curvature of the dome.

The air shimmered briefly as the magic missile revealed Mallena's true form crouched atop the arch, her guise used in the Other no longer needed. Abby recoiled at Mallena's double set of eyes and pincer like mouth.

The Thraxen hissed upon realizing her visibility to the group. "Manta," she spat, studying her adversaries one by one. Her eyes locked on Abby. "You," she roared, standing up. "You will regret the day you followed me." She whipped out her curved blade and fingered its point. "I knew I should have dealt with you when I had the chance."

Abby stood, her body tense. "You're outnumbered, Mallena. If you know what's good for you, you'll leave us in peace."

Mallena bellowed, glaring at Rowen. "You may have bested my underlings in the past, but you are no match for the mighty leader of the Thraxen." She swung an arm wide. "I leave this putrid wood one way and one way only — with the book and with you dead," she threatened, twirling her weapon, stopping it mid-spin to point it directly at Abby.

Finlay reared up on his hind legs like a bear, growling louder than Abby thought possible. He thumped to the ground and sidled up next to her. *Do not leave my side, child.*

Abby stared at the weapon still directed at her. *No problem. That's one crazy bug up there.*

Rowen loosed several arrows in quick succession at Mallena.

To everyone's surprise, she launched herself from the dome, giving the arrows no chance to hit their mark. Leaping high into the air, she landed gracefully outside their protective ring after several flips. Moments later, she disappeared.

Abby gasped in unison with her comrades. "Great," she groaned, "that will be hard to defend against."

Soft clicks sounded all around the group. First near Wren, then Emi, then Rowen. Faster and faster the sounds jumped until pinpointing Mallena's location became impossible.

A storm brewed in Abby's gut. *She's taunting us.*

Cody squealed when a twelve-inch long wound appeared suddenly along his hind leg.

"Co-dy!" Rory rushed to his guide's side, flames roaring from his sword.

Rowen strode toward the center of the group, stringing an arrow. "We shall make this an even battle."

With swift movements Abby could not follow, Rowen shot arrow after arrow into the ground, creating a perimeter around the group. He ended by sinking one into the dirt near Aillig and Wren. "Stay within the ring and she cannot hide from us."

Abby looked nervously around the magical boundary. "Smart thinking, Rowen." She glanced back at Cody, relieved to find Rory inspecting the now-healed wound. She smiled at the Scotsman's ability. *We'd be in a world of trouble if it weren't for that.*

Aillig turned a slow circle. "I refuse to help you further, beast," he shouted in no particular direction.

A hissing whisper replied from beyond the perimeter, "Then you too shall die."

Aillig gulped and hugged the book for dear life. "Now, now, that is unnecessary. I am sure we can make some kind of arrangement."

The hissing continued, jumping from spot to spot, "Death to all Manta. The book will be mine. Shay will be mine."

Abby snorted. "You mean Shaeron's. You're nothing but his hired thug."

A shrill cry trailed into mocking laughter. "The old fool is near his end. Once I unlock the secret of the book, the last thing he will do is bow to my power. I, and I alone will control the Brana. Shay will be mine."

Abby glanced at everyone and held back a gasp when she saw Wren's languishing carriage. Her friend slumped even lower on her staff, her skin dull in the morning sun.

She called out frantically to Finlay. *Have you noticed Wren? She's way worse than even a few minutes ago. Something is really wrong with her.* Helplessness consumed Abby. *I have to do something, but what? Especially with this demented bug stalking us.*

Finlay rubbed against Abby's side. *I feel your despair, child. I too am worried for the girl. Know I would act if a solution were clear.*

Well, Abby pinched the bridge of her nose, *maybe you should at least zap her out of here to some place safe, get her away from Mallena.*

A murmur ran through Abby's mind as her dog worked through the suggestion. *That may be best, but only with her permission.*

Abby wiggled a thumb's up in reply and made her way toward Wren. "Hey, Wren," she whispered as she drew close. A slight breeze and soft thump stopped Abby's forward progress. She looked around, confused. "What was that?"

Wren stiffened in response, gasping.

Mallena's form materialized behind Wren. The Thraxen grabbed her around the waist, pulling her close. She hooked her weapon around Wren's neck and hissed into her ear. "This one appears to be your weakest link."

Rowen cried out, aiming an arrow at Mallena's head.

The Thraxen let out a purring click. "Choose your actions wisely, Manta. You will all die eventually. The question is, who will go first? One wrong move and it will be this one here," she said, jerking Wren for emphasis.

Wren whispered something Abby could not make out.

"What was that, Manta filth? Were you begging me for mercy?" Mallena asked, leaning in.

Wren filled her lungs and found her voice for all to hear. "Only the Keeper of the Land may divine the secrets of the book, and you are not she, though she will come again."

"What? What is this nonsense?" Mallena turned Wren enough to study her face. "Yes, you must be the one I have heard about. The one who knows things. You will certainly serve my purpose." Mallena shifted Wren back to face Aillig. "You," she blinked all four eyes at the old man, "you will give the book to the young hag, and that one," she said, nodding her head at Finlay, "will take us away from here. No tricks."

Mallena howled gleefully when Abby's eyes grew large. "Yes, Manta, that is correct. I am astute enough to understand your mutt's ability." She dug the tip of her blade into Wren's neck, prompting a soft squeak from the girl. "The book," she hissed at Aillig, "give it to me now. Abide my orders and I may let you all live for now."

Aillig sputtered, his eyes uncertain.

"Do you not remember our agreement?" Mallena growled at the man. "You do as I say. Always. I may even let your pathetic heart continue beating."

Wren sighed, "Give me the book."

"Wren, no!" Abby cried. "We can't let her have the book again. And...and I won't let her take you!"

"Please," Wren assured in soft tones, "all will be as is meant." She motioned to Aillig, "Pass me the book."

Aillig pulled the book from his chest and studied its cover.

Abby inched toward the old man. "Don't you dare."

Aillig glanced at Abby, then turned his attention back to Mallena and the small form she imprisoned. With quivering arms, he extended the book forward, his eyes locking with Wren's.

Wren stretched her hands as far as the dangerous restraint on her body would allow. Just as her fingers brushed the underneath of the book, Aillig jerked his arms back a few inches and gulped.

"Never trust a Ratchet," Aillig sneered.

"What did you say?" Mallena roared.

Aillig stood straight. "You heard me, beast."

To everyone's astonishment, the old man heaved the book into the center of the ring.

"Never trust a Ratchet," he said again. Before anyone could react, he dashed away as fast as his old legs would allow and headed toward the forest.

Mallena shrieked, her eyes burning red with fury. "Ratchet!" she screamed. She glanced from Wren to the book. To Abby's dismay, Mallena jabbed the curve of her blade deep into Wren's armpit and shoved her to the ground. Mallena dove for the book. "It belongs to me," she barked.

"Wren!" Abby wept helplessly, watching her friend crumple into an unmoving heap.

Mallena grabbed the Book of Shay with one hand and crouched as if preparing to launch herself into the air.

"Now," Rowen commanded, nodding to Rory.

Just as Mallena pushed off from the ground, two arrows plunked into her chest, followed by a focused stream of fire. She released the book and fell onto her back. Her body writhed from the initial shock of the flames.

Finlay leaped next to the Thraxen and scooped up the book carefully into his mouth before shuffling backward.

Rory strode toward Mallena, his face icy as he pointed the sword at her chest. The intensity of the flames increased, consuming her body completely. Her piercing wails soon faded until the only sound came from the crackling of the fire. Rory summoned the flames back to his sword, revealing but a charred shell.

Everyone stood silent for a moment, shocked.

"Wren!" Abby gasped, running to her friend and falling to her knees.

Rowen kneeled to Wren's other side not a moment later and helped roll her onto her back.

"Oh, Wren," Abby sobbed, inspecting her wound. "Rory! Heal her."

Rowen scooted behind Wren and lifted her head, resting it in his lap. "My love," he whispered, stroking her cheek.

The Scotsman hurried to stand over the trio. The moment he held his sword above Wren, a swath of healing, golden light consumed her.

Abby turned her head to the side and shut her eyes. After several seconds, the light dimmed and she looked back at her friend.

The wound in the pit of her arm healed, Wren drew in raspy, shallow breaths.

"But..." Abby stared up at Rory, confused. "Why isn't she better?" She listened to Wren's breathing again. "She's worse. Why is she worse?"

Wren patted Abby's hand. "Please, do not worry yourself, my friend. There is no cure for what ails me, not even by your binding's gift."

"I...I don't understand, Wren. What's wrong with you? There's got to be a way we can make you better." Abby stifled a whimper. "There just has to be."

Wren reached up with her left hand to cup Rowen's cheek and with her right, she squeezed Abby's fingers. "Look into my Talisman, Abby, there you will find the answer.

Puzzlement filled Abby's mind. *Look into her Talisman?* She leaned across Wren and grabbed her friend's staff. Taking care not to hit anyone with it, Abby angled the walking end away and rotated the stone into view. A deep, black mass swirled inside the gem, only specks of blue remained. Abby whipped her head toward Wren and found her familiar, compassionate eyes waiting.

"It is the sickness," Wren wheezed.

Rowen bent low and touched his forehead to Wren's. He rose with tear-streaked cheeks.

Abby's lip quivered. "But, what does that mean?"

Wren intertwined her fingers with Abby's. "Aster's tree is dying."

Abby stared into her friend's eyes for several silent moments and gasped, understanding flooding her face. She shook her head hard. "No, no, no. It can't be!"

Wren closed and opened her eyes slowly. "And so too will I complete my circle."

Fat teardrops rolled down Abby's face. "No! You can't go!" she choked between uncontrollable sobs.

Wren moved her hand to Abby's face. "Shh, my friend," she paused, taking in a labored breath. "Do not grieve for me. All things must come full circle. It is my time."

Rowen pivoted around to face his binding, love radiating from him. He bent low again and met Wren's forehead. They whispered in unison. "In life and in death..."

Abby's sobbing subsided when she saw the braveness of both Rowen and Wren. She rubbed her thumb along Wren's hand. "I'll never forget you, Wren," she whispered.

Rowen sat up and stroked Wren's hair, watching as her breathing slowed. "The land calls her home, Sister."

Wren's eyes fluttered as she struggled for air. She pulled her hand free from Abby's and beckoned her with a finger.

Abby propped herself on her left elbow and slid in close. "What is it, Wren? Please, don't strain yourself."

Wren smiled lovingly at her friend and when Abby's ear hovered just above her mouth, she breathed her last words, "You are she and she is you. You must believe, Amaray..."

Abby pulled away from her friend, stunned. She burst into tears when Wren's chest rose no more.

***

Abby leaned against Emi's dome entrance and stared into the distance, an emptiness gnawing at her stomach. "I can't believe she's gone," she mumbled to herself, slumping down to the ground. With red-rimmed eyes, she watched Riffin disappear over the tree line, Wren's body tucked in his talons as he and Rowen headed to the Forest of Souls.

Rory approached Abby slowly and motioned at a spot next to her. "May I sit with ye, A-by?"

She nodded, patting the ground.

The Scotsman lowered himself next to Abby. Looking at her out of the corner of his eye, he wrapped a hesitant arm over her shoulder, rubbing it gently.

Abby sighed and without thought, leaned into his warm hold and rested her head against him. She struggled to keep her voice even. "I can't believe it. It happened so fast."

Rory said nothing but continued to rub her shoulder.

"And what's weird is Rowen didn't seem that upset, almost like he expected it. I mean, sure, he cried a little, but since they were bound, I'd think he'd seem more devastated. Maybe it's a 'Shay' thing."

Rory cleared his throat and glanced down at Abby's face. "We all have different ways of expressin' our sorrow. Does no' make the pain another feels any less than our own," he said softly. "But know if ye were taken away from me, I would no' be able to go on. I would be destroyed."

Abby sat up straight and met Rory's eyes. She opened her mouth to speak, but instead continued to hold his gaze. She studied the depths of his intense stare and knew with certainty in that moment the truth it held. *He really does love me.* Before she could lose her nerve, Abby smiled and kissed his cheek, then settled back into the nook of his arm.

The pair sat in silence for several minutes. Abby sighed. "So, what now?"

Rory shrugged. "We wait for Rowen to return. He will know what to do."

Abby echoed the Scotsman's shrug and watched as Finlay ambled toward them, the Book of Shay still nestled in his mouth. He eased himself to the ground and placed the book in front of them. *May I suggest, little one, you study this while we wait. Perhaps there is something we overlooked the first time.*

Abby glanced at Rory. "Finlay thinks we should look at the book again. That maybe we'll find something new. I'd say it's a waste of time, though, considering it's written in some secret language. Even Aillig couldn't figure it out, and that's supposedly his specialty."

Rory reached forward and hefted the book into his lap. He stroked the ornate cover. "Even so, it could no' hurt."

Abby propped herself on a hand and leaned in as Rory thumbed through the opening pages. She stared wide-eyed when he stopped to study a picture of a giant toad much like the one they encountered upon first arriving in Shay. She squinted at the accompanying text and shook her head just as he turned the page. "Wait!" she exclaimed, reaching across to place a restraining hand on his.

"What is it, A-by?"

"You will not believe this," Abby shook her head again, staring at the page. "Heck, even I don't believe it."

Rory suppressed a chuckle, "Well do no' keep me in suspense, Lass. What gives ye such surprise?"

Abby pointed at the toad. "That's called a Blackbelly."

Rory raised a brow. "And how do ye know that?"

"Because I can read every word."

12

Abby sat by herself with the Book of Shay opened in her lap after Rory convinced her she should take some time to explore it. She glanced over her shoulder and smiled at a snoring Finlay, who lay curled in the shade just inside the dome's opening. Perking her ear, Abby picked up on Emi's distant humming from deep within the tunnel. She turned to look out into the clearing. Rory practiced defensive moves with Cody in the distance, the hare jumping back and forth, dodging thrusts of the Scotsman's sword.

She sighed, confused and a bit frustrated by the latest, strange development. *What was it that Wren said about the book? Only its creator could read it?* Abby averted her attention to the tree line, lost in thought. *But that was the Red Queen, aka Amaray.* She replayed Wren's final words in her head. *You are she and she is you. What is that supposed to mean? Did she think I'm supposed to take the place of the Red Queen?* Abby snorted at herself. *I'm just a girl from Nebraska. There's nothing royal about my blood. She couldn't have really expected me to fill the Queen's shoes, could she?* She wrapped a finger around her golden curl and twirled it without thought. *I am part of the Manta tribe though.* She pictured her mother and sister, realizing what it also meant for them. *So, someone in Mom's bloodline came from here. I wonder if they traveled to the Other during the Great Crossing...*

Abby dropped her gaze back to the picture of the Blackbelly toad, then flipped through a handful of pages. *Hmm. It almost reminds me of dad's field guide for birds, like with a species description and interesting facts.* She stopped at the next page. *Hey! It's the fuzzy, orange grass.*

"Sparkseed," she read aloud. *Huh, guess that makes sense*, she thought, picturing the wave of twinkling lights produced when disturbing the grass. She shrugged and continued to read, "The seed head of the Sparkseed enhances eyesight when properly ground and mixed with two parts Goldenglow." *Hmm...good to know, I guess.*

Abby flipped to the front of the book, wondering if there were anything like a table of contents. As she recalled from their first look at the tome, a lavish drawing resembling tree roots bordered the first few, and otherwise blank, pages. She turned to the next page, remembering the tree with grand roots drawn with a metallic gold. *Oh yeah, the words no one could read before.* "The secrets of Shay," she whispered. *Well, Mallena was right about the book holding secrets. Not sure what she thought she'd get from it, but I bet she would have been steaming mad to know it's a catalog of all the plants and animals in Shay. At least, that's what it looks like.*

Abby flipped to the next page. No border. No pictures. Only elegant script.

"To she who bears the gift to read my words. You are now the Keeper of Shay."

Faint whispers pulled Abby's attention from the page. Tingles raced along her spine when the phrase 'you are the next,' and the word 'Keeper,' met her ears in hushed tones. Her heart fluttered before continuing to read aloud from the book.

"As the Keeper, it is your duty to protect every living being in the Land. All life is connected to the Brana, the essence of Shay, and will thrive only when all is in balance. Each being bears a special gift, a special purpose, as is documented in this book. Learn their truths, but know these writings are not all inclusive, new life will emerge over time, as is the way. Become one with them in spirit and continue on in my place. Record all you see and discover, and remember all life is cherished."

Abby reread the passage several times. *The Brana. I swear I've heard that word before. Not sure what it is though, besides 'the essence of Shay.'* She rested her head against the dome entrance and searched her memories. Staring out at Rowen's arrows embedded in the ground, she envisioned the earlier scene. *That's right, Mallena said something about it. That she'd unlock the secret of the book so she could control the Brana.*

A great weight threatened to press down on Abby. She lifted a shoulder, not knowing what to make of it all. Shifting her eyes back to the book, she turned to the next page. A tree root border encircled a paragraph of beautiful script that was begging to be read, but the detailed drawing below sparked a moment of recognition. A wooden box filled the lower portion of the page. An intricate carving of a tree adorned its top. *I've seen that somewhere...*

After staring at the box for several moments, Abby moved on to the script. "Born from the Tree of Life, the Brana ensures the land's connection with all beings. It is the heart of Shay, an entity all its own as is its Mother Tree. Without the other, neither can live. It is the Keeper's bidding to protect them. Should the Mother detect a threat to Shay, it will hide away its child. Only the Keeper may restore the Brana to its proper state."

Well that makes about zero sense. Why does everything always have to be so cryptic?

Abby relaxed her head against the dome again and closed her eyes to concentrate, hoping to sort out what she had just read. As she focused on slow, even breaths, the strange whisper returned.

"Darktree Hollow," it drawled with unnerving force.

Abby snapped her eyes open. "Darktree Hollow?"

As she glanced down at the drawing of the box, images rushed through her mind. A powerful darkness. Blackened trees. Hints of movement all around. A blue glow. Shaeron. And a box. The box.

Abby gasped aloud. "It wasn't a dream?"

"No, it was real," she replied to herself with certainty. "I was there."

She shut the book and jumped when Finlay appeared by her side, bending low in a stretch and smacking his lips.

What is this I hear, child?

Abby scrambled to her feet, hugging the book to her chest. "I know what we have to do now, but I'm not sure how. We need Rowen."

Upon his somber return, Abby waved frantically for Rowen to join the group in the clearing.

"Sister," Rowen approached with tired eyes, "what fills you with such urgency?"

"First off, are you okay?" Abby asked softly. "I'm so, so sorry for what happened. I'm still numb and can only imagine how you must feel."

Rowen lowered himself to the ground to sit with the others, setting his bow to the side. He brushed a hand over a clump of Sparkseed, remaining silent as he watched the glistening lights pop from the seed heads. "Wren was the bravest of Manta. A fierce streak ran through her, yet she held such compassion for others." He flicked another Sparkseed with a single finger before raising his head. "She knew this would happen when we completed Aster's circle, yet she did not falter once in her decision to do so," he said with a weak smile.

Abby's stomach churned. "Wait. Wren knew she'd die if we found Aster?" she paused, shaking her head slowly. "That's got to be one of the most selfless things I've ever heard." She whispered, directing timid eyes at Rowen. "Did you know? Like, before we went to the Howling Mountains?"

Rowen sighed. "My love and I kept no secrets; however, I only realized her impending fate last night. Wren knew I would show resistance in completing Aster's circle were she to tell me." He managed a sorrowful laugh. "She was right. I would have pled with her not to take possession of that tainted Talisman. Wren always had a way of knowing things," he said, first looking at Rory, then turning his head to lock eyes with Abby, "just like she knew the gifts of the Keeper had been bestowed to you, Abby."

A hush fell upon the clearing. Rory looked back and forth between Abby and Rowen. "What does he mean, A-by? Gifts of the Keeper?"

Abby collected her thoughts, thumbing the cover of the book before opening it. "I don't understand much of it, and maybe I don't even believe it yet, I don't know..." she trailed off, flipping to the page with the illustration of the box, "but I've seen this box before," she said, maneuvering the book so everyone could see the picture, "and it's the key to healing the land, stomping out the sickness that took Wren. And I know where it is, but it won't be easy getting it back."

A multitude of emotions swarmed Rowen's face, ending with deep concern. "You've seen the vessel of the Brana?"

Abby bobbed her head, "I have. At first, I thought I remembered a dream, but now I'm certain I had an out-of-body experience."

Rowen leaned forward, his eyes eager. "And do you know where you were when you saw it?"

"Darktree Hollow." Abby frowned with disgust at the name.

Rowen's face hardened. "Shaeron." He fell still for a moment and ran a hand through his hair. "There have been rumors floating around Willow Wood for some time, but I did not want to believe them. So, it is true then, he has somehow stolen the Brana. What can you tell me of your time in Darktree, Sister?"

Abby stared off into the distance as she spoke. "Darkness surrounded me and I'm pretty sure there were dead, black trees everywhere, not to mention a bunch of creepy Thraxen. Then I saw a deep, blue glow. It took me a bit to figure it out, but it was coming from the Stone of Longevity around Shaeron's neck. So, I got as close as I dared, and I could see him trying to open the box. He couldn't though. And he was pretty mad, yelled something about Mallena and the book, then told a bunch of Thraxen to go searching for her." Abby returned her gaze to meet Rowen's. "It makes sense now."

Rowen tipped his head curiously and gestured with his hands for Abby to continue.

"Shaeron thinks the Book of Shay will tell him how to open the box. And Mallena must have thought so too, but she wanted it all to herself. That's why you found

Aillig off on his own. Mallena didn't want to give the book up to Shaeron. Good thing, I guess. Now neither of them will have it." Abby paused and darted her eyes toward the forest. "Hey, speaking of Aillig, shouldn't we have gone after him or something?"

Rory gripped the scabbard laid across his lap. "Do ye want me to go find the scoundrel, A-by?"

At nearly the same moment, Finlay huffed into Abby's mind. *I could stand for a good hunt today. Though I do not care for the taste of you two-footers, the old man would not know otherwise. Perhaps a well-deserved scare is just what he needs.*

Abby focused between Rory and her dog, motioning with her hands for quiet. "Not everyone all at once," she chuckled.

"I take it your guide is as eager as our brother to find Aillig?"

Abby snorted. "More like he wants a good chase, instill a healthy dose of fear into the dirty rat."

Rowen nodded. "As is understandable. But he will not go far, the trees will keep him inside the boundaries of Willow Wood. Because he bears no gifts, I do not see him as an immediate threat. I think we can all agree we have more important issues at hand."

Abby nodded. "Agreed. Like getting back the Brana. But," she paused, "I'm not sure what to do with it once we have it."

Rory gestured toward the Book of Shay. "Perhaps it will tell ye."

"Well, it says only the Keeper can restore the Brana to its proper state." Abby shrugged, "No clue how I'm supposed to do that, but I guess we start by stealing it back. We'll figure it out as we go, I hope."

"But did Wren no' say no one knows where to find Darktree Hollow?" Rory tightened his brow. "How can we expect to get there?"

"Well," Abby replied slowly, "Finlay could take us there if he had a picture to look at or had been there himself, but seeing as how I'm the only one that's seen the creepy place, not much good that will do."

"You are wrong in your assumption, Sister."

Abby scrunched her face. "Huh? What do you mean by that, Rowen?"

"It is well known the Keeper of Redwin's time had many special gifts. For instance, she could communicate with any animal guide, and was the only living Manta to hear the words of the Great Willow." Rowen propped his elbows on his knees and leaned forward with a smile. "Does this sound familiar, Sister?"

Abby chewed on the corner of her lip and wiped the sudden nervousness beading on her palms across her pant legs. "Is that how Wren knew, that for some crazy reason, I'm supposed to be the next Keeper?

Rowen tipped his head. "Yes, Sister, but I would not consider it crazy. We are all destined for great purposes long before we take our first breaths. Though it may scare you now, you must learn to embrace and understand your destiny. Without you, all good in Shay will be lost."

Abby choked back an anxious chuckle. "Nothing like a little pressure, eh?"

Rory reached out to rub Abby's shoulder. "Do no', worry, A-by. I will be by yer side for all ye face. But," he asked, "how will this help us take back the Brana?"

"There is another gift the Keeper of old did not use to her advantage. And I say this sadly for I believe she could have survived her encounter with those determined to take her life."

Abby scowled at the image of Mavis and Tavis striking down the Red Queen. "Faerie magic isn't the easiest thing to escape, especially if you're not expecting it. What could she have possibly done differently?"

"Your words are true on this point, Sister. But had she tapped into the powers of the animal guides of her time, her fate may have been changed."

Abby's jaw went slack as she shook her head. "I don't get it. What do you mean 'tap into the powers of the animal guides?'"

"The Keeper is as one with the creatures of Shay, and her connection is strongest with those who are guides. Imagine Emi living in the time of Redwin. Emi's abilities would also have been the Keeper's abilities. With a simple thought, the Keeper could have summoned weavings of roots to subdue the evil ones." Rowen gauged Abby's reaction. "Do you understand what I am saying, Sister? Think back to all you have experienced upon entering Shay."

Abby leaned back, keeping her eyes on Rowen. Her gaze drifted eventually to a point beyond the Protector as she became lost in thought.

"A-by," Rory prodded gently when she remained silent for several minutes. "Do ye no' see the truth in his words? Though it may be a terrible memory, think of the boulder that crushed yer leg. Could it be ye freed yerself?"

Abby pulled her attention to the Scotsman. "Oh," she gasped softly, playing the scene back in her mind. "I...I thought Guido did it somehow. But, he did tell me he wasn't responsible. I guess he really does have to be touching whatever it is he wants to move."

Rory placed a hand on Abby's knee, giving it a soft squeeze. "Do ye see then? Ye were touchin' the boulder when it moved. Is the only sensible explanation. Ye used Guido's gift to free yerself."

"It is true, Sister. You are the Keeper. Search your soul. Feel your connection with Shay. Believe in yourself. When you do — and you will — I would not be surprised if your abilities grow well beyond that of what history holds."

Abby locked fingers with Rory and drew a long, slow breath. Closing her eyes, she exhaled in kind. *Hey fuzzface,* she projected. *You didn't take us all to the top of the cliff when we went to Amaray's tree, did you?*

No, lass, I did not.

It was me then, wasn't it? I somehow used your power...

This is so, child. Do not be frightened.

Abby added a hint of sass to her inner voice. *I'm not scared!* She paused, softening her tone. *Sorry. It's just, I'm having a hard time believing it all. I mean, why me?*

Why any of us? Perhaps it is sometimes best not to question what you cannot control. It is obvious to me, lass, you were fated to, and chosen for, this role.

Well...maybe, but chosen by who?

That is something we will never know. It could be the Amaray of old knew things as Wren did. But we should not concern ourselves with that. We must focus on the present, on saving the land and all it gives life to. Are you up for the task, little one? You know I will always be by your side.

Abby opened her eyes and nodded. "We better start planning."

***

"I'm not so sure about that, Rowen," Abby said, shaking her head, "we have no idea how many Thraxen there'll be when we get to Darktree Hollow. I think it's much smarter for as few of us as possible to go. Nice and quiet. Sneak in, sneak out."

Rowen leaned forward and clasped his hands together, propping his nose on the tips of his upright index fingers. "I am wary of this plan, Sister. We are stronger as a group."

"Aye, A-by, there is sense in his words. We may no' be able to hide as well, but we can better protect ourselves as a greater number."

Abby sighed. "But that's my point. Do you really think we won't draw attention when a giant owl, over-sized hare, and monstrous dog appear suddenly in the hollow? I see what you guys are saying, but I think we'll have a better chance of retrieving the box if, say, only Rory, Finlay, and I go."

Cody's ears fell limp to either side of his face at the exclusion of his name.

Rowen stared hard at the ground, disapproval in his expression. "No, Sister, I too at least need to be present. Without my gift, how do you expect to see the Thraxen? You would go in blind and I fear you would not find your way home."

Abby began to protest when the whispering voice swirled around her again.

"Sparkseed shows all..."

Abby perked her ears. "Did you guys hear that?"

"Hear what, A-by?"

Abby rolled her eyes at herself. "Of course you didn't," she mumbled, "lucky me with the mystic voice only I can hear." She brushed off her frustration and continued. "Our mystery helper just said 'Sparkseed shows all.'"

Rowen ran a hand through the grass. "This is a curious message but I do not understand how it helps us."

"Hmm." Abby watched the display of sparks as Rowen continued agitating the grass. Running a finger along the edge of the book's cover, a thought popped into Abby's mind. "I wonder," she muttered, flipping to the entry on Sparkseed. She scanned the page and looked up excitedly. "I think I know what the message means, well, maybe."

Rory leaned over, glancing at the drawing. "What did ye find?"

"It says here that if you mix two parts Goldenglow with one-part Sparkseed, it will enhance your eyesight. Who knows, maybe it helps you see the Thraxen." She paused and concentrated on a strange feeling in the pit of her stomach. "Yes," she nodded decisively, "I'm sure that's it."

"While I appreciate this discovery, Sister, we have no way to test it. You would go in with only the hope it works."

"Look," Abby held up a hand, "I know it seems like a long shot, but please, trust me on this. I know I'm right. We'll be able to see any Thraxen that are hiding. It will make it even easier for us to sneak around."

Rowen turned to Rory. "What say you, Brother?"

Rory squeezed Abby's hand. "If A-by believes this is best, then I am no' one to argue. I trust her intuition."

Abby bumped Rory playfully shoulder to shoulder. "Good answer."

Rowen chuckled but resumed a serious face. "Let it be so. But please, you must promise to retreat to safety the moment you sense any danger."

"You don't need to worry, Rowen. I swear, the second we feel we're in trouble, Finlay will zap us back here."

Abby scanned the group and when no further objections presented themselves, she pointed to the book. "All right then, we need to hurry up and make this. Rory," she said, smiling sweetly at the Scotsman, "will you go get a handful of Goldenglow from inside the tree where we sleep?"

Rory stood with enthusiasm and motioned with his head for Cody to follow. "As ye wish, Keeper of the Land." He smiled, wiggled his brow, and bowed dramatically. With a quick turn, he sprinted away, Cody bounding past him.

Abby contained a snort, watching Rory race into the forest. *He's so goofy.* Grinning, Abby noted with surprise a flush rising in her cheeks. *Perfectly goofy I guess, hard not to love that, right?* She glanced at Rowen to find him smiling and cleared her throat, pretending to study the entry. "So, uh, I think we need to grind the ingredients before mixing them, so we'll need a flat rock, or even better, something bowl-like. Any ideas?"

"Indeed, Sister," the Protector answered, rising, "I believe Emi will have what you seek. One moment while I check."

Rowen disappeared into the dome. After no more than a minute, he emerged carrying a wooden object.

"This should suit our need, Sister," he said, holding out what appeared to be a shallow platter formed from woven roots. He passed it to Abby as he lowered himself to the ground.

"Hmm, yeah." Abby ran her hand over the center of the piece. A pretzel-like weaving of roots formed the outer lip of the small tray. Abby marveled at how Emi created a completely flat surface in the center. "Don't know how she made it, but yup, this will be perfect."

The sound of approaching footfalls caught Abby's attention. She glanced up from the tray to find Rory jogging toward her, hands cupped together and held against his midsection. "Here ye are, A-by, as ye requested," he huffed, coming to a stop.

"Awesome, Rory. Thanks," she smiled, "I guess just put it on the tray here."

Rory nodded as he dropped to a knee. Hovering his hands over its surface, he released a handful of Goldenglow onto the wood.

Abby eyeballed the size of the pile. "Okay, so we need twice as much Goldenglow as Sparkseed. Rowen, want to pick us some seed heads?"

The Protector waived an affirmative hand and sought out a clump of grass, stopping at one with plump, fuzzy heads. He glanced at the pile of Goldenglow and pinched off several seed heads with care. "Thank you for your sacrifice," he whispered. Stretching out, he dropped the Sparkseed onto the tray.

"Perfect, thanks, I think it's about right." Abby stared at the plants. "Hmm, okay, so now we need a way to grind this stuff."

"I will do it for ye, A-by," Rory said proudly, pulling out his dirk.

Understanding his intention, Abby set the platter on the ground and swiveled it in front of the Scotsman. "Have at it."

With the blade held upright, Rory gripped its handle firmly at the base. Starting with the Goldenglow, he methodically ground the plant into fine particles. Nodding at his handiwork, he wiped the handle clean along his pants and repeated the process with the Sparkseed. After several minutes of careful grinding, he slid the tray back in front of Abby.

Abby stared at the piles, unsure of how to proceed. "Wonder if we have to make a soup out of it?" After another moment of indecision, she swept the grounds together with the sides of her hands and mixed the ingredients with her fingers. "Hey, look!" she exclaimed, pulling back her hands and pointing at the pile. The plant matter swirled slowly on its own. As Abby watched on with amazement, three small balls formed. "They're like baby Bria," she laughed, picking one up after all movement stopped. She sniffed the creation and with a shrug popped it in her mouth. "Not what I expected," she said, covering her mouth as she chewed, "and it doesn't even taste bad."

With a final swallow, Abby held a second ball in the air and wiggled it at her wolfhound.

Finlay responded by licking his lips and snatching it from the air once Abby tossed it to him.

Rory scooped up the last of the concoction and popped it in his mouth, swallowing it after a single chew. With a grunt, he agreed with Abby's assessment.

Abby glanced from Guide to Protector. "You guys feel different?" Before any response came, Abby rubbed at the bridge of her nose. "Whoa." She blinked her eyes rapidly. "Something's happening." She stared at the treetops in the distance, then turned her attention to the Sparkseed, running a hand over the nearest clump. "Wild. Everything is so vivid. Is it the same for you?" she asked.

Rory managed only a nod, his eyes wide as he looked all around.

Aye, lass. This is indeed a curious enhancement to my vision. I trust in your judgment that this will reveal any Thraxen presence to us, but we do not know how long it will last. I suggest we waste no further time in our departure for Darktree Hollow.

You're right, I didn't think of that. The book says nothing about how long the mixture works.

Abby stood and turned to Rowen. "We have to go now. I'm not sure when this Sparkseed magic will wear off." Abby held out the Book of Shay. "Here. Will you keep this safe for me while we're gone? Maybe have Emi hide it in her chamber? Never know what kind of nonsense Aillig might try."

"Yes, of course, Sister. We will make sure it is left untouched. But please," Rowen said, taking Abby's hand, "be careful and bring everyone back to us safely."

"Don't worry, Rowen, we got this."

Abby swiveled around and reached for Rory, then sunk her other hand into Finlay's coat. "I have no idea what I'm doing, so a little patience if it takes me a bit."

"I have complete faith in ye, A-by."

Abby smiled and closed her eyes, picturing the blackness of the long-dead trees and the unnerving clicks of the insectoids. The memory forced a shiver along her spine. She sighed to herself. *Everyone's counting on me, we have to go there, even if it gives me the heebie-jeebies.* Keeping the image in her mind, Abby shifted her attention to the dog fur clutched in her hand. She reached out mentally until Finlay's warmth wrapped around her. Abby concentrated, shifting her mind's eye back to Darktree Hollow. *Take us there.*

Just as the familiar pull tugged at Abby's being, she whispered to herself. "For Wren..."

13

Abby flicked her eyes open, the sight eliciting a tiny gasp. *I...I can't believe I did it. I really brought us all to Darktree Hollow.*

A deathly stillness surrounded the trio. They stood behind a downed tree, its black, gnarled branches reaching into the gloomy sky. "Everyone crouch down," she whispered.

Rory drew his sword swiftly while following her instruction.

Finlay pressed himself against the barren ground. *A great evil fills this hollow.* He tested the air. *But there is something else. A deep sadness. The land cries for what was.*

Abby shuddered at his thoughts, sensing a great anger building inside her dog. Composing herself, she turned away from the fallen tree and scanned the landscape behind them. She could see no end to the blackened death. Her altered vision intensified the cracks and crevices of every tree. A subtle movement caused her to lock in on a tree off to their right. "Hey," she said with such softness she was not sure her companions would hear her. "Can you see it?" She pointed toward the tree, keeping her hand low and movement restricted. "In the middle of the trunk. I think there's a Thraxen asleep inside it."

Rory stretched forward and focused on the tree. He mouthed a silent affirmation and clenched the handle of his sword tighter.

A mental growl rolled through Abby. *Aye. I see the hideous creature.*

Having a better idea of what to check for now, Abby continued surveying the area. "That's the only one I see back this way," she whispered before pivoting around to look out across their fallen hiding spot.

Rory matched her actions and slid in close, bringing his mouth next to her ear. "Where do we go from here?"

Abby continued to search the trees for any sign of Thraxen, asleep or otherwise. "I only see the one Thraxen behind us. I wonder if most of them are out trying to find Mallena."

Rory considered the thought and nodded. "Aye, is logical."

"Best not let our guard down though, never know what sort of creepies Shaeron has hanging out in this place. But to answer your question, I have no clue where we should go from here."

A cold nose brushed Abby's hand. *Perhaps we start where you saw the box.*

Abby ran her fingers along Finlay's muzzle. *Guess that's as good as any place.*

She leaned close to Rory again. "Let's go to where I saw Shaeron. I'm positive he will have the box on him." Abby thought back to her out-of-body experience. "Yeah, in fact, I remember he put it in a big pouch hanging at his side."

Rory tightened his lips into a thin line. "Will be more difficult to retrieve."

"I know. You're right. But we have to do whatever's needed to get it back. This," she gestured at the fallen tree, "has to stop, no matter what. Hopefully Shaeron won't be at the top of his game since he no longer has the Talisman of Longevity."

Rory glanced over his shoulder towards the sleeping Thraxen. "Do ye think we should leave it, A-by?"

Abby bit her lip and considered. "It'd be nice to have one less bug to worry about, but let's not push it, I think we've been lucky so far. Let's try to keep it that way."

The Scotsman nodded and meshed fingers with Abby. "Let us move on then."

"Okay guys," she whispered, sinking her hand into Finlay's coat, "let's see if I can do this again." Abby closed her eyes and pictured the old man squatting atop the chunk of rotted wood. *Take us there...*

***

Abby cracked an eye. They stood not two feet from the stump she remembered. *Huh, guess I'm getting the hang of this zapping thing.* She flinched when the brief clicking of a Thraxen sounded in the distance. She crouched immediately, pulling Rory down with her as Finlay made himself as small as a giant dog could.

"It came from that way." Rory pointed off to their left.

Abby studied the scattered trees. "I'm not seeing it. You?"

The Scotsman shook his head, pausing when the insect sounds started up again.

Abby flitted her eyes left then right, hoping to find the source of the noise, groaning when it died off seconds later. Realizing a potential mistake, she whipped her head around to scan behind them, afraid they may have left their backs vulnerable. *Whew. That could have been bad.*

"A-by." Rory tugged at her shoulder.

"What's wrong?" she hissed, jerking her head to their front.

"Look, do ye see it?"

Abby tried to follow the invisible line where Rory pointed. "What? Where?"

"Far beyond the largest tree just there," he replied.

Abby leaned into him, craning her neck to see past the tree he indicated. "Oh. Whoa. It's like a giant beaver dam or something. Let's hide behind that big tree, see if we can get a closer look."

When Rory grunted agreement, Abby touched both Guide and Protector, focusing on the chosen spot. Seconds later the three squatted behind the tree.

Abby peered around the trunk, shrinking quickly back. "Thraxen," she mouthed.

Noticing the stark contrast between Finlay's brilliant coat and the dead environment around them, worry filled Abby's mind. *Should have had you roll around in some dirt first.*

Finlay flattened himself to the ground. *Let us control what we can at this moment. Tell me what you see, child.*

Abby peeped to the left side of the tree while Rory poked his head to the right. Ducking back and pressing up against the trunk, she yanked on the Scotsman's shirttail to do the same. "I think I counted five Thraxen. And it looks like that giant thing out there is a hut-like structure made of dead trees," she whispered. "I bet that's Shaeron's hideout. There's three bugs on top of it and one on either side of the entrance, standing guard maybe."

"Do ye think he will have hidden the Brana there, A-by?"

"Mmm, doubt it. I guarantee he keeps it on him. As crazy as he sounded that night, there's no way he'd let it out of his sight. It's got to be in his pouch."

Rory scooted closer to Abby. "Then we must devise a way to remove it from him."

Abby nodded, struggling to come up with a sound plan. "Let's not make this any more complicated than it needs to be. We obviously can't surprise him. The second we step around this tree, the Thraxen will see us. In fact, I kind of can't believe they haven't yet. Anyway, might as well go big. Let's zap out there, maybe half way between here and that cave-thing. I'll yell his name and Rory, you light the place up with your sword. I think we've seen enough proof fire is effective against those nasty bugs. Let's show no mercy, burn the trees if you have to. Who knows? It might actually help them by incinerating the sickness."

"Aye, but how will we take his pouch? I can no' battle the Thraxen and Shaeron at once."

"Well...I know neither of you will like this, but, if you give me your dirk," Abby paused at Rory's facial reaction. "Just wait, listen for a minute," she said. "I need a weapon anyway, so it makes sense for you to give me your blade, right?"

Rory nodded reluctantly.

"Okay, so, you fight the Thraxen, and Finlay and I will take on Shaeron. Once I get close enough, I'll cut the strap holding the pouch, or, who knows, maybe I can even get a hand in it and pull the box out. We'll have to play it by ear. And don't worry, my trusty dog won't let anything bad happen. Isn't that right, fuzzface?"

Finlay growled low. *It is an ambitious plan you have, little one. But at this point, I am of no mind to argue. Let us move quickly before we are discovered. Keep your wits about you, and please, think before you act.*

Abby smiled triumphantly, meeting Rory's eyes. "Finlay says we should go for it, are you good with this?"

Rory stared at Abby. With a long exhale, he fiddled at his waist and presented her his dirk, handle first. "Please be careful, A-by."

Abby accepted the small weapon, and before Rory pulled away, she kissed him on the cheek. "Don't worry, it will be okay. I promise."

After a final peek around the tree, Abby touched Rory's arm. Just as she went to place a hand on Finlay, a curious thought struck her. "I bet I can move us without touching anyone." She removed her hand from Rory. "Let me experiment. You guys be ready for action in about five seconds."

Rory swiveled himself around to face the tree and readied the grip on his sword.

Abby nodded and closed her eyes, establishing a connection with Finlay's mind. She envisioned Rory and the dog standing next to her a safe distance in front of the strange structure. "Go."

***

The trio appeared side by side twenty feet from the hut's opening. The Thraxen standing guard on either end of the entrance let out an ear-piercing shriek. Abby cringed, nudging Rory, "Better get busy with some fire."

Two of the Thraxen on top of the structure wasted no time in somersaulting to the ground to the left of the group while the third held its position on top.

Flames roared to life along Rory's blade, causing the insectoids to recoil. With a flick of his wrist, red-hot spirals shot into the air, snaking round and round until they created a giant, fiery perimeter sixty feet wide.

"Whoa. Smart thinking, Rory," Abby said, seeing the flames sink to the ground to form a protective wall. "Impressive. That will make those bugs think twice."

Rory smiled at the compliment, though his eyes remained hardened as he tracked the Thraxen.

Abby scrutinized the hut. *Maybe he isn't here. You'd think all these alarm calls would have brought him out.* She readied herself and yelled at the top of her lungs. "Hey! Shaeron!"

As Rory shot more flames into the air, the Thraxen stood their ground, hissing and crouching while twirling their curved blades.

Finlay growled suddenly, his hackles at attention.

Abby glanced at her dog, following his gaze to the opening of the structure. "What is it?" When she stopped to focus on the entrance, a pair of icy, blue eyes blinked at her from within the darkness. She gasped. "I've seen those eyes before."

A shaggy, black leg emerged from the darkness, bringing with it an enormous dog. Growling as it exited the hut, it took four even steps and stopped to stand tall. The creature's grand stature rivaled that of Finlay.

Abby gulped, fighting the hypnotic draw of its icy stare.

The dog swiveled its head back, an ear perked toward the hut. As if disinterested in whatever it may have heard, it resumed its questioning gaze at Finlay.

And then Abby heard it when the Thraxen fell silent. Shuffle, shuffle, thump. Shuffle, shuffle, thump. Over and over the noise came until an ancient man in rags emerged from the hut, supporting his efforts with a wooden staff.

Abby gulped again, not realizing how terrified she would be to see him in the flesh. *Shaeron...*

The old man leaned on his walking stick, his hands a reflection of the gnarled branches all around. He lifted his head and studied the trio. "So," he barked, the strength of his voice unexpected for his frail frame, "come for the Brana have you, Manta?"

Though weak in the knees, Abby found her voice. "It was never yours to take. It belongs to Shay. So," she paused, standing up straight, "do us all a favor and give it to me without a fight."

Shaeron laughed himself into a wet, coughing fit. Once it subsided to a crackle, he pointed at Abby. "I will do no such thing. Come and take it if you think you can, little girl. My guide will shred you to pieces should you step any closer."

A tired sigh crept into Abby's mind. *Old fool...*

Abby jerked her head to the left toward Finlay. *Was that you?*

Was what me, child?

The same voice rolled through Abby's mind again. *So, Amaray has come again...*

Realizing this was not her guide speaking, Abby turned her head to stare at the only other source. The giant, black dog.

Ah, yes. It is so.

Abby forced herself to blink away the surprise. *You, you're Eirwen.*

The dog gave a slight bow without breaking eye contact with Finlay.

Wh-why did you call Shaeron an old fool? If you're his guide, aren't you supposed to be loyal to him?

I may be his guide but only by force. He does not understand his decrepit attempt at domination of Shay is about to end. You will have your Brana soon enough...

Wait, you're not going to try to stop us?

No child, I will revel in his fall. And I am much more interested in the beast standing next to you. It...smells familiar.

Abby glanced at Finlay knowing she should not reveal his identity. *Something is off about Eirwen. I think I can feel conflict within her.* She moved her attention back to the black dog and shrugged. *He's of no concern to you.*

We're from the Other, and we just got here a few days ago.

A low rumble rolled from deep in Eirwen's massive chest.

Shaeron thumped her flank with his staff, "Silence, swine." He angled his stick toward Finlay. "Kill that foul beast, now!"

Eirwen flinched when Shaeron smacked her a second time with more force.

Abby sensed vibrations of great turmoil from the black dog.

Eirwen advanced several paces but soon stopped, her body shaking. She arched her back and hacked a single, forceful cough, sending a glob of black goo to the ground. Her eyes narrowed as she bared her teeth. She growled again and slunk to the ground in obvious preparation to launch herself at Finlay.

Finlay! Abby cried. *Try not to hurt her. Something isn't right here. Just hold her off long enough for me to get the Brana. Then maybe we can figure out how to save her.*

Her guide assumed a defensive position. *I do not wish to cause my mother harm, but will do what is needed to keep you safe, child.*

At the same moment, Shaeron pointed at Rory with his stick and called out to the Thraxen. "Kill the boy!"

A flurry of action erupted around Abby. All five Thraxen pivoted to face the Scotsman, cackling with glee. Eirwen shifted off to Abby's left, her gaze never leaving Finlay's tense form, and the old man thumped the ground forcefully with his staff. "You will regret the day you set foot in my hollow, little girl," he said, as he hobbled forward several paces.

Abby gulped, darting her eyes to the left and then right from her guide to her Protector. Her warriors were focused on their advancing adversaries. She looked back to Shaeron. *Okay, Abby, you're on your own with this one.* She scrutinized the aged body inching toward her. *The pouch! Right where I remember. He's so slow, I bet I could run right up to him and cut it free.*

As cries, roars, and shrieks rang out, Shaeron stopped and grinned a toothless grin at Abby. With one hand held in front of himself as high as his body would allow, he pointed the tip of his walking stick directly at her, mumbling strange words

Abby narrowed her eyes. *What the heck is he doing?*

In response to her silent question, a tiny, black shard of wood shot from the tip of Shaeron's staff, zinging straight at Abby.

"Ahh!" Abby jumped to her right, twisting her upper torso away from the path of the missile.

The old man growled and repeated his magical process, this time sending two spikes of wood sailing at Abby's head.

She dropped to the ground, panting as the splinters whooshed by her head. *Guess this creeper means business. Won't be able to get close enough to him at this rate. Got to get that staff away from him somehow.*

Abby brought herself to a crouch and watched Shaeron's movements, flinching at the raucous battle around her. She stole a glance to see Rory holding his own, keeping the Thraxen at bay with the threat of fire. Finlay and Eirwen continued a standoff of growls. Shaeron swung the bottom of his staff forward. As it hung in the air, the tip transformed to a steely, black blade.

Oh great. Abby renewed her grip on the dirk.

Shaeron shuffled toward her, arcing the blade through the air. Gaining ground, he tried to jab Abby's head, but she rolled to her left and hopped to her feet.

"Sorry, but you'll have to do better than that."

Shaeron howled in reply only to fall into another coughing fit, leaving him defenseless.

Abby recognized the opportunity, but her body ignored her brain's request. She groaned. *Come on, this isn't the time to be a chicken. Grab the bag and go!*

A piercing cry broke Abby's internal battle and seconds later, the head of an unfortunate Thraxen rolled past her. With great surprise, Abby darted her eyes from the head, to Shaeron, and back. Without hesitation, she lurched to the side and scooped it up.

"Hey! Shaeron! Got something for you. Catch!" she called wickedly, lobbing it straight at the old man. The moment it left her hands, Abby dashed forward, hoping things would happen as she envisioned.

At the tail end of a cough, Shaeron reacted by dropping his staff and bringing both hands in front of his body. Catching the head, he glared at it and, for a precious moment, shifted his attention to the redheaded warrior.

Abby barreled into Shaeron, knocking him back. As he fell, she wrapped her left hand around the pouch and struck out with the blade, sawing at the leather straps with vigor.

Shaeron roared but could not stop himself from falling to the ground.

A dull snap gave both Abby and the mystic pause.

"Yes!" she exclaimed, glancing at the now-free pouch. She flared her nostrils at the feeble form writhing before her.

Wasting no time, she ran toward Finlay. *I've got it! I've got the pouch.*

Stay back, child. She may strike at any moment.

Abby slowed to a stop a safe distance from the dogs.

Eirwen slid her gaze to Abby, a spasm rolling through the black beast's body. *Child, you must act or I will be forced to do his bidding.*

A moment of sorrow filled Abby. *It's just like with Mavis and Tavis. She's trapped by magic and has no choice...*

Abby frowned, fearing help would not find Eirwen this day. She sprinted the remaining stretch to her guide and upon stopping, slipped the dirk blade-down into the pouch.

"Finlay! Back to Rory!"

The moment Abby grabbed a fistful of fur, they reappeared several feet behind the Scotsman. Abby shifted the worn bag, scrunching it tight into the pit of her arm to free her other hand.

Rory danced from side to side, releasing devastating arcs of flame from his sword.

"Rory! We have to go. Now!" Abby cried, motioning for his hand.

Thraxen shrieked with horror as fire consumed trees all around. Loud pops and snaps sounded everywhere and a tall tree to their left crashed to the ground.

Rory scooted backwards toward his companions and outstretched his free hand, not once looking away from the threat.

Abby suppressed a growing panic. *Finlay, as soon as he reaches us, I want you to take us back. This is too dangerous to count on me getting it right.*

As you wish, child.

Relief flooded through Abby when she latched on to Rory's thumb. "To Willow Wood!"

***

Abby bent over, hands on knees. "Did we really just do that?" She straightened and stared at the pouch now clutched in her left hand.

"Brothers! Sister!"

Abby turned to see Rowen jogging toward them.

"Are you unharmed?"

Abby patted her body, then circled Finlay, ruffling his coat. "Good here. What about you, Rory? You took on five Thraxen all by yourself. Please tell me you're okay."

Rory sheathed his sword slower than normal. Placing a hand on his fighting shoulder, he grimaced when attempting to rotate it. "Save for minor scratches, no harm has come to me. Is easy when yer enemy does no' like fire," he said, pulling his hand from his shoulder when he saw Abby eying him suspiciously.

"That's not a scratch, you've hurt your shoulder."

"Is nothin', Lass."

"Didn't look like nothing to me. Why not just heal yourself?"

"Do no' worry, A-by, me shoulder is fine. And I prefer to save me gift for those in true need." He tipped his head, a shy yet proud smile stretching across his face as he redirected the conversation. "Ye were brave, A-by," he said, pointing to the pouch.

Abby shrugged. "Just doing what had to be done, right?"

"Have you checked inside the pouch yet, Sister?"

Abby turned to Rowen, suppressing a nervous laugh. "Actually, no. Wouldn't that be ironic were the Brana not in it?" She loosened the top of the bag. "Guess we better make sure that wasn't all for nothing." Peeking into the pouch's dark depths, she retrieved the dirk. "Oh yeah, forgot about that," she said, passing it back to Rory. "All right, let's see what you've got for us." Leaning over, Abby gripped the lip of the opening with her left hand and the base of the bag with her right. Shaking it gently, she emptied its contents onto the ground.

An aged, wooden box slid from the bag. Thinking it not quite empty, Abby gave the pouch a final shake. Out popped a black glob of goo. It dangled from the pouch for several seconds and splatted to the ground as Abby recoiled, jumping away. "Eww! That stuff is nasty. No one touch it." She inched forward and laid the bag on top of the offensive mass. Shifting back to the box, Abby pinched a finger on either end and lifted it carefully to inspect for any traces of the evil sludge. "I guess it's okay," she murmured to herself. As she squatted, relaxing into a seated position, Emi, Cody, and Riffin appeared in the clearing, approaching with interest. All around, eager eyes peered at the box. Blowing out a long breath, Abby willed herself confident and picked it up. She gasped, a blanket of deep sadness wrapping around her. The weight of the Brana's losing battle flowed into her, and she choked back the immediate desire to vomit. "It's," she swallowed hard, not finding the words she sought, "Shay. It weeps. It mourns. It fears absolute loss is to come." Fat tears rolled down Abby's cheeks. She craned her neck toward the sky and squeezed her eyes shut. After several silent moments, she called out. "I promise, we will save you."

Abby lowered her head, flicking her eyes open when an immediate warmth radiated from the box. She exhaled slowly, recognizing a calming shift and nodded to herself. "Time to open you." Abby ran a thumb over the intricate carving on the lid. *Just like Amaray's Tree now.* Holding the box up in front of her, she examined its construction. *Looks like it's hinged on this side, so if I push up here...*

Abby's breath caught when the box opened without resistance. She studied its contents. A lining of pale green velvet supported a blackened mass. "This can't possibly be the Brana, can it?" She glanced up, searching Rowen's eyes for an answer. "It's like a shriveled-up heart or something."

"It is, Sister. It is the soul of the land and it is dying."

Abby ran a hand through her curls, images of Wren in her final moments flashing through her mind. "So, we have to heal it. But, I don't know how."

"Perhaps I can heal it with me sword, A-by?"

Abby shrugged. "Somehow I think it will take a little more than that, but let's not discount it." She motioned for the Scotsman to come closer and set the box on the ground in front of her.

Rory freed his sword and concentrated. An immediate swath of yellow glow streamed from the blade, surrounding the Brana. After a long minute, Rory withdrew the healing powers and sheathed his sword.

Abby leaned forward with a frown. "It didn't work."

Finlay flopped down next to Abby. *What of the book, child? Did you see no reference?*

Abby shook her head and jerked a thumb at her dog. "Finlay just asked if the Book of Shay might tell us what to do, but I don't remember seeing anything about saving the Brana from Shaeron's nasty sickness."

"I will retrieve the book for you, Sister; it is at least worth another look."

Abby nodded but a distant whisper stole her attention. She held up a finger, signaling for Rowen to wait, and strained her ears.

"The thirteenth stone will save all..."

"Uh, guys, our whispering mystery helper just told me the thirteenth stone will save all. Like, I guess maybe it will heal the Brana?"

Rowen paced, rubbing his temple. "But there is no thirteenth stone."

Abby drew a deep breath. "Yeah, didn't Wren say Sylvan Myst refused to make the last stone with his brother?" she continued without waiting for a response, "so how can something that doesn't even exist help us heal the Brana?"

The question hung in the air silently for many minutes.

Abby closed her eyes and considered past events, running through everything she could think of that might lead her to an answer. Opening her eyes, her gaze alighted on Rory. She sighed, looking fondly at the scabbard Mrs. MacTavish had passed on to her kin. She looked at the hilt of the Scotsman's sword. "That's it!"

Rory appeared startled. "What is, Lass?"

Abby flapped her hands excitedly, then rubbed her face to calm herself. "Okay, just run with me on this for a minute. I think the thirteenth stone is the Talisman of Healing."

Rowen raised a brow. "Even if this were true, it does not exist."

"Oh, but it does, Rowen. And Rory's sword is proof."

Rory pulled his weapon again, holding the hilt eye level. He stared at the yellow gem. "Ye think this is the thirteenth stone? But A-by, it was created in the Other."

Abby pushed back the frustration building inside her. "Think about it Rory, everything you've been able to do with it. It makes perfect sense now. Sylvan refused to make the last Talisman with Shaeron. It doesn't really matter why, but he did make it, on his own. He made it for Enya. And, who knows, maybe he knew it would end up in Shay someday to serve its intended purpose. I don't know. Again, I don't think it matters. But what does matter is the golden drop is the Talisman of Healing and it's going to save the Brana. Save Shay."

The creases lining Rory's forehead relaxed as he stepped forward. "If ye truly believe, A-by, then I will follow yer heart, always." Rory held the sword out, laid across both palms. "Tell me what do to with it."

Abby smiled, glancing around the group, stopping to lock eyes with Rory. "Well, I think I know what to do now, but it means you must sacrifice your gift. You won't be able to heal people, or...me, anymore," she measured the Scotsman's reaction, "are you willing to give that up?"

Rory lowered himself to one knee without hesitation and extended the sword toward Abby. "If it will save the land and keep ye safe, I freely pass on the gift of the Talisman."

Abby blushed, diverting her gaze toward the box and clearing her throat.

"You are an honorable Protector, Brother," Rowen said, clapping a hand to Rory's shoulder. "But tell us, Sister, what plan do you have?"

"Well," Abby replied, "I think we need to put the Talisman in the box. And then, if I'm right, things will take care of themselves."

"Let us all hope you are right, Sister, in Wren's name."

Rory grunted, his face serious as he retrieved his dirk and set about prying the golden drop from his sword's hilt. With a gentle pop, the Talisman broke free from the sword's hold. Rory cupped it in his hand for several moments.

Abby dropped to a knee next to the Scotsman, "What's wrong, Rory? Are you having second thoughts?"

"Nae, Lass," he said with a slight smile, "was just rememberin' all the good that came from this tiny stone, and thinkin' of all the good yet to come. Here," he continued, dropping the Talisman into Abby's outstretched hand, "time for ye to save Shay."

Abby's eyes warmed at Rory's selflessness as she scooted over to the box. She gazed at the gem, the importance of what she was about to do weighing on her heart.

Finlay nudged her back. *Do you doubt yourself, little one?*

Abby glanced over her shoulder. *Maybe a little. What if I'm wrong?*

Do you remember what I told you when I first found you in the mountainside cave?

Abby stared at the ground, thinking back to what she then considered a terrifying encounter. She craned her neck back to meet Finlay's eye. *To trust myself?*

Aye, Lass. Trust yourself as I trust in you, and all will be as it's meant.

Abby turned back to the wooden receptacle. *Thanks, I needed that.* And without further thought, she set the golden drop next to the lifeless Brana and closed the lid.

"Now what, A-by?"

Abby tucked her legs under and leaned over the box. "Now, we wait."

A hushed silence fell over the clearing as everyone drew in close.

With every passing minute, Abby's confidence frayed as she waited for a sign of any kind. *Please let this work,* she repeated over and over to herself. After an eternity, Abby placed a hand on top of the box. "Oh," she muttered, surprised by the radiating warmth seeping into her skin. "I think something is happening," she said, looking up at everyone. Abby picked up the box and sat back on her haunches. A slight vibration caressed her fingers and on a mental count of three, she opened the lid.

A collective gasp filled the clearing.

"It worked!" Abby exclaimed. "It's amazing," she said, entranced by the deep, emerald glow emanating from the box. She reached inside hesitantly, her fingers brushing the soft lining before wrapping around a smooth, firm stone. She extracted her hand to reveal a glistening gem three times the size of the golden drop. In its rightful state, the Brana winked a brilliant and pleasing green in the sun's rays.

Abby's heart skipped a beat. "I think this is the prettiest thing I've ever seen. But," she paused with a slight grimace, "something still feels off." She placed the Brana back in its box and hopped up, walking over to the tattered pouch. With the toe of her boot, she flipped the bag to the side, revealing the black blob. Abby let out a frustrated sigh. "I hoped healing the Brana would instantly destroy Shaeron's sickness. I should have known it wouldn't be easy."

"Do not despair, Sister. You have healed Shay's soul, but I do not think a wooden box is where it truly belongs. Perhaps this is the missing element.

As Abby stared at Rowen, contemplating his misgivings, a line from the Book of Shay popped into her head. *Born from the Tree of Life...the Mother Tree.* "The Tree of Life!" she blurted. "We have to take the Brana back to where it was created. That's how we stop the sickness, I just know it."

"The Tree of Life, Sister? I have not heard this reference before," Rowen said inquisitively. "Surely you must mean the Great Willow, the grandest of all trees in Shay."

"Actually, no," Abby paused, "we're going to Amaray's tree."

14

The extraordinary company of companions appeared in the middle of the stone circle. Riffin took flight, obeying Rowen's command to patrol the skies. Emi waddled off, inspecting the nearest stone, and Cody hopped outside the ring, ears alert.

Abby unlinked her hands from Finlay and Rory. Stepping back, she shielded her eyes from the sun. She turned slowly, stopping to admire the blossoming tree. "Wow. I think it's grown since the last time we were here."

"Aye, A-by," Rory said, pointing to fresh shoots at the top of the tree.

"I believe you are right, Sister. This gives me great hope. The Tree of Life is finding her way."

Abby smiled. "I almost think I can feel pulsations of joy coming from it. We're definitely on the right track. Just have to figure out what to do with the Brana."

A sudden, warm breeze flowed through the circle, rustling the branches of Amaray's tree, causing a handful of deep red petals to float to the ground.

A soft whisper reached all ears the moment the wind dissipated. "Return the child to its mother…"

Abby's eyes grew large. "You all heard that, right?" She glanced at the Protectors, noting their surprised expressions. "Guess we have our answer. Though, I'm not sure how we're supposed to do it."

"Perhaps if ye hold the stone, A-by, it will tell ye what to do. Ye do seem to have a connection with it."

"Good idea, especially seeing how touching the Talismans always gets a response of some sort. Grab the box for me?" Abby asked, pointing a thumb over her shoulder.

The Scotsman nodded, moving swiftly to stand behind Abby and insert a hand inside her bag. "Here ye are, me lady," he said, bowing before placing the intricate box in Abby's outstretched hands.

Abby suppressed a snort but smiled at Rory appreciatively in return. "Thanks," she said, shifting her full attention to the box. Anticipating the mesmerizing look of the Brana, she lifted the lid and scooped the gem into her palm. The moment she wrapped her fingers tightly around the Brana, the box disintegrated, falling from her other hand to the ground as dusty specks.

"Whaa…" she mumbled. Abby relaxed her right hand to inspect the Brana again, afraid it too would disappear. Tension eased from her shoulders when the gem glistened back at her. She looked rapidly from her hand to the tree and back. "I know what to do," she whispered.

"Did ye say ye know what to do, A-by?"

Abby turned to Rory, exhilaration flushing through her. "Yes, well, it's more of an impression. The tree is calling the Brana to it. I can feel it somehow. Like we're all connected or something. The pull is really strong. I don't think I could resist it even if I wanted to. But don't worry," she continued, reading the worry on his face, "it's a good thing."

"So ye need to take the Brana to the tree?"

"Yes, I…"

A terrifying shriek, followed by a spasm of coughing near the opposite side of the stone circle evoked sharp gasps all around. Abby spun to find the source of the sounds, though she knew what her eyes would behold.

Shaeron, Eirwen, and four Thraxen stood just inside the circle. The old man leaned against the stone nearest him as the uncontrollable cough continued to rack his body.

Rory and Rowen armed themselves, standing protectively in front of Abby. Finlay prowled to the left in a wide arc as Cody and Emi tensed for action to the right. A whistle from Rowen summoned Riffin into a low circle. Abby hoped the Protector thought to command his guide to use his grab-and-drop technique on the Thraxen.

Peering around the young men, Abby glared at Shaeron. "What are you doing here?" she yelled, emphasizing each word as she stepped into clear view. "How did you even get here?"

Shaeron wheezed in the aftermath of his coughing fit. "Foolish child, your beast is not the only one capable of spontaneous travel." The old man hacked a black, wet glob onto the ground, causing Abby to wrinkle her face in disgust. He wiped his mouth with the back of a hand and pointed a crooked finger at her. "Now give me back my box."

Abby narrowed her eyes. "Sorry. Not going to happen. Besides," she added with a smirk, "I don't even have the box."

"Liar!" Shaeron roared with surprising intensity. "Old are my eyes, but I watched your thievery. Give me the box!"

Rory whispered to Abby without taking his eyes from the mystic. "Ye best do what ye need to do, now, before battle overtakes us."

Abby squeezed her hand tight around the Brana, jerking it from view behind her back.

Shaeron grumbled, leaning forward so far on his staff, Abby envisioned him tipping over. "What?" he croaked. "You are hiding something. Give it to me now or feel the wrath of my slaves."

Finlay rushed into Abby's mind. *Child, wait no longer with your actions. To the tree with you.*

A foreboding chill overcame Abby. Taking several slow paces backward, Abby started to turn around, intent on sprinting the twenty feet to the tree. In her peripheral vision, the forms of Eirwen and Shaeron blinked in and out to stand not five feet in front of Finlay. *Oh no!* Abby cried to herself as she hesitated leaving her mighty guide.

Finlay growled warning at her. *Go now before you have no chance.*

Abby gulped, breaking into a run. She pumped her arms and concentrated on not dropping the gem. A strange draw from the tree pulled her along, enhancing her agile movements. Screams and roars broke out behind her as she skidded to a stop under the blooming canopy. Abby whipped around and ducked behind the tree's trunk. She placed her free hand onto the trunk's red bark and the sensation of a magnetic pull latched on to her with force. She jerked her hand back in surprise and stared at the tree.

Sweet whispers floated around her. "A salvation foretold, with hair of fire, a protector to free all, from sickness so dire."

That's the writing from the cave wall. Why is someone singing that to me? Rory is the protector with red hair...

A ferocious howl jerked her attention from the tree. She leaned left to peek around the trunk, afraid of what she might see. As Rory, Rowen, and their guides fought valiantly against the Thraxen, Finlay stood nose to nose with Eirwen. He slunk back several paces into a crouch as if preparing to launch himself.

What Abby saw next filled her with intense horror. Shaeron lifted the bottom of his staff into the air, its tip morphing into a sharp, metal point. The old man gripped the weapon with both hands and directed it straight at Finlay the exact moment the wolfhound leaped toward him.

A scream filled Abby's ears when the blade pierced deep into the dog's chest with deadly accuracy. She realized immediately the scream came from her own lungs. "Finlay!" she cried when her guide howled unnatural sounds tapering into silence.

The dog turned his muzzle to lock eyes with her as he crashed to the ground. *Child. Follow your destiny. Fear not for me.*

Unable to process the scene before her, Abby slumped behind the tree. A heavy weight pressed on her chest and her breaths came short and fast. *This isn't happening,* she repeated over and over to herself, refusing to believe her mighty warrior would ever fall. "Finlay," she whimpered, opening her hand to gaze at the Brana. She looked from the gem to the tree, tears threatening to flow.

Finlay's voice struggled to reach her. *Do what you were meant to, little one. I am with you always...*

Spurred by her guide's urging, Abby pushed herself to her feet. Following her instincts with a brave nod, she placed both hands against the trunk. Instantly, the same, strange sensation encompassed her, forcing her body against the tree. In a moment of panic, Abby turned her face to the side, her cheek mashing against the trunk. She envisioned her body smashed flat, with bark treads decorating her skin, but as quickly as the pull began, she found herself free of its oppressive hold, standing somewhere cold, damp, and pitch black. And completely alone.

Shivers consumed Abby. She gritted her teeth and fought to control them. Frenzied thoughts of her guide prompted a quiet sob. *It can't be.* She called out in her mind. *Finlay? Please answer me! Tell me you're okay.*

No reply.

I need you! I'm scared. I...I don't know where I am. Please, talk to me.

No reply.

The heavy weight returned to Abby's chest, followed by a profound stab of searing pain. She cried out into the darkness. Never had she experienced such agony. The heaviness in her chest subsided as the burning pain seemed to tear away from her body and dissipate. And, in that moment, she knew a piece of her soul was gone forever. Shaeron's evil had claimed another.

Having no care for her surroundings, Abby crumpled to the damp ground and rolled herself into a ball. She sobbed until exhaustion took hold, and her tears abated. Empty and hopeless, she laid still until she could no longer ignore the cold seeping into her bones.

Sitting up, Abby wiped her face and realized she still clutched the Brana tight in her right hand. She stroked the gem, studying its shape with her fingers. A tickling sensation worked its way from the Brana up through Abby's forearm, suddenly reminding her of her plight. "For Finlay. For Wren. For Shay." She drew a slow breath, giving herself a mental pep talk. *All right Abby, pull it together. If you're going to save the world, better start by figuring out where the heck you are. Time for some light.*

Abby shrugged her arms from her bag and pulled it into her lap. With a blind hand, she rummaged through its contents, ever thankful for her father having taught her to always be prepared. "There you are," she whispered, wrapping her fingers around a flashlight. She slipped her bag onto her back again and turned on the light.

The beam cut into the dark environment less than Abby cared for. Though it only illuminated a few feet in front of her, she did not need to guess she sat in a cave of some sort. "Great," she groaned, "always with the caves." She pushed herself to her feet, and after shining the light all around, decided she stood in a tunnel. The sound of water dripping up ahead reached her ears. She stood quietly, listening for additional noises but heard none. "Okay. Time to see where this leads."

Abby inched her way along the tunnel, taking great care to watch her step. The passageway curved to the right with a gentle decline. After a good fifty paces, the tunnel opened into a large cavern. Abby stopped at the threshold, dumbstruck by the scene. She could not surmise how, but the entire cave lit up as if the noon sun hung overhead. She switched off her light and dropped it absentmindedly to the ground. "Whoa," she blurted.

A wide crevice split the cavern in half. Thick tree roots swirled in strange patterns along the ceiling and walls, stopping several feet above the cave floor. Abby gazed beyond the deep chasm. "What is that?" she whispered, confused by a peculiar mass of roots against the far wall.

The mass shifted with a straining crack and pop, causing Abby to flinch. A scratchy voice cut through the otherwise silent cave.

"Who is this that stands before us?"

Surprise filled Abby as she kept her initial response to herself. *That voice sounds familiar...*

"Who is this that stands before us?" the voice commanded.

Abby cleared her throat, doing her best to stay calm. "I...I'm Abby Fletcher. May I ask who you are?"

The mass of roots shifted again, swirling faster and faster until a defined humanoid shape protruded from the wall. "We are the end. We are the beginning. We are the many. We are the few. We are the one. We, are Mantara."

A million thoughts buzzed through Abby's head. *I knew it!*

Abby tensed her muscles and took a step into the cavern. "Do you remember me, from the hollow in the Other? I could use some help."

Abby waited silently for a response. She eyed the crevice of at least fifteen feet, wondering how deep it might be. The cracking of wood pulled her attention back to the Mantara.

"You are the Keeper."

Abby gulped at the reality of the statement. "H-how do you know that?"

"We know all."

"Oh," Abby replied, biting the corner of her lower lip. "I suppose you knew back in the hollow, didn't you?"

"Yesss."

Abby transferred her weight from one leg to the other uncomfortably. "Why didn't you tell me?"

The Mantara ignored her question. "Have you brought us that which was wrongfully taken?"

Abby lifted her chin in surprise. "Do you mean the Brana?"

"Yesss."

"I have." Abby held her hand out to reveal the gem. "But I don't know what I'm supposed to do with it."

"Return it to us."

Abby glanced at the intimidating crack in the ground. "Um. Okay. But how? There's a giant crevice between us. No way can I jump across it."

"You are the Keeper."

Abby furrowed her brow. "Yes, but what does that have to do with getting across that hole?"

"You are the Keeper."

Abby groaned to herself. *Why does it keep saying that! I get it, I'm the Keeper.*

When the Mantara remained silent, Abby considered its words. *So, I'm the Keeper, why should that matter?* An image of Rowen's face popped into her mind, reminding her of their recent conversation. *Of course! Why do I always forget the obvious? I can access and use the gift of any guide I choose!* An empty pit gnawed at her stomach and she let out a tiny sob. *Except for the one that matters. Oh Finlay...*

Abby stared at the chasm. *All right. Be logical, Abby.* She pictured each guide she could think of one by one. *Riffin has super-owl strength. Don't think that will do me much good. Those horses, Tiffa and Daylo. Hmm. I don't even know what they can do so that's no help. And Guido, he can lift and move objects if he touches them, but I don't see how that's any use unless I lifted myself.* She considered this option further but shook her head. *No, that's too weird. There's Cody, but he only talks to plants.*

Though, technically the roots are plants. Abby shrugged. *Why not? Maybe I can sweet talk the roots into helping me.* She imagined the hare conversing with a tree and reached out with her mind. *Hello, roots? Would you please help me cross the dangerous hole in this cave? I'd really appreciate it.* Abby strained her ears, hoping for any sound in reply. After a minute with no response, she scowled. *Well that was a stupid idea, don't know why I bothered. I guess that leaves Emi the Weaver.* Abby gazed up at the roots again and the way they crisscrossed one another to form a tight mesh. *Wait, that's it! Emi can manipulate roots and things. Maybe I can make them move myself!*

Feeling pleased with her deduction, Abby concentrated on Emi. She imagined the strange creature singing her even stranger song. *Weave, weave, stitch, stitch, la-la-la, fix, fix.* Abby reached out with her mind, envisioning Emi standing in the stone circle, then pictured the roots swirling down from the walls to create a walkway for her. For the briefest moment, Abby thought she felt a connection with the Weaver but sighed after several minutes. *Why isn't it working? Everyone's counting on me and I don't know what I'm doing.*

After a moment of pouting, another thought came to mind. *Maybe Cody and Emi just aren't the right guides for this, but who else is there?* Abby did another mental inventory of all the animals she had talked to prior. *Wait. I forgot about Eirwen. I doubt she'd like me tapping into her powers, but she clearly can teleport too. And that's exactly what I need. Maybe I can do it without her even sensing me.* Abby weighed the risks of trying to connect with Shaeron's guide and nodded. *I've got to try.* She pinched her eyes shut and, once a state of calm flowed within her, Abby pictured the black dog and her icy eyes. She imagined standing in the stone circle and placing a hand on Eirwen. With a final effort, Abby searched for a connection. *I can't do this. I don't even feel her anywhere.*

In that same moment, a flood of heat washed over Abby, and her insides filled with a burst of love. She doubled over and shot out a steadying hand.

Lass...

Abby stood with a gasp, twirling around in a circle. *Finlay! Is that you?*

I am here, child.

But you...you died!

Aye, lass, that is so.

But, but now you're not dead?

I live, little one.

But how? I felt your connection with me rip away. It was the worst thing I've ever experienced. Well, next to seeing what that nasty old man did to you. How could you come back from that?

My mother.

Eirwen? She saved you?

In a way, child. It seems she had many gifts, one of which was to heal that which was dead by giving of her own life.

Abby stood speechless.

Moments after Shaeron drove his hideous staff into my heart, Rory struck him down dead. The others finished off the Thraxen, leaving only my mother. Rowen drove an arrow into her chest. She collapsed next to me, and for one frozen moment before the darkness took me, we connected. She knew I was her pup. She had never wanted any of what had been forced upon her and desperately needed to do an act of good before going full circle. She promised to bring me back. One moment I was fading away, there was nothing, only quiet. And then, my eyes opened and I could feel your frustration.

Tears flooded Abby's cheeks. *Oh, Finlay. I wouldn't have been able to go on without you. I can't explain how full my heart is now to hear you, to know you're okay.*

Aye, lass, it is good to hear you too. But now, you have a job to do. You must focus.

Abby glared at the crevice. *I need you. Can't you come and help me?*

No, lass, you must do this on your own. Believe in yourself as I believe in you.

Abby wiped a stray tear from her face and nodded. *Okay. You're right. I can do this, now I know you're with me. Just need to borrow a little magic from you.*

Borrow away, lass, and hurry back to us.

Abby hopped up and down, then rotated her shoulders. *Okay, let's do this.* She wrapped her mind around her guide and pictured herself standing on the other side of the chasm. A second later she appeared there with a giant smile. *Sweet. I love you, Finlay.*

Finlay chuckled back. *I love you too, little one.*

Abby strode toward the Mantara and held the Brana out in front of her. "Now what?"

The giant mass of roots creaked and groaned. "Give it and yourself to us."

Abby shuddered and backed up. "Um, what do you mean give myself to you?"

"You must become one with Shay."

"Become one with Shay?" Abby squeaked.

"Yesss. Only then will your transition to Keeper be complete."

Abby's stomach lurched. *Can I really trust the Mantara? What if they turn me into a glob of roots?* She thought back to their first encounter with the strange entity in the hollow. Finlay urged the group to trust his sense and indeed no harm came to them. *Finlay was right then and, hopefully, I will be right now. Looks like this is the only way to set things right for Shay. I can't let the Manta tribe down.*

Abby stepped in closer. "Okay. What do I need to do?"

A single root snaked out from the Mantara, hovering eye level with Abby. It split slowly into two shoots. The first lowered to Abby's opened hand and wrapped gently around the Brana. The second slithered up her arm to rest flush with her temple.

The Brana pulsed a beautiful green in tune with Abby's heartbeat. She gazed at the gem, transfixed, holding as still as she could. Comforting warmth passed from her hand cupping the Brana to the tip of the root against her forehead.

The Mantara lifted the jewel into the air. Abby watched in awe as the mass of roots seemed to part, reeling the Brana in toward it. Seconds later the gem disappeared from sight, tucked away inside the entity. The chamber rumbled and a warm wind whipped up from the chasm.

"Yesss," the Mantara sighed, releasing the root from Abby's head.

Whispers floated throughout the cavern. "The Keeper has come and banished all evil. Shay is whole again." The mysterious voices drifted away as one. "Amaray is free at last. Be at peace, our Queen."

What do they mean Amaray is free at last? We completed the old Keeper's circle...didn't we?

The wind flowed around Abby, faster and faster, wrapping her in a warm blanket, lifting her off her toes and turning her around. She giggled with delight, and when her feet made contact with the ground again, the wind subsided and a misty form materialized in front of her.

Abby squinted, perplexed by the happenings. *That looks like...*

"Hello, dear Abby."

"You...you're the Red Queen."

"Yes, my brave dear."

Abby studied the elegant woman floating before her. Though only a ghostly likeness, she could see exhaustion on the Queen's face.

"You have traveled far and overcome many adversities. I am so very proud of you, young Amaray."

Abby could not help but smile, though a mixture of confusing emotions filled her. "Thank you," she managed to whisper. "But why?"

"Why what, dear Abby?"

"Why me? Why am I the next Keeper? I'm just a girl from Nebraska."

The ethereal woman smiled and reached out a misty hand to caress Abby's face. "My dear, you are most special. From the moment before you cried your first breath you were destined to follow in my path. Have no doubt in yourself, my child, for all is as is meant to be."

Abby raised her eyebrows. "So, did I really do it then? Shay will heal and the Manta are safe again?"

"Yes, dear Abby. And you have set me free from my binding chains. I am forever grateful."

The Queen floated backward, rising slowly. "The time has come for me to move on."

"But wait, I have so many things I want to ask you!" Abby cried as the misty form disintegrated.

"Open your heart to love, young Abby. Love for the people, love for the land, and love for he who would stand beside you."

Abby stared in silence, soaking in the Queen's words. *Love for he who would stand beside me...*

As the Queen was but a faint image, she motioned to Abby as if blowing a kiss. "I leave you with one last thing. Farewell, young Amaray..."

A gust of warm wind flowed over Abby, lifting her hair from her shoulders. A strange tingling danced across her entire body. And then, the Queen vanished.

Abby held her hands out to examine them. *I feel...different.*

A sudden shift in the roots yanked Abby from her thoughts.

"We are whole again," croaked the Mantara. "Find your way home, you must, Amaray."

Joy bubbled from Abby as she pictured Finlay and called out for his gift.

15

Abby appeared next to the thriving tree. She surveyed the circle, her heart torn by the vision of death among those she loved. "Finlay!" she cried when the wolfhound perked his head toward her. His mighty frame thundered across the distance separating them, and Abby flung herself into his soft coat after he slowed to a stop.

Oh Finlay, Abby wept happily, *what would I ever do without you? Never die again. That's an order, mister.* She pulled herself away and grasped his muzzle. *It's good to see you.*

Finlay ran a wet tongue along Abby's cheek. *As with you, little one.* The dog swiveled his head to the side and inspected Abby. *It seems we both have had a big day.*

Abby scrunched her face. *Well, yeah, of course. But why are you looking at me like that?*

Motion to Abby's side caught her attention. She pivoted to find Rory staring at her, jaw hanging low.

"Uh, you're apt to catch a fly, Rory," she snorted. "Hey," she added, snapping a finger in front of the Scotsman's face when he did not respond, "what's with you? Why are you staring at me like that?"

Rory gulped hard and pointed a finger at her. "A-by, yer hair. What happened to ye?"

"Wait, what? What's wrong with my hair?" Abby replied, glancing at her shoulder. "Holy cow!" she said, pulling a lock in front of her. Fiery red curls fell through her fingers. She whirled in a circle as if able to see herself from all angles. Coming to a halt, she pulled handfuls of hair around either side of her face. All red, all her own. "This can't be." She paused to think of the last words the Queen said before disappearing. "She did this?" And then the prophecy carved into the cave wall appeared in her mind. *A salvation foretold, with hair of fire, a protector to free all, from sickness so dire.* "With hair of fire," she whispered.

Oblivious to movement around her, Abby continued to stare in dismay at her transformed hair.

"Sister?" Rowen placed a gentle hand on Abby's shoulder.

Abby released her curls, turning to him. "Huh? Oh, hey Rowen, what's up?"

"You have visitors," he replied with a smile, sweeping his arm toward the outer edge of the circle.

Abby looked out beyond the stones to see dozens of people, her people, filing into the circle curiously, one by one. Young and old, all dressed in similar Manta garb, men with bow and arrows, and all the women with golden curls. With more confident steps once inside the sacred monument, everyone approached Abby with wide eyes.

"It is true then," said a stout man with a husky voice, "the black curse is gone, and our Queen has come again."

Whispers passed from person to person and to Abby's surprise, every Manta dropped to a knee. "Our Queen," they hailed in unison.

Overwhelmed, Abby stood speechless, unable to understand what was happening until Finlay's soothing voice caressed her mind. *It is as they say, little one. You are the Guardian of Shay. I would say it is fitting now you are their Red Queen.*

Abby choked on her thoughts. *The Red Queen? I...I think I'm going to need some time to process that, but I promise I'll do my best.*

Finlay dropped to his haunches in front of Abby, lowering himself on one leg. *I know you will, my Queen.*

A single tear crept from Abby's eye, and she wiped it with the back of a hand.

Seeing Finlay's gesture, Rory stepped forward, taking Abby's fingers in his own. With none of his usual dramatics, Rory dropped to a knee and smiled sweetly. "Me Queen."

Abby gazed into his eyes and a sudden rush of emotion churned inside her. "There's something we need to go do, that is, if you want to come with me," she blurted.

"Aye, A-by, I will follow ye anywhere."

Abby gripped the Scotsman's hand and gave him a tug to stand.

Rory grinned his goofy grin and hopped to his feet.

Abby stretched to meet his ear. "I think I need to say something to everyone first. Would be a bit rude to up and leave," she whispered.

Rory nodded, standing proudly next to the girl with wild, red curls.

Abby turned to face the small gathering of Manta. "Um, hi everyone," she said with a quick wave, hoping her cheeks would not match her hair. "What you're saying is true. The mystic Shaeron is dead and the sickness he inflicted on the land is banished. And I," Abby paused, giving her head a small shake of disbelief, "well, I am privileged to be the next Keeper of Shay."

The Manta roared, clapping with passion.

When the sounds of celebration tapered, Abby scanned the crowd, making eye contact with each person. "This is all new, and well, a little scary to me, but I give you my oath I will cherish the land and do all in my power to protect it and its people. Please," she continued motioning upward with her hands, "there is no need to bow to me, we are all one."

Glancing at one another, the Manta rose slowly. When everyone stood as equals, a petite girl of only seven scooted forward to stand in front of Abby, eyes directed at the ground.

Abby smiled sweetly and lifted the girl's chin. "Don't be shy; did you want to ask me something?"

The girl nodded quickly while clutching her stomach. "I am most hungry, Amaray. We have found no Bria for days."

Abby frowned inside. *These poor people have probably been starving. How could I not even think of that?* Abby circled an arm around the young Manta's shoulders. "We will find you something to eat, something for everyone. Hold tight for a minute."

The girl smiled shyly and dashed back to her mother's open arms.

Abby knelt and placed her hands on the ground. An instant connection with the land flowed through her fingers. She closed her eyes and pictured an endless supply of food for the Manta. A squeal of delight snapped her from the image.

"Bria!" shouted the little girl as she pointed at the tree.

Abby stood and turned to see what reaped such excitement. "Amazing," she whispered. No longer did Amaray's tree bear velvety blossoms. Tens of hundreds of Bria pulsed in place of blooms.

"May we have one?" the girl asked with eager eyes.

"Of course, little one, perhaps Rowen will help you," Abby said, looking at the Protector.

"It would be my pleasure, my Queen."

Rowen plucked the lowest Bria from the tree and handed it to the child.

To Abby's surprise, moments later a new Bria formed in its place.

Rory stared in amazement at the tree. "If what our eyes see is true, A-by, this is certainly a blessin'. The Manta shall never know hunger again."

"I have a feeling you're right," Abby replied, watching as Rowen continued handing out Bria.

She grabbed the Scotsman's hand and pulled him with her toward Finlay. "Hey, fuzzface. Rory and I need to go take care of something," she said, scratching the dog under the chin, "but we won't be gone long. Watch over everything for us?"

Finlay pressed the side of his muzzle against Abby's chest. *Aye, lass, I will keep a watchful eye.*

Good doggie, I can always count on you.

Laughter rumbled in the dog's chest. *Aye. And lass, I approve of your decision.*

Abby eyed Finlay suspiciously. *My decision? What? You mean you know where we're going?*

Of course, child, a good doggie knows all.

Abby rolled her eyes and readjusted her grip on Rory's hand. "Ready?" she asked, looking up at the handsome, young man and, upon a nod of his head, she reached out for Finlay's magic and envisioned their destination.

***

"The Great Willow?" Rory said with surprise. "What are we doin' here, A-by?"

Abby ran her hands along the enormous trunk. "This is a special place. Wren told me a story of sorts about it once."

Rory tipped his head inquisitively.

"When I ran off with the Brana, I got sucked inside the tree, I guess, and ended up in a big cave. It must have been below the tree or something. Anyway, while I was down there, I ran into the Mantara again." Abby paused when Rory mouthed a surprised 'oh' at her. She laughed in response. "I know, right? I definitely wasn't expecting that. Anyway, the Mantara took the Brana from me and it healed the land. But it also freed the original Queen. And get this, she floated out of this chasm and talked to me."

Rory's eyes grew wide. "That's amazin' A-by. What did she say?"

"Well," Abby started with hesitation, "she said lots of things, but the most important thing she said was I needed to open my heart to love. Love for the people, love for the land, and," Abby stopped to draw a breath and grab her courage, "love for he who would stand beside me."

Rory remained attentive, showing no reaction in his eyes but his cheeks betrayed his true response.

Abby blushed too and gazed at the ground, picking at the hem of her shirt. "So, here's the thing," she said, meeting Rory's stare slowly. "I know how you feel about me, and even though we haven't really known each other long, well," she paused, knowing she spoke the truth, "I love you too."

A grand grin stretched across Rory's face, filling Abby's heart. "Yer right, A-by, this will forever be a special place. The place where I won yer heart."

"You won my heart long before we ever stood beneath the Great Willow, Rory, but," she continued rapidly, trying to mask her embarrassment, "that's not why this is a special place. This is where the Manta perform the binding ritual," she ended in a near whisper.

"Bindin' ritual?"

"Yeah, don't you remember hearing Wren call me your binding a couple times? You know, like where you promise yourselves to one another?"

"Aye, like husband and wife?"

Abby gulped. "Yes, like husband and wife, except the Manta call it binding, but," she went on, feeling embarrassed and averting her eyes, "don't expect to be making babies any time soon."

Rory's cheeks flamed as he cleared his throat. "Oh, aye, I mean nae, Lass. I would niver..." He reached out and interlocked fingers with Abby, his awkward expression subsiding. "If ye are sayin' ye want to and are sure, A-by, how do we do this bindin' ritual?"

"I've never been more sure, Rory. I know in my heart we are meant to be together." Abby breathed evenly as she held the Scotsman's gaze. "I think I remember the words Wren told me, but I don't know if there's more to it." She glanced at the Great Willow hoping for guidance. "Maybe we should hold hands," she said, giving his fingers a squeeze, "and, I don't know," she added with a shrug, "put our other hands on the tree?"

Rory nodded. "Whatever ye see as best."

Abby bit her upper lip and placed her free hand on the Great Willow, watching as Rory copied her movements.

She searched her memories, smiling sadly to herself as an image of Wren filled her mind. "Okay, I'm pretty sure I have the words right. I'll repeat them a couple times first so you can memorize them too, then we need to say them in unison."

Warmth radiated from Rory's face as he smiled and gave Abby an understanding nod.

"Okay, here goes."

Abby recited the words at a slow and steady pace. "All that was, all that is, all that will be. Bound by touch, bound by soul, bound by eternity." After glancing at Rory, she repeated the phrasing. When she finished for the second time, a strange sense of fulfillment flowed from the tree's rough, outer shell through Abby's body. She stole a peek at Rory and raised her eyebrows as if to ask if he were ready.

A goofy grin answered her and, with a quick nod of her head, the duo spoke in harmony until the cascade of words ended with silence.

Abby expelled a short breath and glanced at Rory, wondering if she had guessed wrong about how the Manta perform the ritual after nothing spectacular seemed to happen. She leaned hard against the tree with the palm of her right hand. "Maybe..." a sharp crackle cut through Abby's thought. The sound gave way to a new sensation. "Uh, what's happening?" Abby exclaimed when her right hand sank into the Great Willow's trunk. She looked frantically to Rory to see his left hand suffering the same fate. They both lurched forward, now wrist-deep in the tree.

"Is it hurtin' ye, A-by? Are ye in pain?"

Abby shook her head. "No, no, I'm fine. Actually, it feels pretty good, nice and warm, tickles a little, maybe. What about you?"

"Aye, yer description is accurate."

A warm, red glow seeped from the cracks in the bark, streaming along their arms and swirling rapidly to envelop them.

Rory turned to Abby with raised eyebrows. She tightened her hold on Rory's hand and grinned in response, knowing this must be part of the ritual. After they reveled in the comfort of the glow for only moments, the tree creaked and, in a snap, the light disappeared.

An ancient voice whispered to Abby. "In life and in death, forever as one..."

The pair stumbled suddenly backward, the tree's hold on them released.

They both gaped at their hands, then turned to each other with wide eyes.

"A-by! What is it?"

"I...I don't know, but it sure is cool!" Abby exclaimed, studying the adornment covering the top of her hand and running several inches up her wrist. Like the roots of most trees in Shay snaking along the ground, deep red, raised lines branched out from the top of her hand, weaving their way around her wrist. Abby flexed her fingers, smiling with fascination as the lines wriggled with her movements.

"Is most peculiar, A-by. What do ye think it is for?"

"No clue, but I'm feeling incredibly happy about it." Abby stared at Rory. "This will sound weird," she paused, uncertain how to explain her thoughts, "I almost think I can sense your emotions."

Rory held Abby's gaze, his face lighting up with recognition after several moments. "Ye're right. Is like I can feel a piece of ye within meself."

Abby snorted. "They weren't kidding about it being a binding ritual."

The Scotsman stepped in close. "Aye, my Queen. Will take some gettin' used to but I much like carryin' ye with me."

Abby tried to hide her blush by staring at the ground. "So, um, now that it looks like it's official, there's one last thing we need to do."

"What might that be, A-by?" Rory asked softly, running his fingers through her curls.

Abby raised her head and met Rory's loving eyes. "This," she whispered, grabbing his braids and pulling him into a sweet, soft, binding kiss.

Butterflies soared in Abby's stomach, and she willed herself not to become lost in the moment. She released her grasp on Rory and stepped back.

The Scotsman grinned wildly, as if his brain were in the atmosphere. "What do we do now, me love?"

Abby chuckled. "Well, we've checked saving the world off our list, but we probably need to make sure there aren't any more Thraxen lurking about. You know, see that everyone's safe. And I have a lot of reading to do, things to learn. I have a feeling it's going to take a while." Abby paused and slapped a hand to her forehead. "My family! Well, er, our family. We have to bring them here."

The color drained from Rory's face at the mention of those beyond the portal.

"Rory, what's wrong. You look a bit ill."

"Yer faither," he said with a hard swallow. "Me love, should I have no' asked his permission?"

Abby held back a giggle and gazed at her proper Scotsman. "I wouldn't worry about it, honest. Considering the circumstances, everyone will understand. So," she said, motioning toward the Rose, "think you can still open portals with your Talisman?"

Rory pursed his lips and considered her question. "Aye. Me gut says it is so."

Abby smiled, thinking of all the amazing experiences she'd been through with Rory and Finlay by her side, and all the incredible unknowns yet to come. "Okay then," she said lifting onto her tiptoes and touching her forehead to Rory's. "Let's bring our family home."

My fellow story lovers, many humble thanks for following Abby on her grand adventure. I hope you enjoyed reading the Red King Trilogy as much as I loved writing it.

Though this circle is complete, it is just the beginning.

If you liked, loved, or even did not care for the Talisman of Darktree Hollow, please consider leaving a review at your favorite online retailer.

I love hearing from readers. Feel free to reach out to me at:

redkingtrilogy@gmail.com

www.facebook.com/TheRedKingTrilogy

Twitter: @finlayforever

www.ingramcontent.com/pod-product-compliance
Lightning Source LLC
Chambersburg PA
CBHW031151120726
47905CB00006B/1908